I'd been thinking the same thing. For a reality TV show, nothing seemed to be real at all. Adultery, pretend contestants, phony death threats . . .

I turned away from the craziness, headed toward the hot tub. "Maybe we should talk."

"About?"

"Us. That on-camera kiss today."

The corner of his lip curved up in a smile. "The audience will eat that stuff up, don't you think? We are pretend contestants, remember?"

"Of course. Pretend." Only there was nothing pretend about that kiss. He knew it. I knew it. Question was, what were we going to do about it?

I leaned on the edge of the hot tub. I dipped my hand into the water, swirled it around. With a loud yelp, I suddenly yanked it out of the water while jumping backwards, nearly knocking Bobby over. He steadied me, but I couldn't stop shaking.

"Nina, what's wrong?"

I pointed a shaking, dripping finger toward the hot tub. "Someone . . . someone's in there."

"What?" He reached into the water, searching with his arm.

His face paled as a body rose to the surface.

**Nina Quinn Mysteries by
Heather Webber**

Heather Webber

TROUBLE in BLOOM

AVON BOOKS
An Imprint of HarperCollinsPublishers

This is a work of fiction. Names, characters, places, and incidents are products of the author's imagination or are used fictitiously and are not to be construed as real. Any resemblance to actual events, locales, organizations, or persons, living or dead, is entirely coincidental.

AVON BOOKS
An Imprint of HarperCollins*Publishers*
10 East 53rd Street
New York, New York 10022-5299

Copyright © 2007 by Heather Webber
ISBN: 978-0-06-112971-1
ISBN-10: 0-06-112971-2
www.avonmystery.com

First Avon Books paperback printing: May 2007

Avon Trademark Reg. U.S. Pat. Off. and in Other Countries,
Marca Registrada, Hecho en U.S.A.
HarperCollins® is a registered trademark of HarperCollins Publishers.

Printed in the U.S.A.

10 9 8 7 6 5 4 3 2 1

Acknowledgments

A big thanks to Sarah Durand, my fabulous editor, for pushing me to push myself. Thanks, too, to the whole Avon staff for all the hard work they do behind the scenes.

Thanks and hugs to Jacky Sach, agent extraordinaire.

Huge thanks to my critique group, Shelley Galloway, Cathy Liggett, Julie Stone, and author-in-waiting Hilda Lindner Knepp, for everything. Thank you to Laura Bradford for her continuous cheerleading, keen eyes, and honesty. And a very special thanks to Sharon Short for being a great roomie, brainstorming genius, and road-trippin' buddy. You guys are the best.

TROUBLE in BLOOM

One

Thou, Nina Colette Ceceri Quinn, shall never, ever, resort to a bad comb-over if thou should happen to go bald.

I hoped I wouldn't, but if I did, this commandment would zoom to the top of my personal list fast. Right up there with never wearing dark socks—or any socks for that matter—with sandals and never letting the hair on my upper lip grow to the point where someone thinks I have a moustache.

Some things in life were just a given.

Horrendous was the only way to describe the comb-over on Willie Sala. Five thin greasy clumps of dark brown hair swooped from his left ear to his right, hugging his shiny head for dear life.

Maybe five-five, 160 pounds, Willie also had the darkest, beadiest eyes I'd ever seen.

Fortunately, he had good teeth. A girl could overlook a lot for good teeth.

Willie Sala was the producer/director of the local TV reality show *Hitched or Ditched*, which filmed right here in Ohio. Forget *WKRP*, HoD was currently Cincinnati's claim to fame. Sad as that was to say.

It was a show where couples signed up to test their relationships. Ultimately, the home audience would decide whether contestants should get hitched . . . or ditch each other.

I glanced to my right. The man sitting next to me in the Cracker Jack–sized conference room at the HoD studio was tall with shoulder-length wavy blond hair and broad shoulders—an overall great build. Beautiful light blue eyes crinkled at the corners from good humor, and his lips were tantalizingly kissable. The Florida sun had bronzed his fair skin to golden perfection. He was the epitome of the all-American boy next door.

It helped that he was calm, confident, gorgeous, sexy, and good in bed.

His name was Bobby MacKenna, and I knew about that bed part because I'd slept with him.

Notice the past tense?

He looked over, caught me ogling and winked. He'd been raised in Texas and had the wink down pat.

Bobby and I happened to be one of the couples on this week's show. Mario and Perry were the other couple. The four of us, along with HoD's boyishly charming host, Thad Cochran, and a handful of TV people, listened to Willie bark about being "real" on TV yet "dramatic" enough to keep viewers tuned in every night.

My life leaned toward dramatic, so I didn't think I'd have trouble with that part.

The "real" part might be a problem. Seeing as how Bobby and I were pretend contestants, here on the show under-cover to help Bobby's lawyer cousin nail Willie for sexual harassment.

"We want to see everything." Willie spoke in short stac-cato bursts, a rapid-fire verbal machine gun. "Little things. Washing dishes, to work, to fights. We love fights." His weasely voice bounced off the cracked mushroom-colored walls, but the smarmy edge was undercut by the dark in-dustrial carpet so old it was probably laid in 1932, when the studio was built. "And sex! Lots of sex too! A ratings booster if there ever was one."

Bobby's eyebrows waggled.

Danger! Danger!

It would be hazardous to my mental state to pick up our sex life where it had left off.

Just over six weeks ago Bobby had left Ohio to take a job as an elementary school principal in Tampa, Florida, and it hadn't been any bond with me that brought him back. Mac, his grandfather, had fallen and injured his hip and needed Bobby's help finding long-term care.

Murky would be a good way to describe the relationship between Bobby and me right now. There were still feelings between us. His move hadn't changed that. I'd fallen for him hard and fast soon after the breakup with my ex-husband Kevin Quinn. And because I'd been so confused about my sudden feelings, Bobby had gone ahead and taken his dream job in Florida. We'd agreed that a long-distance relationship wouldn't be fair to either of us.

Which was true.

But now he was back in town—on a temporary leave of absence to help Mac, and to do the show.

And to use Bobby for sex while he was here would be wrong.

Wrong, wrong, wrong.

Or so I told myself to keep sane.

I'd thrown a serious pity party for a good solid month when Bobby first left. Then I woke up one morning wondering who the hell I was. What defined me? What did I really want out of life? I burned with questions I'd never taken the time to figure out. All I knew was, I didn't like who I'd become, all mopey and depressed.

So here I was, currently on day ten of a serious self-discovery quest. With resolutions for a healthier lifestyle, some serious self-examination, and most important: no men.

The whole kit and frustrating caboodle.

The no men part had been fairly easy with Bobby gone. But now he was suddenly back in my life.

As if that alone weren't bad enough, we also had to pretend to be engaged in front of the whole Cincinnati viewing area.

Fate?

My temples throbbed. Pondering fate gave me headaches.

Willie stood while the rest of us sat. He jabbed his finger in the air to punctuate his choppy speech. "For four days cameras will record parts of your normal lives. Each night you'll come here to play *Rendezvous*." He wiped a bead of sweat from his head, dislodging one section of his combover. It flopped down over his forehead like a wilting daisy.

Rendezvous was HoD's ripped-off version of the *Newlywed Game*. It was filmed several hours before actual broadcast, in order to edit out any bleeps or blunders.

Thad Cochran, the picture-perfect host of HoD, motioned to Willie's wilting hair while saying to us, "Be honest with your answers, people. The truth always comes out in the end." He had a deep cleft in his chin that bobbed when he talked.

Willie pushed the errant hair back onto his moist head. It stuck without a fight. "I'll be up front. Big name executives will be in and out of the studio all week. HoD is going national. We must make this week a good one. Nothing can go wrong. Got it?"

Great. Added pressure.

One of Willie's assistants poked her head in the door and said, "Mr. Sala, Mrs. Sala is here."

A sultry feminine voice said, "Willie, sweetheart, may I have a moment?"

I craned my neck to see what kind of woman would marry that kind of man.

She stood in the doorway. Six feet of perfection. Long

ebony hair, dark exotic eyes, flawless olive skin, curves in all the right places.

Perry, one of the other contestants, leaned in toward me. He had a smooth deep voice full of inflection. It rose and fell as he spoke. "That's Genevieve Hidalgo Sala, Willie's brand-spanking new wife." His eyes sparkled. They were a shade of gray-green I'd never seen before. "She's also the new hostess of the show. She's Vanna to Thad's Pat Sajak." His pale eyebrows arched, lifting his whole forehead a half inch. "Wonder how she got that job, wink, wink, nudge, nudge."

Ooh, that was an interesting tidbit. "What happened to Jessica Ayers?" I whispered, playing dumb. After being abruptly fired eight weeks ago, Jessica Ayers claimed she'd been sexually harassed by Willie while on set, and hired Bobby's cousin Josh, a two-bit sleazeball lawyer, to file a lawsuit.

"Oh, that! Well, I've heard—"

"Perry, stop gossiping," Mario chastised.

With dark hair, dark eyes, and beautiful mocha-colored skin, Mario was Perry's significant other. Partner? I wasn't sure of the proper term these days for gay lovers. In the few hours I'd known the two of them, they seemed headed toward ditched, in my opinion. Mario was a stick in the mud. He hadn't stopped griping at Perry since they arrived, nitpicking about this, nagging about that. He kind of reminded me of my mother.

"We'll talk later," Perry whispered.

I'd make a point of it. Curiosity burned. Did he know anything that could help Josh's case? After all, that was why I was here.

Participating in this torture.

All because of a favor. One Bobby promised Josh in order to get off the phone when we'd been, ah, indisposed.

True, I probably could have finagled my way out of doing the show. However, I felt as though Bobby and I had *both* made the promise to Josh that day, and if there's one commandment I strictly adhere to, it's keeping my promises.

And, since the HoD cameras would be following me during the day, it would be great—free—PR for my landscaping company.

But, I confess, I'd had another motive to do the show. I'd wanted to have this week with Bobby. To see if I had made the right decision in letting him go. To see if we were well and truly over for good.

That had been my grand plan, at least. Unfortunately, it had only taken two minutes of seeing him again to know I'd probably made the biggest mistake of my life by breaking things off with him.

I loved him. Simple as that. I loved him, and I'd let him go.

But I'd made my decision, and now I had to live with it. There was no other option. I couldn't ask him to come back—being a principal was his dream job. And I couldn't leave Ohio. This was where my family was, my job, my friends.

It was clear I was just going to have to suck it up, live with the decisions I'd made, stay strong, and get through this week without falling back into that dark hole I'd been in after he left.

This week would be all about self-preservation. Of keeping my distance from him, physically and emotionally. Easier said than done, though, because I wanted nothing more than to fling myself at him.

Another reason why self-discovery could only be a good thing for me.

"Give me a minute," Willie said to all of us as he walked over to his wife. Genevieve towered over him by a good four inches. He kissed her hand (Perry *awwwed*) and led her into the hallway, closing the door behind them.

Bobby brought his head close to mine. He smelled good, a little bit laundry detergent, a little bit of coffee, a little bit of just . . . him. It was a scent I couldn't quite describe, but it did funny things to my stomach.

"This is going to be fun," he murmured.

The way my stomach flippity-flopped, this was going to be cruel and unusual punishment, spending a week with him, pretending to be his fiancée. "What doesn't kill us."

"You'll cave."

He'd already tried to get me into his bed twice since being back.

"Nope."

A lazy grin crept across his face. "Oh, you will."

I had a sinking feeling he might be right. I was weak where he was concerned.

Since I had goals for my mental health, I needed to stay strong about the sex part. *Wrong, wrong, wrong to use him,* I told myself again. But it would be so easy to give in . . .

Wrong!

Perry leaned in. "What are you mumbling about?"

My cheeks flamed. If he only knew. "Nothing, really."

His eyebrows dipped. "You bipolar?"

I laughed. "No." Glancing at Bobby, I easily saw him naked in my mind's eye. Suddenly warm, I tugged on my shirt collar. "Ever been on a diet, Perry?"

"Have I ever." He patted a slightly rounded stomach.

"And could use one again," Mario put in, clearly eavesdropping.

Perry rolled his eyes. "Ignore him, he's nervous. He's always crabby when he's nervous. Go on."

"Well, you know that feeling of wanting something really badly but not being able to have it?"

Solemnly, he nodded.

"Let's just say I need a cookie."

He squeezed my hand, seeming to know I wasn't talking about cheating on my low-carb diet. I'd just started it, hoping to lose a couple of pounds, and it was killing me.

As was the no-sex thing.

Self-discovery was a bitch.

"You know what you need?" Perry asked.

"What's that?"

"A little makeover. Something to spruce you up a bit. Make you feel better."

"It will do wonders," Mario piped in.

Ordinarily, I would have turned him down flat. But that was the old Nina. The new Nina took a second. "No way."

Perry picked up a lock of my dull brown hair. "Really?"

"Is it that bad?" I went cross-eyed trying to look at the piece he held.

Mario leaned forward, looked at me. "Yes."

"But you probably think everyone's hair is bad." He had that kind of air about him.

Perry nodded. "She's right about that."

Mario pointed at my head. "But yours especially needs help."

"Come on," Perry urged. "The makeover's on me." He slid a business card over to me. "Come in tomorrow afternoon and I'll squeeze you in. By tomorrow night you'll be one hot *mamacita*."

I looked at the card: PERRY OWENS, STYLIST. He worked at Azure, a hip downtown salon I'd heard ads for on the radio.

Being a hot *mamacita* had to be good for anyone's self-discovery. But . . . "I can't tomorrow afternoon. Work."

"Tuesday, then?"

I hemmed. I hawed. I agreed. "All right. It's a deal." All in the name of self-discovery. I tucked his card into my backpack and leaned back in my chair as Thad stood up, paced the tiny room.

About forty, Thad didn't look like a stereotypical low-budget game show host. No slick hair, slick smile, or slick way of talking. He was more Mr. Rogers than Wink Martindale. He had a pristine reputation, was big into charities and family. Yet, he hosted a game show with questions like,

"If you and your significant other were playing strip poker, what item of clothing would your partner remove first?"

Maybe that's why Thad thrived as a host of HoD. He wasn't the norm. He brought fresh-faced sincerity to the show.

While we waited for Willie, Thad explained there would be several taped interviews while we were at the studio today, and then tomorrow, Monday morning, bright and early, we'd each meet our cameraman and field producer.

Since the show was low-budget, our houses only had one camera, in the bedroom (they'd put one in my living room, since it was currently being used as my master bedroom). The installation process hadn't bothered me all that much. What were a few more holes in the walls of my house when half my living room ceiling was missing due to a leak in the upstairs master bath?

I was having serious construction issues. Absentee workers, mostly. I could only imagine what my mother had done to scare them away. She was currently in charge of the remodeling, and I debated firing her. Not that I'd hired her, but still. Enough was enough.

Thad stopped pacing, put his hands on the back of a chair belonging to a blonde production assistant who'd been making eyes at Bobby the whole time we'd been sitting there.

I tried not to jump across the table and strangle her. I told myself she should be grateful for my new self and accompanying newfound restraint.

Thad's voice rose and fell as he spoke. "During the week, online votes from home viewers will be tallied and will ultimately determine who should be hitched and who should be ditched. On Friday night, everyone will meet back here for the results show, which will be broadcast live."

Raised voices carried through the door. We all quieted as Willie Sala loudly told his new wife to mind her own business, and she told him she'd damn well do what she pleased.

So much for newlywedded bliss. Sounded like they were on the road to ditched.

Thad cleared his throat. "Okay, people. That's it for now."

One of the crew looked at his clipboard. "Mario? You're first for the interviews. Follow me."

The room pretty much cleared out, leaving Bobby, me, and Perry alone.

Now would be a great time to question him about Jessica Ayers, but before I could, he asked, "You're here to test your relationship . . . who's having the doubts?"

"Me," Bobby and I said at the same time.

With dipped eyebrows, Perry said, "I'd say you two came to the right place."

"I think maybe she's just using me for sex, Perry," Bobby said. "I'm hoping this week will answer that question."

Perry's mouth popped open.

I glared at Bobby.

He winked at me.

Damn that wink!

I cleared my throat. "Well, he won't have to worry about me using him this week, because he'll be sleeping alone. I need a clear mind . . . for the show."

Bobby's gaze landed on my lips. "Is that so?"

Hot. In. Here.

"Yes." I cleared my throat again. "Absolutely."

"Ah." Perry laughed. "The cookie."

"Cookie?" Bobby asked.

"It's nothing," I said quickly.

There was a good chance Bobby already knew how badly I wanted him. He didn't need confirmation.

The door opened and Thad came in. He smiled and said, "Forgot some papers." He picked up a folder and looked at me. "Aren't you that landscaper? The one-day lady?"

That was me, in a nutshell. I tried not to be annoyed at the way he'd phrased it. I was supposed to be Zen about things now. When I figured out what Zen was, I'd probably be better off. "Yes."

"That's you?" Perry's eyes lit.

Afraid of what he'd heard about me, I nodded. It hadn't been admiration in his voice.

Thad rested his files on the table. "My wife would love to speak to you about a makeover for her parents next spring. She's been talking about it ever since she heard you'd be on the show."

"Have her call me." I fished a business card out of my leather backpack-style purse.

"Nina's the best there is." The pride in Bobby's voice nearly stole my last shred of willpower. If he winked now, I was a goner.

"That's good to know," Thad said. He stopped on his way out the door. "Do you give discounts by any chance?"

Perry rolled his eyes.

"I'm sure we can work something out." Have a look at me—Nina Colette Agreeable Ceceri Quinn. Maybe this self-discovery stuff was kicking in.

As Thad walked out, Perry leaned in, his eyes wide. "Did you really dig up a dead body once? Do tell."

I'd opened Taken by Surprise, Garden Designs, a few years ago, and business had taken off. My company specialized in surprise garden makeovers. We completely changed someone's yard in one day, usually as a gift to an unsuspecting loved one. It took a lot of planning and hard work, but the end results were usually worth it. Plus, I had some of the best people working for me, despite their criminal pasts.

Occasionally I fell across a dead body or two during a job. It wasn't something I liked talking about, and I really wished everyone would just forget about it.

"Digging up? Only once." I looked around, tried to change the subject. "You know, a new coat of paint in this room would do wonders. And maybe a plant or two."

"Oh wait!" Perry snapped his fingers. "Didn't a guy have a heart attack and die from the surprise? When was that? Last month?"

I winced. "Two months." He was referring to Russ Grabinsky, a former client. Kind of.

The door swung open. I breathed a sigh of relief. No more talk of dead bodies, thank God.

Much to my surprise, Genevieve Sala waltzed in and introduced herself. A handsome man followed her in, maybe six feet tall, brown hair professionally styled, thirtyish years old, salon tan, and bright white perfect teeth. Veneers, I was sure of it. He wore expensive jeans, a mint green with baby blue stripes button-down, and a brown suede blazer.

My father would call him a dandy.

I think these days men like him were referred to as metrosexuals.

He looked vaguely familiar.

"This," Genevieve introduced, "is Carson Keyes. He's the entertainment reporter for Channel 18."

Aha! I knew I'd seen him somewhere before. The local Fox affiliate, Channel 18 was my favorite station for their ten o'clock newscast. I was an early-to-bed kind of girl.

"Are you here for your Friday 'Behind the Scenes' segment?" Perry asked Carson.

"Yes," Genevieve answered for him. "Except we've arranged with Channel 18 to do a segment every night this week! It's great PR."

Carson grinned. "The audience will love it." He asked us a few preliminary questions, and closed his notebook just as one of the production assistants came in, a package in her hand. It was the same woman who'd been making goo-goo eyes at Bobby.

"Mrs. Sala, this just arrived for you via special messenger."

"Oh?" Genevieve ripped open the envelope, pulled out a piece of paper. The color drained from her face. The note slipped from her fingers onto the table.

START SAYING YOUR GOOD-BYES. YOU'RE ABOUT TO DIE.

Genevieve quickly snatched the paper from the table. "No one saw that. Do you hear me?"

Carson Keyes was already taking notes.

Bobby rose. "I think the police should be notified."

Genevieve crumpled the paper, held it in a tightly closed fist. "It's none of your business," she said to all of us. "I'll deal with this."

"Do you know who sent it?" Carson asked, a gleam in his reporter's eye.

Perceptive, Genevieve picked up on his intent. "You cannot do a report on this, Carson!"

"Genevieve, it's my job to report news, and this is news. Big news."

She let out a small cry and fled the room. Carson followed her out, asking if he could see the note and if there had been other threats.

After a good five minutes, Perry said, "Do we call the police?"

I looked at Bobby.

"I think it's in Genevieve's hands now," he said.

We sat in silence for a minute. Then Perry inched his chair closer to mine.

Oh no. I needed to escape before the conversation returned to dead bodies and how many I'd dug up. "I'm, uh, going to find a drink." I made a run for it, leaving Bobby and Perry alone. I prayed the conversation wouldn't return to cookies.

As I wandered, I wondered who'd want to see Genevieve dead.

My immediate thought was Jessica Ayers. After all, Genevieve had taken her place on the show.

She'd been upset enough to file a sexual harassment suit—was she upset enough to threaten murder?

Wait.

It was none of my business. The old me would be bursting with curiosity, the need to know.

Okay, the new me was too.

I had a feeling it would take quite some time to change such ingrained personality traits.

At a T in the hallway, I turned right. Down this way, there were several offices, including Willie's.

My father would have called Willie smarmy. I would have agreed with him.

The door was wide open, the lights off. What would it hurt to look around?

I moseyed to Willie's desk to have a little look-see. A framed wedding picture of him and Genevieve sat catty-cornered, almost teetering off the edge. I wondered if Willie knew how friendly his wife had been with Carson Keyes—who had a very nice head of hair *and* nice teeth.

If I were Willie, I'd be worried.

Maybe not as worried about that as hearing his wife had received a death threat . . .

Had it been her first?

None of my business, I reminded myself.

I reached for the frame, but froze when I heard something.

Dropping to the ground, I crouched beneath the desk, keeping out of sight.

After a heart-pounding minute, I realized voices were coming from the private bathroom behind me.

I duck-walked closer, curious. I listened but couldn't tell who was in there, just that there were two of them. Male and female.

The thick wool carpet absorbed my footsteps as I inched toward the door, my thighs burning. I peeked through the crack.

Genevieve.

Doing what she damn well pleased.

With Thad Cochran.

Naked.

Two

"Are you sure it was Genevieve and Thad? Not Carson Keyes?"

"It was Thad all right. I'd have recognized that dimple anywhere. What a phony he is! You know," I pointed out impatiently, "the gas pedal is on the right."

"You've been driving too much with Maria and Ana."

Maria, my sister. Ana, my cousin. Both drove like hyped-up six-year-olds on a go-cart track. Their car insurance premiums were sky-high and both were on a first name basis with "Rock" from Dollie's Auto Body. I think Ana even dated Rock once, which wasn't saying much, because Ana dated everyone.

I fiddled with the radio, stopped on a John Denver song.

Bobby's eyebrow arched.

"What?"

"John Denver?"

"There's nothing wrong with John Denver."

He laughed, then reverted back to our conversation. "If you want some excitement, I'll take you out on my Harley some time."

My seat belt nearly strangled me as I turned in my seat. "You have a Harley?"

The blinker on the dash flickered as he changed lanes. "There's a lot you don't know about me."

Mr. Boy-Next-Door Bobby MacKenna had a bad boy side? This I had to hear, because I didn't believe it for a second. "Like what?"

"Maybe you'll never know." He smiled, lips closed. It caused a dimple to pop out near the curve of his cheek. It reminded me of Thad's Michael Douglas cleft.

"I can't believe I fell for Thad's Mr. Good Guy act. I'm so disappointed in him. It's like, like . . . " I motioned to the radio. "Like finding out John Denver cheated on Annie."

"John Denver did cheat on Annie."

I gasped. "Really?"

Bobby nodded. "That's what I heard."

"I'm depressed now."

"I can cheer you up," he said softly.

My blood pressure spiked. I chose to ignore him for the sake of my sanity.

Traffic on 75 north slowed near the Jim Beam plant. A drink would have been nice right about now. The old me wouldn't have thought so, but the new me was making strides.

I picked lint off my dark pants. "You know me a little better than Thad does."

"A lot better."

"I am not sleeping with you."

"Did I ask?" He grinned again. Damn that dimple.

"Well, no."

"Then what are you getting so worked up about?"

I powered down the window, letting the autumn air cool me down.

He laughed. "You'll cave."

The subject needed to be reestablished immediately. "Genevieve certainly didn't seem too worried about that death threat."

"Maybe Thad was consoling her."

I laughed. "Gives new meaning to consolation prize."

Bobby smirked. "Or . . . "

"What?"

"What happens if Carson Keyes reports that new hostess Genevieve Hidalgo Sala received a death threat on the set of *Hitched or Ditched*?"

Shifting in my seat, I took a good look at him. "Ratings for *Hitched or Ditched* go through the roof, just in time to ink the deal with the major network."

"Exactly."

Traffic slowed to a crawl near the Lockland Split. I took a deep breath. "Do you think Genevieve's that manipulative?"

"Without a doubt."

"It would explain about her not wanting the cops involved too."

Bobby nodded. "I think, as Genevieve said, we should just mind our own business where she's concerned, and stay out of it."

"Do you think Genevieve and Thad sleeping together affects Josh's case at all?"

Bobby glanced at me. "Maybe. Maybe not. I'm not sure what Josh is hoping for us to accomplish. I can't imagine we'll learn anything in a week."

"Perry seemed to know a lot. I can probably get more information from him."

"Louisa didn't seem to mind telling me about Willie Sala's bad marriage. Seems Genevieve and Willie have been fighting a lot these days. I'll see what else I can get out of her."

I didn't like the sounds of that last sentence. "Louisa?"

"The production assistant. The cute one with the brown eyes, long blonde curly hair, nice lips."

The one that had been eyeballing him during the meeting. I grit my teeth, trying not to be insanely jealous because he thought she was cute. *I* was very sure she was a no-good tramp. "She must hear everything."

He smiled as if knowing, just knowing, what he was doing to me. "I have to tell you, this is a lot more fun than new teacher meetings and planning sessions."

"Don't go turning all Frank Hardy on me."

"Tell the truth, you had a poster of Shaun Cassidy on your wall as a kid."

"Two," I said, laughing. "Maria had three."

He turned serious, his lips thinning, his eyes narrowing.

"What?" I asked.

"That. Your laugh. I've missed it."

"Oh." Deep breath. *Take a deep breath, Nina.* I could handle the joking, the teasing. It was these brief moments of seriousness I had trouble with.

Bobby exited the highway at Tylersville, turned right. "I'll call Josh in the morning, let him know what we've turned up so far. Did Willie hit on you at all? That would help solidify Josh's case."

I accepted *his* change of subject. HoD was safe ground. "Nope. Not a single person did."

"You sound depressed about that."

Fiddling with the radio, I pretended to pout. "It hurts a girl's ego, you know."

He laughed as he turned onto my street, the heart of the Mill, aka the Gossip Mill, located on the outskirts of Freedom, Ohio.

Maple tree branches heavy with fire engine red leaves canopied the street, shading it from the late afternoon October sun.

A brand new FOR SALE sign sat in the yard across the street from my house. The previous owner had died during the summer, a tragic accident.

"You have company," Bobby said.

I wasn't surprised. I always had company.

My mother's car sat in my driveway.

Celeste Madeline Chambeau Ceceri had been around a lot lately. She was in charge of the reconstruction of my house, since the renovation of my bathroom—a gift from her—had sent my second floor plummeting through the ceiling onto the first floor.

That had been months ago, and à la Humpty Dumpty, my house still wasn't put back together again.

My front door opened and my mother waved. "I've made dinner!"

Inside, she kissed our cheeks. "Do tell everything!" she gushed. "Did you meet that dreamy Thad Cochran? Is he just as cute in person as he is on TV? He's just so . . . *Sigh.*"

She'd scratch Genevieve Sala's eyes out if she knew. "He's something. Where's Dad?" I asked, hooking my backpack purse on the rack near the cat clock with the creepy eyes and swaying tail. The clock had been a gift from my stepson Riley years ago, and I didn't dare part with it even though it gave me the heebies.

"Late class."

My father, a retired history professor, recently went back to work, teaching part-time at Freedom Community College.

He says because retirement was boring.

My gut says it was to keep from killing my mother. She was a lot to handle 24/7.

Bobby pulled out a counter stool, sat, poked at the grapes sitting in a Tupperware bowl on the island.

"Honestly, *chérie*, I couldn't be happier. He drove me crazy being at home all day. I need my space."

"*Your* space." I laughed.

She gave me the Ceceri Evil Eye. "Yes, my space. I've been working on Tam's baby shower. I haven't the time to baby-sit your father."

Plucking a grape from the stem, I said, "I don't think Tam wants a baby shower." Tam Oliver, my right-hand woman at work, wasn't big on surprises. In fact, she hated them. "The baby's already seven weeks old. She probably already has what she needs."

"*Pah.* She'll love it."

I wasn't so sure.

As my mother dished out chicken alfredo, she caught me staring at the huge hole in my living room ceiling.

It was hard to miss. The contractor had to widen the original gap to fix the second floor floorboards. A job that was supposed to take two weeks. It had been almost eight now.

"The crew will be here in the morning with the drywall," she said.

"I'll believe it when I see it."

She turned, but I could have sworn I heard her mutter, "Me too."

Never a good sign.

I looked at my plate with longing.

"Eat," she urged.

"I shouldn't. It's pasta."

"And?"

"I'm on a low-carb diet."

"You, *chérie*, do not need a diet."

"Really? Look at this." I grabbed a love handle, jiggled.

She gasped. "Where'd *that* come from?"

I'd eaten a lot in the month before I'd sunk to the depths of self-discovery. "Cookie dough."

Eyes wide, she snatched my plate, scraped my food into the garbage disposal. "I'll make you a salad."

Bobby leaned over, whispered, "You look great. Better than ever."

"You've been in the sun too much."

"We could always skip dinner," he whispered in my ear. "Go straight to dessert."

All I could think about was cookies and how long it had been since I'd had one.

My cheeks flushed. Skipping dinner suddenly sounded like a great idea. I caught his eye. He winked.

I caved. "Mom—"

"Yes, *chérie?*"

The back door opened and Riley marched in, my ex-husband Kevin on his heels.

Drats! "Never mind."

Bobby jabbed his fork into his pasta.

I plucked another grape. "You two are home early."

Grunting, Riley headed upstairs.

It had been almost seven months since I'd found lipstick on Kevin's boxers—a shade that wasn't mine. He'd moved out, but left behind the one thing I really cared about: fifteen-year-old Riley. It'd had been Kevin's idea to have Riley live with me, but it had been Riley's decision, which made me happier than I could put into words. We had our moments of strife, but overall, we'd been getting along great.

On the whole, I was a decent stepmom. Riley's mother had died when he was a toddler, and I knew he still missed her each and every day. As much as my mother annoyed me on occasion, I couldn't imagine life without her—so I could only imagine the pain Riley had been through in his young life.

"Smells good," Kevin said to my mother as if he was still her son-in-law.

"Hmmph," my mother said. She still hadn't forgiven him for cheating on me.

I'd come to terms with it, and had even kinda-sorta begun to think we could rekindle a friendship, which was why he was allowed to come into the house without knocking. Well, when he was with Riley.

Much to my dismay, Kevin and Bobby *had* become friends. Friendlier on Kevin's part since Bobby had moved.

"Since he's home, does Riley know how to play cribbage?" she asked me. "I need to learn if I'm ever going to beat Donatelli at the weekly match. A couple hours of practice should do it." Donatelli Cabrera, my next door neighbor and quasi-grandfather. He was known for his ability to ferret out the littlest piece of gossip and dole it out at the Mill's weekly cribbage game like penny candy. "Just how late are you planning on staying?" I asked.

She shook a ladle at me. "Are you trying to get rid of your mama?"

"I'd never!" I forked a tomato, stared at it. Blah.

"That's what I thought."

"Where's Tony?" Kevin asked her, scooping chicken alfredo onto a plate.

I took the plate away from him. There were still some limits to our friendship. "*You're* not staying."

"Hmmph," he said.

Bobby eyed the phone. "I should probably check on my grandfather."

"Oh!" my mom cried. "How's Mac doing? I haven't spoken to him in a couple of days. How's Jasmine?"

Jasmine was the nurse my mother had found to help care for Mac during his rehabilitation.

"She's great, but she quit yesterday."

My mother looked horrified. "Quit?"

"Mac likes to touch."

My mother's cheek twitched. A nervous tic.

"But I'm checking into homes for him. At eighty-five, a bad hip, and no nearby relatives, it's time."

Looking longingly at the pasta, Kevin said, "Tell him his twenty bucks is in the mail."

"Football?" Bobby asked.

Kevin nodded.

"You should never bet against Mac."

"I know that now. You could have warned me before."

I looked between the two of them. "You know Mac?" I said to Kevin.

"From way back."

"What's that supposed to mean?"

My mother cut into the conversation—she never liked

being left out for long. "Tony's at school," she said, giving Kevin back his plate. She shrugged at me. "We can't let him starve."

Kevin grinned while I said, "Yes, we can."

"Manners, *chérie*."

I speared a cucumber and gritted my teeth.

"School?" Kevin repeated.

"Teaching part-time." Mom ladled another scoop of sauce on his plate.

I grinned. "Because Mom needs her space."

Kevin's fork stopped in midair. "*Her* space?"

"Exactly," I said.

My mother gave us both the evil eye.

Smiling, Bobby buttered a roll and kept quiet.

Butter. Rolls. *Mmmm.*

Dieting sucked.

"Why's Riley in a mood?" I asked.

Kevin twirled linguine. "I had to bail on dinner."

Now that I really looked at him, I noticed dark circles hung like half-moons under his green eyes. He looked horrible. Pale skin, bloodshot eyes, wild hair. I wondered what was so important that he'd ditch Riley, but figured I didn't have the right to ask since our divorce.

"I got called in for duty tonight," he said, as if he were now the Amazing Kreskin.

I wondered if all my thoughts were so transparent. That wouldn't be so good. I glanced at Bobby. Nope, not good at all.

"Who died?" my mother asked, sounding suspiciously like my cousin Ana, who had a morbid fascination with death. Ana loved hanging out with Kevin, a homicide detective.

"No one that I know of," Kevin said, his mouth full. "I've been doing a little undercover work."

Hah. That's what he told me when he'd actually been cheating with his partner, Ginger Ho. Er, Barlow. Detective Ginger Barlow. I wondered if karma was coming back around to kick her in the patooski.

"Hey," I said to him. "Hypothetical question. If someone should receive a death threat and doesn't want to call the police, should witnesses call?"

Both Kevin's eyebrows arched and his fork stopped halfway to his mouth, then fell out of his fingers. It landed on his plate with a clatter as he leaned back, eyed me. "Nina . . . "

"What?" I said. "It's hypothetical."

"Who got a death threat?" my mother cried. "Not Thad!"

"Hypothetical," I singsonged.

"Not you!" My mother came around the counter, pulled me into a bear hug.

"Can't. Breathe."

She let me go.

"It's not me. It's hypothetical." Everyone looked at me. "Okay! Genevieve Sala got one, but she doesn't want to go to the police, and we're not sure if she sent it to herself for ratings."

"Genevieve who?" my mother asked.

"The new hostess of *Hitched or Ditched*," Bobby said, leaning against the counter.

"I didn't know the show had a new hostess," she said.

"Me either," Kevin said. "And actually how are you involved with that show?"

Uh-oh.

"They're on it!" My mother grinned. "Isn't that great?"

"Wonderful," Kevin said, shoving his plate aside.

I didn't think now was the time to get into the whole undercover thing with him, and I was going to kill my mother for making it seem as though we were real contestants when she knew quite well we weren't.

"So?" I said to him.

He knew what I was talking about. "If she won't go to the police, there's nothing much we can do."

"Maybe that's what she's hoping for. If news leaks out to the media, ratings will soar."

"You really think it's for ratings?" my mother asked.

I nodded.

"That's brilliant!"

It really was. However, if anyone found out what Genevieve had done, it could be the end of the network deal.

"What if it's not fake?" Kevin asked.

My mother made the sign of the cross even though she hadn't set foot in a church in over thirty years.

I was saved from answering as the back door swung open and Mr. Cabrera hobbled in, carrying a poker chip carousel. He was still recovering from a recent broken ankle, and despite the chill, he wore a short-sleeved, button-down collared shirt covered in swans that, with beaks together, created a heart shape. His on-off girlfriend, my nemesis, Brickhouse Krauss, had bought it for him. She strode in behind him. Right now they were on again.

"Donatelli! Ursula! Glad you could make it." My mother dished up two more plates. "Where's the cribbage board?"

Mr. Cabrera shook Kevin's and Bobby's hands, kissed my cheek, and sat on a stool at the end of the kitchen island.

"Cribbage is so yesterday," he said, sounding like he'd been hanging out with Riley too much, which was true. Riley adored the old man.

Brickhouse sat down next to him, clucked. She did that a lot—clucked. Like a stout, German, brick-shaped chicken.

"Donatelli's been on a Hold 'em kick for a week now," she said.

"Riley's been teaching me." Mr. Cabrera poured two glasses of white wine.

Wine? There was wine around, and I hadn't self-medicated yet?

"Pass me that, would you?" I said to Mr. Cabrera, not caring if it was on my diet or not. Priorities and all.

"Riley's playing poker?" Kevin asked, sounding worried.

"Mostly on his computer." I filled a wineglass to the rim.

Bobby took the bottle from me and filled himself a glass as well.

Kevin's eyebrows dipped. "Not for money, I hope."

"Nah," Mr. Cabrera said around a mouthful of pasta. "I'd have heard about that."

Brickhouse clucked. "He would. Nosiest man I know."

"Hey!"

She patted his arm. "Said in love, pookie."

I tried not to toss my . . . tomato.

Brickhouse and I had a . . . strained relationship. She'd been my high school English teacher, and we'd hated each other.

I'd done a mini makeover of her landominium's backyard last spring and kinda-sorta set her up with Mr. Cabrera, who kinda-sorta had a way with women.

Meaning he usually killed them.

Not on purpose, of course. He was cursed—his girlfriends all seemed to die while dating him. Usually of natural causes. Most recently from a tragic accident. Only Brickhouse seemed immune to the curse, in fact only becoming sick when she wasn't dating Mr. Cabrera.

Brickhouse had also been helping me out at work, filling in for Tam while she was out on maternity leave. Now that Tam was back at work part-time, Brickhouse worked for me a couple of days a week.

Dare I say I was getting used to having her around?

I daren't. I'd need a few more glasses of wine before I'd lose my mind like that.

"I need to get going." Bobby set his empty glass on the island.

"Me too." Kevin stood.

I kept my glass with me. "I'll walk you out."

"Aww, that's so sweet of you," Kevin said. "And here I thought I might not be welcome anymore."

"Not you," I growled.

He grinned.

"Where's the kid?" Mr. Cabrera said. "Maybe he wants to play some poker with us."

"Upstairs." I headed toward the front door, trying to keep up with Bobby, who suddenly decided he wanted to sprint.

"Tell me the truth," I said, hugging my wineglass. "You moved to Florida to get away from my family."

"Your family's great," he said as Mr. Cabrera's footsteps echoed on the hardwood stairs behind us.

They were pains in my tuchkus, my family, but I loved them. "You can borrow them any time you want."

"I'll trade you for Mac."

"Um, thanks but no thanks." Mac was a geriatric handful.

"That's what I thought." His gaze dropped to my lips, but he didn't lean in. After a second he turned and started down the front steps.

I wasn't disappointed. I wasn't.

Okay, I was.

I watched as he got in his car and drove away.

"Trouble?" Kevin asked from behind me.

Turning, I glared at him. I was a good glarer-er—I'd learned it from my mother. "Don't start."

Mr. Cabrera came downstairs. Riley came down behind him wearing a plastic red visor and enormous dark sunglasses.

He grinned bigger than my mother every Bastille Day and shuffled cards between his hands like he'd been born at the MGM Grand. "Let's shuffle up and deal!" He strolled into the kitchen.

I looked at Kevin. He looked at me. I think we were both

seeing Riley in prison stripes playing a peanut game with a cellmate named Rosie.

"You were saying something about trouble?" I asked.

Kevin rolled his eyes but couldn't stop the grin. "Don't start."

Three

"Did you sleep with him yet?"

Leave it to my cousin Ana, who also happened to be my best friend, to get straight to the point. I sat at my desk, played Spider Solitaire with one hand and held the phone with the other. "No."

"Wow. You've lasted longer than I thought you would."

"Thanks for the vote of support."

"Look, Nina, I love you to pieces, but depriving yourself of a man, and not just any man, but Bobby 'Hubba Hubba' MacKenna? That's just crazy."

I couldn't help but smile. "How's Dr. Feelgood?"

My gaze wandered over to the twosome sitting across from me. Watching. Filming. It was unnerving to say the least. I was supposed to pretend they weren't there, to speak only when spoken to. I had to wonder what they were thinking, and if anyone cared about this phone call or whether I won a computer game.

Nelson Kunkle was the name of my cameraman, Roxie Lewis my field producer. Roxie looked to be in her midtwenties. She was a bit on the chubby side, had her red hair cut Peter Pan style, and wore blue framed glasses that accentuated her bright blue eyes. Nelson, "Call me Nels," reminded me of the candlestick from *Beauty and the Beast*.

Tall, skinny, big lips, big eyebrows, and close-set eyes.

I fought off a yawn. I'd been up late watching Carson Keyes's report on Genevieve's death threat and how he was the only reporter behind the scenes, so stay tuned all week.

Then I'd lain in my sofa bed, pondering (a) when I was going to get my bedroom back; (b) whether Genevieve's death threat was real; (c) if it was a valid threat, then who had sent it; and (d) if I was strong enough to keep my hands off Bobby this week. I'd barely gotten any sleep.

"I wish you'd stop calling him that," Ana said. "His name is Johan."

I knew his name. He'd treated Riley's sprained wrist over the summer and had been permanently attached to Ana ever since.

It was time for an amputation, in my opinion. He was much too needy. I'd barely spent any time with my cousin at all lately.

Talk about needy.

This is what self-discovery had come to.

"Well?" I said.

She sighed. I could hear noise in the background—Ana was a probation officer and had a tiny cubicle in a small office at the courthouse. Things could get pretty rowdy once in a while. "We broke up."

"Really?"

"You don't have to sound so excited by it."

"Me? Excited? Nev—"

"I know you didn't like him."

"Like, shmike. It's not my place—"

"You're such a crappy liar." I heard the smile in her voice.

"I know. What happened?"

Her long drawn-out sigh came across the line. "Whenever I was naked I felt like he was examining me with his eyes. You know, checking my moles and stuff like that."

"So he definitely had to go."

"Definitely. If he's looking at moles instead of other things, it wasn't going to work."

I could see how that would irritate.

"How about a movie tonight?" she asked.

"Can't. I'll be down at the HoD studio."

"That's right! You're a stahh! Are the camera people there?"

"Sitting right across from me." I lost my hand of Spider Solitaire. I cursed under my breath and clicked out of it.

"How weird is that?"

"Weird. Want to come tonight?" I asked.

"And meet Thad Cochran! Yes!"

I'd have to warn her about Thad. "Better yet, you'll meet Carson Keyes."

Roxie perked up, took notes. I could imagine the editing needing to happen before tonight's eleven o'clock airing of the show.

When Ana didn't say anything, I started to worry we'd been cut off. "Ana? You there?"

She sighed heavily. "Carson Keyes? Seriously?"

"Yep. He's doing a week-long piece on the show."

She started coughing. Wheezing.

"You okay?"

"Just . . . an asthma . . . attack."

"You don't have asthma."

In a stage whisper she said, "I've got to get my hair done. Carson Keyes. Whoo-eee."

So much for any heartbreak over Dr. Feelgood.

"Oh!" Ana added, "make sure they don't air you saying that asthma part, okay? I could get fired."

I looked at Roxie. "Ana asks that you don't use that last part, my asthma comment."

Roxie gave me a thumbs-up.

"I'll pick you up at five," I told Ana.

"I can drive."

"No!"

"Fine. Oh!" She coughed. "I'm sending someone over later on today. Sweet kid."

"I don't need anyone, Ana. It's almost winter—"

"Just humor me," she said, and clicked off.

All but three of my employees had been "sent over" by Ana. They were a great group, criminal backgrounds and all. Honestly, I don't know what I'd do without them.

There had been some changes at TBS in the last month. I'd cut back on the workload, sticking solely to one major makeover a week and one mini per week. Business had picked up so fast over the last year I found I couldn't keep up. It was too much. Everyone had been overworked and overextended. Rather than expanding the company, I'd opted to cut back on my projects, though I did have a side project in mind for Deanna Parks, a high-energy, up-and-coming designer who had worked for me a couple of years now. Overall, I wanted to keep my small business small.

The new schedule had been working out great. I'd hired two new part-time contractors to help out Kit Pipe, my overworked head foreman. He'd been enjoying having his own little crew. And of course, I still occasionally hired out, mostly to Ignacio Martinez, a floating contractor who provided a team of manual laborers when the going got tough.

Unfortunately, business was going to drop off soon due to the weather. I had outdoor projects lined up through the middle of November, and several indoor designs planned throughout the colder months. My full-timers would stay on, but my part-timers would only work on an as-needed basis.

Until winter kicked in, I'd keep everyone around. There was always a lot of preparation to do for spring—maintenance on the tools, the equipment, things of that nature.

"When do people start coming in?" Roxie asked.

"On Mondays? Around nine or so."

"Is it true all your employees are ex-cons?"

"Not all." I opened the bottom drawer of my desk in need of a chocolate fix, despite my diet. Or maybe because of it.

I stared into the empty drawer.

No Almond Joys.

Ever since I'd met Bobby last spring, he'd been sending me my favorite candy bar. Right up until he left for Florida.

Breaking up sucked.

"Harvey and Shay have clean records, and as far as I know Ursula Krauss hasn't been arrested for anything. Yet." Shay Oshwalter and Harvey Goosey were the new hires. They'd fast become Kit groupies. It was hard not to—Kit had a way about him.

"Ursula Krauss?"

"To know her is to love her," I said. "You'll meet her on Wednesday. She works for me part-time, two days a week."

"But everyone else?" Roxie said.

I shrugged.

"That's seven people out of ten."

"I believe in second chances."

"Oh, that's good. That last part will be a good sound bite." She jotted something in a small spiral bound notebook. "You got that, right?" she asked Nels.

"Right." Nels dropped the camera from his eye. "Is it always this boring around here?"

I smiled. "No. Enjoy it while it lasts."

He looked like he didn't believe me. Poor guy.

I double-checked my schedule for the day. Office meeting at nine-thirty, then a finalization meeting with Pippi Lowther at eleven-thirty. The rest of the afternoon was fairly free, though I hoped to have a much needed conversation with Deanna.

The chimes on the front door rang out. "Hello! Anyone

here? Well, of course there's someone here, the door's un-locked, and the lights are on! Nina?"

Speak of the devil. I looked at the camera. "Deanna Parks."

Deanna appeared in the doorway, looking young and fresh, with her blonde hair loosely pulled back, full make-up, and a cute little knee-length pencil skirt and beautiful cashmere wrap sweater.

"Oh!" she said. "I forgot about the filming."

My foot.

"I brought doughnuts!"

I noticed Nels sat a little straighter. I hoped because Deanna was adorable, and not for the doughnuts.

Though *I'd* perked right up at the smell. My stomach growled. Maybe I could self-discover without being on a diet.

Then I looked down and saw the tummy roll hanging over my jeans. I tried to suck it in, but it didn't budge.

I really needed to go shopping for some looser shirts.

Or actually start exercising.

"Ready for the meeting?" Deanna asked.

"Not yet. Still waiting for the others."

"Where's Tam?" Deanna asked, mugging for the camera.

"Don't know." I came around my desk. Out in the recep-tion area, I checked the calendar on Tam's workspace. She was supposed to be in at seven-thirty. I hoped everything was okay. Tam was usually the first one in, the last one out.

"Want me to call her?" Deanna asked.

"Not yet. We'll give her some time."

"I'm going to put these delicious Krispy Kreme dough-nuts in the conference room," she said into the camera as if doing a commercial spot.

I tried not to laugh—or to whimper. I bet there was a glazed doughnut in that box . . . "Oh," I said to her. "Can I have some time with you this afternoon?"

Panic widened Deanna's eyes. "With me?"

"Yes."

"Why?"

"I just have some ideas I want to run by you."

The fear fled from her eyes, replaced with curiosity. "I have a meeting with Derrick Brandt at the nursery, but should be back by three. I can stick around till four at the latest, but then I have to pick up Lucah at day care."

"Three's fine. Shouldn't take too long."

Kit sauntered in, the chimes jangling his arrival.

Roxie backed up, whether in fear or because Kit's six-foot-five, 250-pound frame took up a lot of room, I wasn't sure.

Despite his somewhat unconventional looks and line-backer height and weight, Kit had a boy-next-door kind of face. Except for now. Now it looked like a serial-killer-next-door kind of face.

He glared into the camera, narrowing his eyes. I fully expected a growl out of him, like one of those WWE wrestlers.

"Kit, this is Roxie and Nels, the *Hitched or Ditched* people."

"Pleasure," he mumbled.

Roxie took another step back. Kit usually had a way with women, but today he seemed grumpy. Not his normal self at all.

I took a good look at him. "What's wrong with you?"

My peripheral vision caught Nels circling, his large camera perched on his shoulder. There were no state of the art cameras for HoD, no fancy fluffy booms, no frills.

"Nothing," he growled.

"Pale. Dark circles. Looks like you lost some weight." I stood on tiptoes and pressed my palm to his forehead. "No fever."

"He's *lost* weight?" Roxie whispered in shock.

Kit glared some more, and she took another step back. He lowered my hand. "I'm not sick."

"What's wrong, then?"

Shaking his head, he scowled. The skull tattoo on his bald head glistened.

All right. I'd let it go.

"Tam called my cell," he said. "She's not coming in. Baby's got the sniffles."

Why hadn't Tam called me? I made a mental note to call her, to check on baby Nic, my somewhat namesake. Her "Nicolette" was derived from my middle name, Colette. After a rocky final trimester, Nic had been born a healthy seven pounds, six ounces, and was now seven weeks old. I wondered if Tam knew about the party my mother was planning. I figured she did. There was little Tam didn't know about around here.

"I should probably call Ursula to fill in." Oddly, I felt no dread about it.

Was I getting used to having Brickhouse around?

What was the world coming to?

Kit leaned on the edge of the desk, eyeing Roxie. "I already spoke to her."

Roxie frantically pointed at me, trying to redirect his attention away from the camera.

"You're supposed to look natural," I told him.

Kit grinned, which made him look somewhat healthier. Somewhat.

The chimes on the front door clanged as it slammed open. A big black four-legged drooling blur barreled down on me.

I braced myself; Roxie screamed and jumped on Tam's desk; Nels cursed; and Kit just kept on grinning.

I was glad to see he was feeling better—just in time for me to kill him.

BeBe, Kit's English mastiff, jumped into my arms, crushed me against the water cooler, and slurped my face with her big drool-covered doggy tongue.

"Gross," Nels said from where he'd taken cover beside the water cooler.

"That's disgusting," Roxie echoed.

Kit whistled sharply, and BeBe abandoned me. She dropped to his feet, her tail thrashing against his leg. Anyone else would have been on their ass.

Ursula "Brickhouse" Krauss stood in the doorway, leash in hand, smiling like a short, white-haired, brick-shaped German Wicked Witch of the West. Only with a cluck instead of a cackle.

I looked between her and Kit, wiped the slime from my face and said, "Do I want to know why BeBe's here? Haven't we already gone through this?"

BeBe was a great dog, but she wasn't supposed to be there. At work.

Drooling on me.

"Ach," Brickhouse said. "She's a good girl. Aren't you, my good little schnitzel?"

BeBe wagged her tail so hard, I was sure Kit would be bruised tomorrow.

"See?" Brickhouse said to me.

I glared at Kit.

"Ursula dogsits for me a couple times a week." He bent over, like a giant sequoia toppling, and flopped BeBe's ears back and forth. "Since she's filling in for Tam—"

"You dogsit?" How come I didn't know about this?

"Three days a week." Brickhouse wagged a finger, much like BeBe wagged her tail. "Today is one of those days. So, if you want me to fill in for Tam, you must take BeBe also."

"Is that a dog?" Roxie asked, climbing down from the desk. Good thing Tam wasn't there. Claws would've flown for sure—Tam is highly territorial about her space. I checked to make sure Sassy, Tam's prized African violet, was okay. She was, basking under a heat lamp set to go on and off throughout the day so Sassy received the proper amount of light.

Kit grinned. "She bites."

Roxie darted behind Nels.

"Oh, she does not!" I said. "BeBe is a good . . . dog." I refused to say the word "schnitzel."

"The meeting?" Deanna reminded from the conference room doorway. "We've got to go over the Towle project, and Nina," she looked at her watch, "you need to leave in ninety minutes to finalize plans with Pippi." For all her nuttiness, Deanna was a stickler for details and time management.

Thank goodness one of us was. It was one of the reasons why I needed to talk to her this afternoon. She was perfect for the job I had in mind.

"We'll be right in," I said.

BeBe's tail thumped happily. I patted her head. "All right. She can stay. But just for today. If Tam's still out tomorrow, then you'll have to find a doggy day care, or leave her with Daisy."

Kit's eyes had been tattooed with dark liner years ago. At the mention of Daisy's name, they narrowed into thin black slits.

I raised an eyebrow. "Not Daisy?"

"Who's Daisy?" Roxie asked, stepping forward, notebook in hand.

"Who're you?" Brickhouse poked Roxie's arm.

"Hey!" She swatted Brickhouse's hand. "No touching."

BeBe growled and lurched to her feet. Brickhouse thumped her back. "That's my good schnitzel."

Roxie took a step back. "Is . . . is she dangerous?"

I looked at Brickhouse. "Very."

"No, not her! The dog!"

"Oh, I think you have more to worry about with Mrs. Krauss."

Brickhouse clucked in agreement.

Roxie stepped back. Smart girl. I made introductions as the phone rang.

Brickhouse answered it. "Hold on one second," she said to the caller. "Kit? Daisy."

Kit growled. He really was grumpy today, and call me Kreskin, but I had the feeling it had to do with Daisy.

Daisy was Kit's live-in girlfriend. If not for the phone calls and occasional hickey on Kit's neck, I'd wonder if she truly existed. Not one of us had ever met her.

Roxie backed off, held up a palm in surrender. "Later. Later is fine."

Brickhouse held out the phone. Kit shook his head. "Sorry," she said, "he's in a meeting right now . . . "

"So, Daisy?" I said to him.

"Not now, Nina."

"Meeting, people?" Deanna tapped a foot, but managed to smile for the camera. "We don't have all day!"

"Coming," I said.

Marty came into the office, looked at the camera, ducked his head and headed straight for the conference room.

"Who was that?" Roxie asked.

"Marty Johnson."

She jotted something else in that notebook of hers. I could only imagine what.

"Bored?" I asked Nels.

"Exhausted."

I smiled. "Welcome to my world."

As Kit and I sat down at the conference table, Deanna said, "I'm so glad you're back together with Bobby."

Wistfully I stared at the doughnut box.

She gushed. "He's so dreamy!"

Did she realize the camera wasn't on?

"Yeah, *dreamy*," Marty mocked her.

She threw a pencil at his head.

Definitely never boring around here.

At work, only Kit, Brickhouse, and Tam (because she finds out everything anyway) knew about the charade. Everyone else thought Bobby and I were back together.

"Yeah," Kit said, waggling his eyebrows. "The way he looks at you . . . He's so in loooove."

"Oh, that's good," Roxie said from the doorway. "Did you get that?" she asked Nels.

Please no, please no, please no.

Nels nodded. "Yep."

Ah, screw it. I reached for a doughnut.

Four

Our meeting ran late, but everything looked to be on track for the mini makeover at Lowther House, a très upscale retirement home in nearby Lebanon. I packed up my design boards, and was feeling guilty about the two doughnuts I'd scoffed down.

Maybe I would start exercising. How bad could it be? I enjoyed gym class as a kid, and loved playing soccer and volleyball while in high school. I could huff and puff my way to a toned body again, but knew I didn't have the motivation to do it on my own.

I found Kit hunched over his desk, scowling at paperwork.

Over my shoulder I spotted Nels raiding the fridge. Roxie was off trying to figure out who Daisy was.

The coast was clear.

"I'm thinking about exercising, Kit."

He didn't even look up. "You?"

"Yes, me."

I dropped into the chair across from his desk. He shared an office with Deanna, but she was still in the conference room. I was excited to talk to her later—I hoped she was open to my idea.

"I've put on a few pounds in the last month," I explained.

"You say?" he said in a way that made me think he'd noticed. "How few?"

"Ten."

Okay, it was fifteen, but who was counting?

"So, really fifteen?"

"I hate you."

He finally looked up, laughed. "You want the name of my trainer?"

"I was hoping."

"His name is Duke."

"Is that his first or last name?"

"People don't ask him questions like that." He jotted down a phone number, handed it to me. "I'll give him a call, let him know you'll be getting in touch. And good luck," he added. "You'll need it."

"Why?"

"You'll see."

Suddenly I didn't want to exercise anymore, but then I remembered the doughnuts.

"Well, okay then. Thanks." I left him in his office, wandered back into mine and plopped into my chair. I was worried about Kit. There was such sadness in his eyes.

Nels sat down across from me as the TBS line rang. I heard Brickhouse pick it up, mumble a few words, then disconnect with a polite, "Have a good day."

She was never that polite to me.

My office was suddenly filled with the sounds of Madonna's "Like a Virgin."

Nels shot me a question with his eyes.

"My cell phone." I rummaged through my backpack for it. "Interesting ring tone."

"My cousin Ana has a sick sense of humor. She programmed it, and I don't know how to change it. Do you?"

Rather evilly, he smiled. "Nope."

I didn't believe him for a minute. Or Riley either, who'd said the same thing. One of these days I was going to find the time to stop by the kiosk at the mall where I'd gotten the phone and have someone fix it.

I finally located my phone at the bottom of my backpack, shut Madonna up by flipping it open.

"Is Carson Keyes single?" Ana asked without waiting for me to say hello.

"I don't know. He isn't married. Well, he doesn't wear a ring."

She tsked. "Well, even if he was it's not like that's stopped me before."

"True."

"A little more off the bottom," Ana said. "I'm feeling frisky today."

"What?"

"Not you. Angie."

I pushed papers aside, picked up my pen and started doodling on my blotter. "Angie?"

"Only the best hairdresser in the world."

"Oh."

"And thanks for not commenting on that frisky part."

Out of the corner of my eye I saw that Brickhouse was now standing next to Nels. "Hold on," I said to Ana.

Brickhouse clucked. "That was Pippi Lowther on the phone. She needs to cancel today. I rescheduled for tomorrow afternoon. Someone died."

"What?"

"At Lowther House."

"Oh." I didn't know any of the residents. "Thanks for letting me know."

I held the phone between my ear and my shoulder and jotted *Pippi* on my desk calendar for tomorrow. Right next to *Perry*. I'd have to call and cancel my appointment with him. "Ana?"

"Did I hear that someone died?"

"Don't get excited. It was just one of the residents of the retirement home where I'm doing a mini."

"Was it murder?"

"I doubt it. People there are old. Old people die. Naturally."

"Or it's made to look natural."

"I gotta go," I said before she could launch into a history of famous serial killers.

"Just keep an eye out when you're there."

"Good-bye!"

Glancing down at the blotter, I spotted Perry's name again . . . And my afternoon was suddenly free. I grabbed my phone.

A perky receptionist at Azure answered. "I'm sorry," she said, "but our stylists aren't allowed to accept calls. Do you wish to leave a message?"

"Do you know if he has any appointments open for this afternoon? Can you ask him? Tell him it's for Nina?"

"I'm not sure . . . "

"Please? If you could see my hair you'd understand."

"Please hold." Every woman understood bad hair days. Or years, as was apparently my case.

A second later she came back on the line. "He says to come in as soon as possible."

I glanced at the clock. "I'll be there in twenty minutes."

"Do you drive like that all the time?" Roxie clung to her little notebook. Her pale skin had lost all hint of color.

"Are you going to be okay?"

"Need to sit down."

I helped her into a chair in Azure's reception area. I noticed two men sitting near the Wi-Fi table. One had a camera just like Nels's.

Nels spotted them too. "What are you doing here, George, Joe?"

"George? Joe?" I asked.

"They work for *Hitched or Ditched* too."

"Ah." That made sense. They were probably Perry's team.

"Working," the cameraman said.

"Working?" Nels parroted.

"Perry Owens."

Nels looked at me. "Are you coming to see Perry?"

I nodded.

"You could have told us."

"Does it matter?"

He grumbled. "Not really. Just like to be prepared."

"Ugh, I feel sick," Roxie moaned.

"Oh, my driving wasn't that bad!" I snapped.

Her eyebrows dipped, she slapped a hand over her mouth and lurched for the bathroom door.

"Was it?" I asked Nels.

"Nah. She gets carsick."

"Don't field producers need to be in cars a lot?"

Nels shrugged.

"Nina!" Perry rushed over and kissed both my cheeks. "I'm so glad you came by." He walked a circle around me, finger to his lips. "I cannot wait to get my hands on you."

Nels hefted his camera, aimed.

"Uh," George warned, starting to stand.

"You!" A cute little thing came bustling out from behind the desk, snapping her fingers. She was maybe five-one, five-two tops, with wide eyes, great cheekbones, and an angular haircut that accented her features. She wore black from neck to toe.

George sat. Grinned.

"Me?" Nels said.

"Yes, you. No filming. Azure prohibits it."

Nels glared at me.

"What? I didn't know."

"I'll take care of it, Justine," Perry cooed to the outraged receptionist. To Nels, he said, "Nina will be out in no time."

"How long is no time?" Nels asked.

"A little while. Relax, read a magazine, nap."

Nels slumped into the vacant chair next to George.

Perry whispered to me, "You've got two hours of freedom, at least."

"Really?"

Leading me around the frosted glass partition, he motioned to a chair, and I slid into it. With the flair of a toreador, he slipped a silky black cape around my shoulders, fastened it at my neck.

"You're so lucky you don't have to be filmed all day." I used the mirror to look at him.

"So I've heard. Mario's already called three times about his crew. They're following him all over the courthouse—even to the bathroom."

"Courthouse? What does he do?"

"Court stenographer."

"I'm surprised the county okayed the filming."

"The judge Mario works most for is up for reelection."

"That explains it."

He nodded. "Okay." His fingers dove into my hair. "For color, I'm seeing honeycomb with a hint of oatmeal."

"Perry," I said. "English."

"Don't tell me you're a virgin? Your hair! Your hair!" he quickly explained at my look of shock.

For a second there I was reminded of the last person who'd asked me if I was a virgin. I'd ended up digging up her body. I didn't think I should share that story with Perry.

I forced out a laugh to hide my sudden discomfort. "As pure as the driven snow."

He squealed with glee. "I'll be right back."

Azure had many styling stations zigzagged across the room—most filled. I spotted a familiar face on the other side of the room and nearly fell out of my chair.

Perry came back, all smiles as he set down two bowls and a handful of foil sheets.

"Is that Genevieve Sala over there?" I asked.

"Comes in every week."

"Is that how you know so much about her?"

Running the end of a comb over my scalp, he separated hair. "There are no secrets here."

I'd remember that.

Perry pulled a section of hair up, slipped a foil over it and slathered on what looked to be butterscotch pudding.

"What's she saying about the threat?"

"All a misunderstanding. A prank."

"Did you see the news last night?"

"Never miss it. That Carson Keyes is one good-lookin' man." He grinned. "Don't tell Mario I said that."

"My lips are sealed."

"I hear Genevieve's been bombarded with calls from reporters all day. She only took the one from E.T."

"*Entertainment Tonight*? Wow. Word travels fast."

"Almost like they were tipped off. Why else would they care two whits about a low-budget Cincinnati game show? Though, the country does love a good scandal, and the behind-the-scenes stuff on this show has the makings of one."

I met his gaze in the mirror. "So, you think the note's a fake too?"

"Faker than her D cups."

"Really? Those are fake? They look so real."

"Good surgeon, sugar pie."

Perry added more goop, more foils. I tried not to look. Or to worry. Worry was what the old Nina would do.

I unclenched my hands, folded them in my lap. "Do you know what happened with Jessica? Did she quit?"

"Fired. Faster than Mario after—" He grinned. "That's TMI."

I laughed.

Goop oozed off his paintbrush-thingy. "Genevieve. That's what happened to Jessica Ayers."

"What do you mean?"

He leaned in. "Do you want the cover story or the real story?"

"Real, of course."

"Thad was teaching an improv class at U.C. this past summer when he met Genevieve."

"A student?"

"You got it. Thad introduced Genevieve to Willie—at her request. Willie fell head over heels. They were married within a month. It took just about that long for Thad and Genevieve to convince Willie she had more potential than Jessica to sell the show to the major networks. Jess is all fluff, no substance. I don't think Willie knows what hit him."

"You think Genevieve married him just to get on the show?"

"Without a doubt."

Foil stuck out all over my head. I tried not to look. "Do you think he knows she used him?"

"Rumor is they've been fighting a lot. Could be Genevieve's shine has worn clear off."

The romantic in me asked, "Do you think she ever loved him?"

Perry laughed. "Sugar, in their world they only love themselves. There are already rumors about affairs, but no one's naming names."

Including me.

"Although Gen would have to be crazy to cheat on Willie."

I glanced over at her. She didn't look crazy, but I'd seen her cheating with my own eyes. "Why's that?"

Perry separated more hair. Just how many foils was he going to use?

"She has a lot to lose," he said, "if Willie ever found out."

"Besides her job, you mean?"

"There was an ironclad prenup, and from what I hear, Genevieve was a maid at the Westin until she married Willie."

"Willie actually has money? Everything I've seen about the show is low-budget."

"He doesn't have money now, but when that network deal goes through, he'll be rolling in the dough."

"So Genevieve is his meal ticket?"

"Genevieve and Thad. They have amazing chemistry. Just sizzle together. The good boy/bad girl stuff."

I'd seen their sizzle with my own eyes, and wished I could forget it.

"Perry, what would you say if I told you that Jessica Ayers was filing a sexual harassment case against Willie Sala?"

He finished putting another foil in my hair. Just like that, I resembled one of my mother's Easter hams. I unclenched my hands again. So much for not worrying.

"I'd say she was lying, Nina."

Five

"Honeycomb" turned out to be a soft honey brown, about three shades lighter than my normal color, and the "oatmeal" was the barest hint of blonde.

I couldn't stop looking at myself in the mirror.

I didn't recognize me.

It wasn't just the hair. It was the newly waxed eyebrows, the manicure, the pedicure, and the makeup too. I actually had on lip gloss.

Lip gloss!

And, God help me, I actually liked it.

My mother was going to freak out.

And my sister Maria too. I put earplugs on my mental shopping list.

And not only did I not recognize myself, Nels and Roxie had actually looked right past me when I finally emerged from Azure's inner sanctum.

An hour later, back at the office, they still stared as though someone had played a trick on them and the old me would march into my office to boot out the imposter.

No one else had seen me yet. Brickhouse had been out walking BeBe when we'd gotten back, Deanna was still at the nursery, and everyone else had left for the day.

I finished up some paperwork, flipped through a Burpee's

catalog for inspiration for a mini scheduled next spring. I kept having a vision of a garden. A peaceful, fragrant space with trickling water and a hammock. I doodled my initial impressions on a drawing pad. Somehow I'd work it into one of my designs.

Glancing over at Roxie and Nels, I noticed Nels nodding off. His head kept drooping forward, then jerking upright.

"Why don't you two go get some lunch? I'm just going to be doing paperwork until meeting with Deanna at three." I slid open my desk drawer, pulled out a couple of take-out menus for nearby restaurants.

They looked at each other, then Roxie stood up and snatched the menus out of my hand. I think she still blamed me for her carsickness. She'd been okay on the way home, though, thanks to a quick run to Walgreens for some Dramamine. Too bad my sister Maria hadn't been around—she always has some on hand to use as impromptu sleeping pills, despite warnings from everyone about proper usage.

"Should we order in?" Roxie asked Nels.

He looked at me.

"Really, I'm not going anywhere. I'm going to work on a design, then meet with Deanna. After that I'm going to head home to get ready for tonight. Bo-ring."

"Okay, okay!" he said. "We'll go out. But we'll be back soon. And if Bobby calls—"

"Don't tell us," Roxie said. "If we don't know, then we won't care."

"Okay."

She tipped her head, looked at me. "I like that eye shadow."

"Majestic purple."

"It goes well with your eyes. Makes them not so . . . "

"Muddy?"

"I was thinking moldy."

My eyes were a dark green that bordered on brown. Unfortunately, moldy was an apt description. "Thanks. I think."

BeBe's bark announced Brickhouse's return before the

chimes on the door. I heard her cluck—I assumed at Roxie and Nels. "Going somewhere?"

"Lunch?" Roxie answered. It came out as a question rather than a statement. It was clear to me Brickhouse Krauss terrified her.

"Ach. Not very professional, are you?"

I walked to the doorway. "Stop scaring the poor girl, Mrs. Krauss."

BeBe strained at her leash until Brickhouse finally let go. BeBe galloped over to me, threw her paws on my shoulders and slobbered my face.

Brickhouse turned toward me. "Scare? Me? I'd nev—"

The pair made their escape as Brickhouse froze, staring at me. I'd known the woman for fifteen years, and I'd never seen her speechless. Until now.

I pushed BeBe off of me, rubbed her ears.

Brickhouse finally found her voice. "What the hell happened to you?"

I laughed. I couldn't help it. "Perry."

"Your mama's going to have a heart attack. You better call and warn her."

I probably should, I thought.

She stepped closer, inspecting. "It's about time, Nina Ceceri, that you started acting like a girl."

I rolled my eyes. "Don't go getting all nice on me now."

She clucked. "Ach. I don't do nice."

"I'm aware."

Her lip twitched and she smiled. Brickhouse Krauss actually smiled. At me. Miracles never ceased.

"Come, BeBe," she said. "Some of us have work to do."

I closed my door and went back to my desk. I played a game of FreeCell and lost. Then I waited five minutes—just long enough to know that Roxie and Nels were well and truly gone—and flipped open my phone. I'd been waiting all day to make this call, but had to get rid of Roxie and Nels first.

Tam's home phone rang and rang until it finally went to voice mail. "Tam? It's Nina. Are you there? The camera people aren't here right now, so if you're there, please pick up. Is Nic really sick? Or a—"

"She's fine, Nina," Tam said, picking up. "I didn't mean to worry you."

I hadn't really believed Nic was sick, so I hadn't been too worried. "What's going on?"

She sighed. "Those cameras. I can't deal with them."

"Why? Wait. You don't have any outstanding warrants, do you?"

"No! Well, not that I know of." Her cultured drawl was part Queen Elizabeth, part Lil' Abner. She had regal diction with a good ol' southern girl accent.

I tapped a pencil on my desk blotter, opened my bottom drawer for an Almond Joy.

Empty.

I kept forgetting. And I wished I wouldn't. Every time I saw that empty drawer, it made me want to cry.

I am so not a crier.

Maybe the new me was. Would that be so bad?

"Then what?" I asked.

"There are . . . people, Nina. People I'd rather not have know where I am. If they saw me on TV . . . "

"Tam!"

"Let's just say I hacked into someone's computer a few years ago," she explained, "and they still haven't forgiven me."

"Are you in danger? Does Ian know?"

Ian Phillips was Tam's live-in love, but not the father of Tam's baby. Nic's dad was in jail on bigamy charges, and I doubted he even knew of her existence. If Tam had her way, Nic would probably grow up thinking Ian was her dad. And I think Ian wanted it that way too. Ian had recently switched from the FBI to the DEA, taking a job that would give him more free time at home. Tam, who had a law-enforcement phobia, hadn't quite reconciled herself to living with the law quite yet.

This could be part of the reason they hadn't made wedding plans.

"I'm not in danger if they don't know where I am! Which is why I can't be on TV. I'm sorry, Nina, but I just can't come in this week."

"It's all right." My goodness, I didn't even want to think about life without Tam in it. She was like the little sister I'd always wanted. Not the bratty spoiled one I actually had. Over the years Tam had become part of my family—everyone had welcomed her with open arms. "The whole somebody's-after-you thing is freaking me out, but if you're not worried . . ."

"I'm not."

"You sure?"

"Positive."

"Okay."

"And Nina?"

"Yeah?"

"Could you please tell your mom I don't need a baby shower? Break it to her gently—I don't want to hurt her feelings. I have everything I need. It would feel wrong to get any more."

I doodled a cake onto my blotter, imagined it was German chocolate with extra coconut. "So, you did know."

She laughed. "Don't I always?"

"I tried to tell her that."

"She is stubborn. Just like someone else I know."

I heard the chimes out front. "I don't know who you're talking about."

"Right."

"I'll see what I can do," I said.

Brickhouse poked her head in the door. "Someone here to see you."

"Who?"

"Jeff Dannon."

"Who?"

I heard a young male voice say, "Ana sent me."

Tam must've heard.

"Are you laughing?" I said to her. "Do I need to remind you Sassy is here at my mercy?"

"You wouldn't!"

"'Bye!" I flipped the phone closed, looked at Brickhouse. "Tam will probably be calling back in a minute."

Brickhouse clucked and turned away.

"Jeff, you can come on in!" I probably should have gotten up to meet him at the door, but I was feeling lazy. Not a good sign the morning training session I'd scheduled with Duke would go well.

Jeff came in, and I did a double take. He was cute. Seriously cute. Much too young for me, but I wasn't blind. Dark hair, light eyes, olive skin that had the look of a perpetual tan. He shook my hand and sat down in the ancient wing chair facing my desk.

"Um, Ms. Bertoli sent me. She thought you could, um, maybe, uh, help me out. Get a job."

I knew why Ana sent him. She was a sucker for good-looking younger guys. "I don't suppose you have any experience?"

He shook his head.

"What were you arrested for?"

"Petty theft."

I was going to kill Ana.

"I don't—"

"Ms. Quinn, I'm a hard worker. Strong." He showed me his bicep.

Yep. He was strong.

"I made a mistake and now no one will hire me."

I took a deep breath. Ana wasn't the only sucker in the Ceceri family tree. My weakness was for sob stories.

As I thought about it, this was my chance to implement a

key element in my self-discovery quest: saying no. Wasn't I supposed to be changing? Doing things I normally wouldn't? Wasn't I freshly waxed and coiffed?

"Please?" he said with eyes that reminded me of BeBe.

"Oh, all right. But just part-time."

I was weak, and this self-discovery stuff was hard. Damn hard.

"Part-time is okay. I just went back to school anyway."

"School's good. What year?"

"Junior."

"That makes you, what? Twenty?"

"Almost twenty-one. December birthday."

I nodded, easily seeing him with Deanna. "See Mrs. Krauss on your way out to get some paperwork. You'll be working under Kit. You'll get your orders from him, you'll do everything he tells you. Got it?"

He nodded.

"Except for anything to do with his dog! Just say no to that."

"Okay."

"Come in tomorrow to meet everyone, and you'll start Wednesday. Be here at six-thirty."

"Okay." His leg bounced.

"You can go now."

He jumped up, held out his hand. "Thanks."

"You're welcome."

Ana owed me big-time.

Six

An hour later Deanna couldn't stop staring at me. "You look so . . . pretty."

I didn't want to think about how she thought I'd looked before.

"Thank you," I said again. It was the fourth time she'd told me. I doodled a cupcake next to the cake on my blotter.

Nels and Roxie sat in the corner. Nels had his head tipped back and was napping (I think it *had* been the doughnuts that perked him up that morning). Roxie was engrossed in a Sudoko puzzle book.

Deanna fidgeted.

I dropped my pencil into the cup. "Do you know how I've been making changes around here lately? Cutting back the schedule?"

"Yes?" She clasped her hands together, one thumb making nervous sweeps over the other.

"I've been thinking that there's really not a need for two designers to work on the surprise makeovers full-time."

Her eyes widened. "You're firing me?"

"What?"

"I knew it! I just knew it." She jumped up, tugged on her pencil skirt.

I leaned forward. "Deanna, wait. You don't understand."

"I had a feeling this was coming. That's fine. Really, it's fine. I mean, I'd been thinking about moving on anyway."

"Deanna—wait. Moving on?"

"To another company. For more experience, you know."

"No." My jaw set. "I didn't know."

"This is probably for the best. Really."

I slumped back in my chair. This hadn't been what I intended at all. I'd been about to promote her, give her more design freedom, and now she was quitting? Or was I firing her?

"Deanna, I don't want you to leave," I said.

"Well, I can't stay knowing that you don't want me."

"I never said that."

"It was implied."

"No it wasn't."

She looked at Roxie. "Wasn't it implied?"

Roxie peered over the rim of her glasses. "Kind of."

I gave her the Ceceri Evil Eye. She shrank back and covered her face with her puzzle book. "It wasn't," I said to Deanna.

"I have an interview at The Grass Is Always Greener on Friday. I'll be okay."

Hurt flooded me. "You have an interview scheduled?"

"I had a feeling this was coming."

"Nothing was coming!"

"I'll get my things and go."

The phone rang. I heard Brickhouse pick it up.

I would have argued but I was too upset. An interview. With The Grass Is Always Greener, one of the top landscaping design firms in the area. That was just downright traitorous. And besides, asking her to hear me out was something the old me would do.

"Fine. If that's what you feel you have to do."

"It is."

I let her go.

The intercom on my desk buzzed. "What?"

"Temper, temper, Nina Ceceri."

I rubbed my suddenly aching temples.

"Riley's on line one."

"Thank you." I picked up the phone. The cord stretched as I walked around my desk, and I kicked the door closed with my foot. Nels snorted awake.

The crackled noise from a TV set came through the line as I said, "Riley?"

"Hey."

"What's wrong?" I dropped into my chair, swiveled to look out the window. The garden showplace in the back looked beautiful. Abundant fall flowers glowed.

He must have muted the TV because I didn't hear it anymore. "Why's something have to be wrong?"

"You never call."

"Oh. Right. Well, I was just on my way to Mrs. Greeble's to do some yard work—"

"Don't charge her too much, you know she's on a pension," I reminded him.

"I *know*," he said. "I just thought I'd call and warn you."

Warn me? "About what?"

The intercom buzzed again. I swiveled. "Hold on, Riley. Yes?" I said to Brickhouse.

"Carson Keyes is here to see you."

My gaze zipped to Roxie. "Why?"

"For his behind-the-scene piece, remember?"

Nope. I'd forgotten.

"Okay," I said to Brickhouse. "Show him in please. Riley? Warn me?"

"About the picketers."

I sat upright. Somehow I'd gotten the cord tangled around my neck. I fought to get free. Hands tugged, elbows flew.

My office door swung open and Carson Keyes walked in, took one look at me and signaled his cameraman to start filming.

Grrr.

I held up a finger to him, finished unraveling myself and said to Riley, "What picketers?"

"Two guys with signs that say 'Reality TV Is Evil.' "

Chocolate. I needed chocolate. I opened the bottom desk drawer, saw it was empty—damn it—and slammed it closed.

"That's not the worst part," Riley said.

"How can it possibly be worse?"

"The construction guys actually showed up today."

"But that's good news!" Images of me sleeping in my own bed soothed me.

"Um, not really. They refuse to cross the picket line. Something about union rules."

On edge, I grit my teeth.

I pumped Riley for more information, but he didn't know much else so I hung up. Picketers. Great.

Looking at Carson, I gave him what I hoped was a reassuring smile, and held out my hand.

As he shook it I couldn't help but think about Ana and what she'd do to me if she found out Carson was here in my office and she wasn't.

I'd probably be keeping this little tidbit to myself.

After introducing him to Roxie and Nels, I asked him and his cameraman to have a seat.

"Did I hear something about picketing?" he asked.

"At my house. Something about reality TV being evil."

"I spoke with Mario Gibbens earlier, and he too had picketers at his place. The footage will be in my report tonight." He tapped something into his BlackBerry, and I wondered if footage of my house would be on the news tonight too.

"Did you interview them?"

He nodded, tucked his BlackBerry into the inside pocket of his tailored suit coat. "Activists for a morality TV group."

"Oh."

Was *Hitched or Ditched* immoral? Maybe I needed a quick brush-up on current vices because I didn't think so.

Carson leaned forward, smiled. "Do you mind if I ask you a few questions off camera? Then do a little filming?"

"Not at all."

Carson seemed like your everyday average guy, and not the most popular TV reporter in Cincinnati. I thought for sure he'd be carrying around a big ego, but he seemed humble and down to earth. I worried about Ana's chances with him—or rather, his chances with her. She enjoyed the narcissistic type.

His questions ranged from why I was doing the show—I came up with a doozy of an answer about long-distance relationships and everlasting love—to how I met Bobby, to if the home audience actually voted for Bobby and me to get hitched, would we?

"Tough one," I said.

"But isn't that why you're doing the show?"

"Well, yes." I was stuck. If I said yes, that Bobby and I would get married, then all of southern Ohio, northern Kentucky, and eastern Indiana would be expecting a wedding. It could bloom out of control.

If I said no, everyone would wonder why we were on the show in the first place. And I couldn't very well explain about Josh Drake and his cockamamie idea to get dirt on Willie Sala for a lawsuit, now could I?

"You're just going to have to wait and see," I hedged.

He smiled. "Said like a woman trying to evade a question."

"Said like a woman who would like the audience to keep tuning in."

He laughed. "Good point."

"Thank you. Now, can I ask you a couple of questions?"

"Me? Why?"

"Curiosity."

Amusement lit his eyes. "Okay."

"Do you have a girlfriend?"

He took a second to respond. "No."

That had been a very pregnant second. A lot was hidden in that second. That second put me on edge. "Recently dumped?" I fished.

"Nope."

"Want a girlfriend?" This would tell me a lot. One, if he was gay. I hadn't thought of that until his pause. Being a very popular TV personality, he might not want the world to know his sexual preference. Two, if Ana had a chance at all.

"I'm open to it. Why? You're not—"

"Me? No! My cousin."

He looked relieved. I didn't take it personally. The old me might have, but the new me was slightly more confident thanks to the makeover.

"She'll be at the filming tonight," I said.

"You'll have to introduce me."

"This could be a whole piece for you. Matchmaking behind the scenes of *Hitched or Ditched*. You two could be the next couple on the show."

"That's not a bad idea." Out came the BlackBerry again.

I didn't warn him Ana was anti-long-term.

"You know," I said, "you're cute, you're good at your job, have a good personality—why are you still here?"

"Here?"

"In Cincinnati? Why not Hollywood, the mecca for all entertainment reporters?"

He shrugged. "I like it here. There's something about being a big fish in a little pond I find appealing."

Was that a little arrogance poking through? Maybe there was hope for him and Ana yet.

Seven

"Sure enough, there were picketers," I said to Ana, trying to focus on driving. It was tough. I was still mad. "Two of them. Didn't say a word to me, just walked in little circles in my front yard." There had been a camera crew there too, compliments of Carson Keyes. I didn't mention to her I'd spent nearly an hour with him that afternoon.

Ana would kill me.

She touched my hair. I slapped her hand away. "That Perry's a genius," she gushed. "I love the sweeping bangs. Gorgeous. Just gorgeous. He might actually rival Angie. And that's saying something."

We drove across the Norwood Lateral and headed to 71 south and the Edwards Road exit, which would lead us to the HoD studio.

"Are you listening to me rant? What good is ranting if you don't listen?"

"Shush. Let me look at you. Those eyebrows! The arch is perfect. And your scar is completely hidden. Why didn't you do this before now?"

I'd had a little run-in with a freight train a while back that left me with a scar on my forehead. The makeup artist at Azure taught me how to cover it with concealer. Who knew?

I shrugged. "I don't know."

I wasn't ready to tell Ana about my self-discovery quest just yet. And not just Ana. Anyone. I had to do this on my own for a little while.

"You look so great. You look better than me!"

I raised a freshly waxed eyebrow.

"All right. Almost as good as me. What did your mother say?"

"I haven't seen her."

"She's going to have heart failure."

"She'll be all right." I waited a beat. "I need to get rid of them. How?"

"Who?"

"The picketers! How's my house supposed to get done if the construction guys won't cross the picket line?" I took the ramp to 71 south.

She dug through her purse. "You met Carson yesterday, right? Is he as cute in person?"

"Ana!"

"Stop worrying, Nina."

I took a deep breath. She was right. I needed to stop worrying so much. So what? There were a couple of guys picketing my house. Big deal. They'd eventually go away. The construction crew could work then.

And being a pretend fiancée to Bobby wouldn't be so bad.

And everything at work would be okay.

And I was being delusional, which was breaking a top commandment.

"Are you nervous about tonight?" she asked as she applied clear lip gloss.

"A little."

"About being on TV?"

"About Bobby."

"Ah. He's hot."

"I don't need the reminder." I changed lanes, sped up.

Roxie and Nels had ditched me at four, to head down to the studio with the day's footage. For a while I was free of cameras. I wondered if higher-budgeted shows had those car cams. Right now I thanked my lucky stars Willie Sala was a cheapskate.

"As soon as the show ends and he finds Mac a place to live, Bobby will go back to Florida. Which, I hope, will be sooner rather than later. I can't hold out much longer."

"I don't know why you're holding out at all."

"My sanity."

"Oh that. Right."

"You're not helping." I exited the highway, turned left.

"Sorry."

Her smile told me she wasn't sorry at all. I didn't hold it against her. She just wanted me to be happy—and she believed Bobby made me happy.

Which he did. But it wasn't as easy as that.

"Do you want to do a little undercover work tonight?" I asked.

"I'm hoping I'll be under covers with Carson by the end of the night."

I rolled my eyes. "How about getting a date first?" Carson didn't strike me as a one-night-stand kind of guy. "Maybe play hard to get?"

"Yes, *Mom*."

I thought about Ana's mother. "Don't make me call Aunt Rosa." Though I wasn't all that sure Aunt Rosa wouldn't take Ana's side. The apple and the tree.

Great. I'd gone and done it again. I moved "stop using revised clichés" to the top of my self-discovery to-do list.

Ana pointed with the wand of her lip gloss. "You wouldn't."

"Tempt me."

"Fine. What do you want me to do?"

I explained about Willie, Genevieve, and Thad. "Just keep your eyes open."

"This could be fun!"

"You absolutely can't say anything to Carson Keyes. I don't think Josh Drake wants the sexual harassment case publicized yet."

I pulled into the *Hitched or Ditched* lot, found a space near the back. The security guard let us in, and someone with a clipboard directed us to the first floor studio.

Ana spotted Carson Keyes bent over a folder and made a beeline toward him, sashaying in her four-inch heels.

I looked around for Bobby but didn't see him on set. I took a minute to soak it all in. The design was very similar to the *Newlywed Game*. Two booths sat side by side, where the contestants would sit. But instead of a lectern for Thad, there was a heart-shaped hot tub, like you'd see in an ad for the Poconos. I walked over to it. Steam rose and the water bubbled.

For a second I let myself remember the time Bobby and I had driven down to Gatlinburg, Tennessee, for a weekend getaway. There'd been a hot tub in our hotel room. We'd made good use of it.

"Nina?"

I spun.

Bobby stood there, eyes narrowed. "Is that you?"

"Hi." I tucked my hair behind my ear.

His gaze traveled me up and down, darkening with each trip. Finally, it rested on my lips.

I gulped.

"You look amazing."

"Thanks."

"Really amazing."

Okay, I'd had it with people saying that. "What was I before? Chopped liver?"

He laughed. "Not at all. You've always been·beautiful. This . . . this just puts the shine on the diamond."

I turned back to the hot tub. My. Heart. Ached. "Well, if that wasn't the cheesiest line I've ever heard." I was proud my voice stayed strong despite the lump in my throat.

His chest brushed my back as he came up behind me. "Cheesy, but true." He dipped his thumb in the water, then slid it over the back of my hand. "Remember Gatlinburg?"

I sidestepped away from him, my face flushed. And not from the steam. "No."

Blue eyes sparkled. "Liar."

Where was Ana? Both she and Carson had disappeared. Great. I did spot Perry and Mario across the room and practically sprinted for them.

"See? What did I tell you?" I heard Perry gushing to Mario, an artist in awe of his masterpiece.

I was never happier to see people in my whole life.

Perry kissed both my cheeks. "Doesn't she look gorgeous?" Perry asked Bobby, whose body heat practically seared my silk shirt.

"More than."

Mario nodded, approving. "Delectable."

"Stop it, you guys! I can't take so many compliments in one day."

"Well, sugar, you better get used to it," Perry said.

I wondered if I could. It was just . . . weird.

"Ms. Quinn?"

A short, slim redhead introduced herself. "I'm Sherry Cochran. Thad's wife? He spoke to you about doing a makeover?"

"Oh hi." I made introductions.

She shifted on her kitten heels. "I was hoping we could talk for a minute tonight after the taping."

"All right." I wondered if I could worm any information out of her regarding Jessica Ayers and why she'd been fired. It would be nice if she could confirm what Perry had heard so I could call Josh and have this whole charade over and done with.

Wait. I'd forgotten about the contract I'd signed with

HoD. With or without the case against Willie, I was obligated under contract to see the show through.

Great.

I made plans with Sherry to meet in Thad's dressing room after the show and watched her walk away.

"I'm going to go say hi to Louisa," Bobby said. "Be right back."

I tried not to be jealous. Tried really hard.

"She's not much of a looker," Mario said.

"Who, that Louisa?" I asked, taking heart.

"Oh sugar," Perry consoled, "Bobby only has eyes for you. No need to worry."

"Me? Worried?"

Mario put an arm around me. "I was talking about Sherry Cochran."

"Oh." I wouldn't have called her attractive, but she wasn't unattractive, either. She was just . . . plain. I wondered if she had any idea her husband was a cheating louse. Which reminded me of Kevin. Which reminded me of home. "Could you believe those picketers?"

Mario fingered my new bangs. "Great job," he told Perry.

"Thank you, thank you."

It was a good thing I didn't have an aversion to touchy-feely people. "Hello? Picketers?"

"Oh, they'll be gone soon enough." Mario leaned in close, looked to be inspecting my pores. "We just need to wait them out."

Said like a man who didn't have construction workers refusing to cross a picket line.

The next hour was a blur of makeup and run-throughs. At 6:55 Thad came out in a robe and dropped it in a dramatic show, revealing an itty-bitty Speedo. He climbed into the hot tub. The cleft in his chin looked even deeper tonight, and I wondered if the makeup people had shadowed it.

Next to me, Bobby leaned in. "You sure you don't remember Gatlinburg?"

I remembered all too well Bobby slipping into the hot tub with nothing on at all. "Nope."

He grinned. "Maybe I'll have to remind you sometime."

Was it me or was it hot under these lights?

Genevieve Hidalgo Sala came out in a bikini and heels. I immediately determined she'd had all sorts of plastic surgery, because I was being catty and didn't care whatsoever if it was on my self-discovery list or not.

As I took a closer look, though, I saw she looked rather skittish, her eyes on the wild side. Without a doubt she looked terrified.

Looking left, I noticed Carson directing his cameraman to film Genevieve.

Was her fright an act for the news camera, to keep the story on the air?

If it was, she was a good actress.

The overdone theme music came up, and before I knew it, Perry and I were backstage in a soundproof closet while Mario and Bobby answered questions about us.

"Have you heard anything else about Genevieve?" I asked him.

"The drama queen, you mean?"

"You think she's acting?"

"Better than Dustin Hoffman in *Tootsie*."

Laughing, I said, "Do you have a straight brother by any chance? I have this cousin . . . "

"The smokin' hot vixen in the killer heels throwing herself at Carson Keyes?"

"That'd be her."

"Sugar, I was thinking about leaving Mario for her."

I smiled. "I'll let her know."

"Give her my card—I'd love to get my hands on her hair."

The closet door creaked open. "Nina, Perry. It's time," Louisa said to us, then mumbled something into the headset she wore.

My stomach did nervous cartwheels as we stepped onto

the set and took our seats, me next to Bobby, Perry next to Mario. Bobby held two large white cards facedown in his lap, as did Mario.

Mind you, there were no points kept. The questions were solely for the home audience to get to know us better and to judge whether we should be together or not.

It would have been nice to get something out of this charade—a TV or a stereo like the real *Newlywed Game*.

Perched on the edge of the hot tub, Genevieve held out a card. Thad read it carefully. "Perry, what was Mario wearing the first time you met him?"

Oh my God, I thought. What was I wearing the day I met Bobby for the first time? It had been last spring, in his office at the high school . . .

I didn't even hear Perry's answer—just knew he'd gotten it wrong by the pout on Mario's face.

"Nina," Thad said. "What was Bobby wearing the first time you met him?"

Wait. What was *Bobby* wearing? Easy. "A cheesy sixties style suit, snakeskin cowboy boots."

Bobby held up a sign. It said, SUIT. Fake applause filled the studio. Bobby whispered, "And you don't remember Gatlinburg. Right."

I avoided eye contact, but I could practically feel Bobby preening next to me.

Genevieve flipped the cards, and Thad read the question silently, making a show of looking bashful. Before seeing him with Genevieve in Willie's bathroom, I would have bought his good ol' boy act. Not anymore.

"Nina," Thad purred, "if Bobby were writing a book on his bedroom experience, would it be a boring how-to manual, a hot, steamy romance, or a rip-roarin' sensory stimulating thriller?"

Oh. My. God.

Next to me, Bobby shook, as if he were trying to hold in a laugh. Glad he found this so amusing.

I glanced over at Perry. He was watching me, totally engrossed.

Ana wasn't to be seen, the rear of the set in shadow.

Thad had a bemused look on his face.

Genevieve was no help either. She kept looking left and right as though she expected someone to jump out of the corner and bump her off.

I thought that a bit overdramatic of her.

"Nina?" Thad prompted.

All I kept thinking about was my mother. How she was going to watch this show. And Riley! And oh, God, Brickhouse and Mr. Cabrera!

"Nina?" Thad said.

Wincing, I said, "I'll, uh, go with hot and steamy."

Bobby held up the sign. ROMANCE had been his answer. More applause filled the space, echoed.

"Kiss her," Perry urged.

I wanted to throttle that Perry.

Bobby cupped the back of my head and pulled me toward him. He kissed me full on the mouth, then let me go.

Out of the corner of my eye I saw Ana stepping into the dim light across the set, fanning herself. Carson stood behind her while his cameraman aimed the camera at Perry as he answered correctly too—a how-to manual. Poor Perry.

The set dimmed as we broke to get ready for the next round.

I needed air.

Ana was busy flirting with Carson Keyes, and Bobby looked like he wanted to talk about Gatlinburg some more. I hightailed it out of there.

Someone had used a brick to prop open a side door. Cigarette butts littered the ground. I walked along the side of the building, out of the way of anyone coming out for a smoke, and leaned against the brick facade.

The crisp autumn night cooled me right down. I didn't

know how I was going to last a week with Bobby kissing me like that.

A quick lap around the building to clear my mind, and I'd go back in and pray there wouldn't be any more sex questions.

A girl could only take so much.

Dried leaves crunched beneath my shoes—boring pumps I'd pulled out of the back of my closet.

Wait. When did I start caring if my pumps were boring? It was a disconcerting thought, to say the least.

Light flooded a corner office, and I couldn't help but look in as I passed by—I was nosy by nature. Through thin miniblinds I spotted Willie Sala. I dropped down out of sight and speculated.

It looked to be some sort of storage room. I peeked in again. He seemed to be waiting for someone. I slipped over to the other side of the window so I could see the door to the office. It didn't take long for it to swing open—or for the woman to jump into Willie's waiting arms.

His snakelike voice slithered through the window. "It will all be over by Friday, darling." Then he kissed her, and I tried not to get grossed out. After all, this was Willie Sala, comb-over king. But the woman kissing him wasn't his wife.

It was Sherry Cochran.

Eight

Bright and early the next morning I met Duke at the gym.

I didn't do bright and early well. Rubbing my eyes, I tried to focus.

"Did you eat?" he asked me. Solid muscle, he stood six feet tall and what seemed like six feet wide.

The gym was relatively empty at five in the morning, and I was beyond grateful for the privacy. "A low-carb blueberry muffin."

"Don't skimp on the carbs in the morning. You need your energy if you're going to work with me." He stood, hands behind his back, feet spread shoulder width apart, military style. Put the man in cammos and he would scare the pee out of any new recruit. "Get your protein too."

I didn't realize I was clenching my fists until my palms started to ache. Little half-moon fingernail impressions marred my skin.

Inhaling, I reminded myself there was nothing wrong with change, with trying something new. It wasn't scary—it was just unexplored.

What was scary was Duke.

Duke was a crew-cut Mack truck, and I sensed he was about to roll over me. Splat.

"We'll start with taking some measurements, do some stretching, and then move to the treadmill to see what's in you," he said.

"Um, the treadmill? Really? There's a reason I don't use escalators."

"No excuses."

I think the muscles in his face had muscles. His cheeks didn't wobble when he talked, and he'd either had Botox or his forehead was made of granite.

I leaned toward granite.

As he measured, weighed me, and wrote everything down for posterity, I couldn't help but think about Sherry Cochran and Willie Sala. Together. Last night.

I shuddered.

Duke barked out a laugh. "Don't worry. You'll be warmed up in no time."

I wondered how Kit knew Duke, and if Kit secretly hated me.

As we stretched muscles I never knew I had, my mind went back to Sherry and how she'd stood me up last night. I'd waited nearly half an hour in Thad's office for her to show. She never did.

I had a good idea where she might have been, but I wasn't going there looking for her. No way. No how. I had a weak stomach.

It was nearly impossible not to think about the death threats and whether they were real. If so, they could be related to the whole love quadrangle going on over at HoD. Or to Jessica Ayers.

Odds were, however, they had been faked.

I sat on the floor in my baggy tee and saggy shorts, my legs stretched out in a V shape. I tried to touch the toe of my left foot, but my back cramped.

"Now the other side," Duke ordered, touching his toe with ease. "Stretch it, stretch it. Bend with your waist, don't strain your neck."

Ana—who hadn't gone home with Carson last night, but did have a date after tonight's taping—had speculated that Thad and Sherry and Willie and Genevieve were swingers.

I supposed it was possible, but I didn't believe it. The meeting between Willie and Sherry had seemed too clandestine, and the timing . . . when everyone else was on the set? What better time to sneak away?

"Now put your feet together and reach."

Yep, Kit hated me.

Now that I knew Willie was in fact the cheating type, I wouldn't put sexual harassment beyond him, but had he actually harassed Jessica? Or had she trumped up this charge as revenge for being bumped off the show by Willie's new wife?

I hated that I'd been sucked into this situation. My mind couldn't just leave things be. My nosiness had taken over, and I wanted answers.

Not your business, my inner voice reminded me. That voice had been fairly quiet since I ventured into self-discovery. I'd missed it.

Duke led me to the treadmill.

Exercising had seemed so desirable yesterday, but now I wasn't as gung-ho. Perhaps self-acceptance was what I truly needed to learn. Over time I could get used to my tummy roll. "I'm not so sure about this, Duke. Mr. Duke? Sir?"

Duke placed his hands on his hips. Muscles flexed. His tone brooked no argument. "I'm sure."

I argued anyway. "Really. I don't do well with objects in motion."

"Get on. Now."

I quickly jumped onto the treadmill and wondered why I paid Duke so much just to be bossed around—I could get that from my sister Maria for free. He clipped a lead line onto me. "For safety." He pressed the On button. The treadmill hummed, and I started walking.

Okay, this wasn't so bad. Change wasn't hard at all! Why was I so worried? Self-discovery was good! I was walking my way to a firmer, fitter bod—

Duke pushed *3* on the keypad. The treadmill sped up. I picked up my pace and tightened my grip on the safety rails.

Not so bad. Piece of cake.

Mmm. Cake. A little digital calorie counter had just hit 100. How long would I have to walk to earn a piece of German chocolate cake?

After fifteen minutes at *3*, Duke bumped it up to *4.5* and said, "Jog."

"What?" Sweat dripped down the side of my face. I didn't dare let go of the rails to wipe it away.

"Jog!"

The treadmill sped up. I broke into a jog. Like a racetrack dog chasing after a stuffed bunny, I imagined a big, ooey, gooey piece of cake in front of me . . . until Duke jumped in front of the treadmill, bursting my cake bubble.

Suddenly I didn't feel much like running anymore.

"Pump your arms!" he ordered.

My arms? That meant I'd have to let go of the rails.

Duke sidestepped, and I swear the piece of cake returned, floating where his head had been. It was all the incentive I needed.

I let go of the safety rail and . . . jogged.

I was doing it! Jogging!

German chocolate cake, here I come!

I looked over at Duke, smiled.

Suddenly, everything woozily tilted off-kilter. My feet flew out from under me and my arms flailed as I went flying off the back of the treadmill, crashing onto the floor. The lead line came with me, shutting down the machine.

I landed on my butt and collapsed in a heap.

Duke hovered over me like the angel of death. "Maybe you're right. The treadmill isn't for you."

* * *

I walked into chaos at TBS. BeBe greeted me at the door, all slobbery kisses and drool. I looked at Kit.

He gawked at me.

Right. The makeover. I'd forgotten.

Roxie and Nels were there, and Roxie was in a snit. "Where were you this morning?"

Right. I was supposed to meet them at home, but I'd come straight there from Duke's torture chamber—after showering.

"Sorry," I said. "I was off meeting Bobby for a secret rendezvous."

Roxie's eyes bulged.

"I'm kidding," I said. "I was . . . somewhere else."

"Where?"

"Somewhere."

"Ach," Brickhouse broke in. "Enough. She's not going to tell you, and it's none of your business anyway."

Roxie folded her arms.

Kit smiled. "How was that somewhere?"

"I thought you liked me."

He laughed. It was good to see him laugh. He still didn't look well. He looked . . .

Wait.

He looked like I did right after Bobby had left.

Had Daisy left? Was their relationship that far gone? I'd known it was on the rocks, but never suspected it had gotten so bad.

BeBe licked my hand. Since Kit was down in the dumps, I decided not to make an issue of BeBe. Looked like TBS had officially become a doggy day care. I wondered if I needed a license for that.

"Did you really fire Deanna?" Kit asked, sipping coffee from a pink LIVE! WITH REGIS & KELLY mug.

"What? No!"

Brickhouse said, "Then why is she leaving?"

My stomach knotted. "You'll have to ask her."

"What about Weekend Warrior?" Kit asked.

Weekend Warrior was my innovative design project, specifically created for Deanna's talents. "I don't know. I didn't get a chance to tell Deanna about it."

Brickhouse clucked. "Maybe you should. Maybe then she wouldn't leave."

I rubbed BeBe's head. She looked up at me, all big brown eyes and adoration. It did my heart good. Being a doggy day care wasn't so bad. "She made her choice."

"Ach. Stubborn."

"Yes, she is."

"Not her." Brickhouse folded her arms. "You."

"Hey, I tried explaining, and she wouldn't let me get a word in edgewise. Right?" I asked Roxie, because Nels had been in dreamland.

Roxie nodded. "It's true."

"In fact," I added, "did you all know Deanna already had an interview scheduled at The Grass Is Always Greener for Friday?"

Kit finally broke the stunned silence by saying, "Sorry, Nina." By the look in his eye, I think he finally understood.

"What was I supposed to do?" I asked them.

"Ach. That Deanna is so stubborn."

I smiled. It was as close to sympathy as I was going to get from Brickhouse. "Well, let's not dwell. We all have work to do."

I walked over to the coffeepot, took a deep breath and poured a mug. "What?" I asked at Kit's and Brickhouse's stares.

"Coffee?" Kit said. "Are we out of Dr Pepper?"

"Ach. I just stocked some."

"I just wanted to try coffee," I said. "No big deal."

Brickhouse clucked. "She's gone and lost her mind. First the hair, now coffee. What's next? A new wardrobe?"

"The hair rocks," Kit said, smiling.

"Thanks." I was glad Perry wasn't there to gloat. And I didn't mention to Brickhouse the shopping trip he had talked me into. We were going to meet later that week.

I leaned against the doorjamb to my office, holding the mug tight, letting its warmth sink into my hands. I could get used to that feeling, especially now that temperatures were dropping like the autumn leaves outside.

"Kit, I hired you a helping hand. He'll be here later on to meet everyone and turn in his paperwork. Ana sent him over. Ursula, if you could run the usual checks, that'd be great. Roxie, Nels, we have a road trip today, so, Roxie, if you need to take some medicine, do it now."

She dove for her purse as the phone rang. Brickhouse answered it. "Taken by Surprise, this is Ursula. Mmm-hmm. Hold on." She looked at me. "Sherry Cochran, line one."

"I'll take it in my office." Since wherever I went now included Nels and Roxie, they were on my heels as I entered my office, set my mug on the desk—still not having taken a sip—and picked up the phone. "This is Nina Quinn," I said. In the reception area, I could hear Kit and Brickhouse gossiping about Deanna. I covered the phone with one hand. "Can you close that?" I asked Nels, motioning to the door with my elbow.

With the door shut, I focused on the conversation.

"I'm so sorry I missed our appointment, Ms. Quinn."

"Nina, please."

"I was . . . delayed, then I completely forgot. My memory isn't what it used to be."

I tried in vain to erase the image of what had delayed her. No luck.

Willie's "It will all be over by Friday" was suddenly stuck in my head. It sounded so ominous, so sinister, especially in light of the death threats.

"It's all right," I assured her. "I didn't wait long."

"I was hoping to reschedule our appointment. I'd really

like to get the ball rolling on a spring makeover for my parents."

"This is a good time to start planning. Would you like to make an appointment to come in, throw some ideas around?"

"That would be wonderful."

I clicked open the computerized schedule book. Winter was my main planning time for next season. Most makeovers for spring would be booked in the next few months. There were always exceptions, though, especially where my family was concerned.

Roxie gestured frantically.

"Could you hold on?" I asked Sherry.

"Sure."

I covered the phone with my hand.

In a stage whisper, Roxie said, "Is it possible to set one up this week? So we can film it? It would be great for the show, and some free advertising for you."

Most of my publicity lately had been negative, what with stumbling across dead bodies and such. It would be nice to have a positive spin for once.

I nodded and squinted at the computer screen. "Mrs. Co-chran?"

"Sherry."

"How about Friday, Sherry, around one?"

"Actually, Friday's not good for me."

I wondered why and if it had anything to do with Willie's prediction. "Thursday?" I asked. "Ten o'clock?"

"That would be wonderful."

We said our good-byes and hung up. I tapped her name into the computer, clicked Save, and picked up the phone to call home.

Where my mother should have been. I hadn't seen or heard from her, which was odd. I suspected she'd watched the show last night . . . She'd have seen my makeover. What did it mean that she hadn't called?

My home phone rang and rang and finally clicked over to voice mail.

I dialed her cell.

It went straight to voice mail. "I need to talk to you," I said. "Give me a call."

The warm mug soothed me. I held it to my lips.

"Are you ever going to drink that?" Roxie asked.

"I'm thinking about it."

"Why wouldn't you?" Nels asked.

"I don't like coffee."

They looked at each other, then looked at me, eyebrows all squiggled.

"Long story," I said.

Roxie looked over the rim of her blue glasses at me. "Just so long as there's a reason."

"There is."

"Good. I was afraid that hair dye steeped a little too long."

I smiled. Roxie had moxie. I liked that about her.

"You can do it," Nels urged.

I could. The new me definitely could. I took a sip. The coffee burned a bitter path to my stomach. "Uck."

"Well, first," Roxie said, "you probably should have blown on it before taking a big gulp like that. Second, did you add cream? Sugar?"

I shook my head.

Roxie elbowed Nels. "Go grab some. And check to see if there's any cinnamon out there too."

For the first time, I wondered if they were related. They treated each other like beleaguered siblings.

Nels came back and dumped sugar packets, little cream containers, a Kroger brand canister of cinnamon, and a stirrer on my desk.

Roxie stepped up, ripped open two packets of sugar, dumped them into my mug, popped the tops of two creamers and poured those in as well. She stirred, then sprinkled a little cinnamon on top. "Try that."

This time I blew across the top of the mug before taking a hesitant sip. My eyebrow arched. "Not bad!"

She preened. "I was a barista at Starbucks during college. I can make any coffee taste better. Even the dreck you serve here."

"Dreck?"

"You should really be grinding your own beans."

"Ah."

Strains of "Like a Virgin" filled the office. Nels sang along. I flipped open my cell phone when I recognized Ana's number. "Hey," I said.

"Why's your mother avoiding you?"

"She's avoiding me?" This was news. Usually I avoided her.

"I think so. She called me to find out why you need to talk to her."

If my mother had resorted to calling Ana, then she was really avoiding me. "I'll never figure my mother out."

"Your mother?" Roxie piped in. "She's worried you're mad about the construction being delayed because of the picketers." At my stunned look, she added, "I spoke with her this morning when we couldn't find you."

"Who's that?" Ana asked.

"Roxie," I said.

"What?" Roxie answered.

"Not you," I said to her. "Ana."

"What?" Ana said.

"Stop!" I cried. "I'm getting a headache." Not only that, but I was starting to ache all over from my morning with Duke. And I had it to look forward to again tomorrow morning.

"Ana, Roxie says Mom's avoiding me because of the construction guys not being able to work."

"Oh! I forgot about Roxie and Nels. Tell them I said hi!"

I rolled my eyes. "Ana says hi."

"She's nice," Roxie said, pulling out a Sudoko puzzle book.

"Is she single?" Nels asked.

"No," I lied. There was no way I was going there.

"Ana, just tell my mom that I need to talk to her about Tam."

"Is Tam okay?"

I looked at the camera perched on Nels's shoulder. I'd yet to determine how he decided what to film. "She's good. Any word from, um . . . " The camera whirred. "You know."

"No. We still have plans for tonight, though. I've got a late court case, so I'll meet you down there."

"Do you really? Or do you just want your own car so you can leave separately?"

She laughed—but didn't answer.

"Oh, your mother is in love with your new look," she said. "I told her all about Perry, and I think she wants you to marry him."

"Did you tell her about Mario?"

"She didn't care. Oh! Look at the time. I've got to get to court—'bye!"

As soon as I hung up, Roxie leaned forward on her seat. "I've noticed Bobby never calls. Is that normal? Don't you two talk during the day? Actually, he hasn't been around either. How do you maintain a relationship?"

I looked into the camera, then glanced down into the murky coffee mug and focused on the flecks of cinnamon stuck to the ceramic. "We, ah, have a special relationship."

"True love that doesn't need to be validated every two seconds?" Roxie asked.

Forcing a smile, the coffee churning in my upset stomach, I said, "Exactly."

Nine

"Where are we? Oz?" Roxie asked.

I'd taken 63 east off 75 north. After the correctional facility, farmland bordered the road on both sides. Looked like most everything had been harvested already, the soil freshly turned, dark and rich.

"Don't get up here much, huh?"

She shook her head.

"You're missing out."

"On what? Life?" she muttered.

I smiled. If she grew up in the city, then this would seem like another world to her. Rolling meadows, dairy farms, houses set miles apart.

If we continued straight, we'd hit civilization again in downtown Lebanon, famous for its old-fashioned charm, but I turned left onto a gravel driveway and drove it for a good mile.

Ash trees in golden glory lined the main drive, and Lowther House finally came into view.

"Wow," Roxie said.

I agreed.

It was stunning. A two story Georgian-style colonial mansion complete with pillars out front, Lowther House was a residential facility for the retired set. Almost innlike, it offered its residents amenities other facilities could only dream of. A concierge, for one. In-house doctors. Private chefs. It was the best of the best, as the quarter-million *per year* price tag suggested.

From the front the house didn't seem so elaborate, but I knew from an earlier tour that four additions had been added to the main house. The lower level's floor plan looked like the Pentagon's, complete with a courtyard in the center of it all.

We parked near the elaborate fountain, a bronze fleur de lis, and passed under beautiful stone columns as we walked up the front steps of the main entrance. I'd called ahead to inform Pippi about the cameras, and she'd been thrilled. She was a closet reality TV junkie and a huge fan of *Hitched or Ditched*.

Though I knew the code for the front door, I spoke into an intercom and was buzzed in.

Pippi met us in the grand foyer. Such a quaint term, foyer. This foyer was two stories of square white panels. Beautiful impressionist artwork splashed the walls with color, breaking the monotony of the white. A wide walnut staircase rose up and branched left and right, curving up to the second floor. It was nothing short of spectacular and looked like something out of *Gone with the Wind*.

I half expected to see Scarlet come running down, dressed in velvet drapes. The evil part of me had always wanted to see her fall down those stairs. I never could stand that Scarlet O'Hara.

Pippi kissed my cheeks. A little thing, she stood about five feet tall. She had a slender build, most of her weight probably coming from her hair, which was gray and pulled into a full bun atop her head.

She looked like a doppelganger for the grandma from the Tweety Bird cartoons, only a tad bit younger.

Pippi pinched Nels's cheeks, told Roxie she loved her glasses. "Please, please tell me Thad Cochran is just as adorable in real life as he is on TV." Her voice was whiskey rough with a hint of southern charm.

"You sound like my mother," I said.

Pippi looped her arm through mine. "Obviously a woman of impeccable taste."

Though Pippi looked grandmotherly, she reeked of cigarette smoke. I also spotted a tiny heart tattoo at the nape of her neck, peeking out from under a lace collar.

I couldn't help but like her.

"So, Thad?" she asked.

"He's cute."

"And married," Roxie piped in.

Like that mattered, I thought. I wondered if Sherry knew about his behind-the-scenes action with Genevieve Hidalgo Sala. Or if Willie knew, for that matter. Could that have been what propelled Willie and Sherry into each other's arms?

"I'm so sorry to hear about your resident who passed on," I said.

"Yes, me too. Poor Gaye Goldwin passed away after a long battle with colon cancer. Awful, awful disease."

"I'm sorry," I said again, though I'd never met Mrs. Goldwin.

"The doctors here at Lowther House made her last days as comfortable as possible. She was at peace. But enough of the drear and gloom. I'm very excited for the makeover. This place needs a little perking up. Come, let's go upstairs to the atrium."

She led us up the stairs, down a lushly carpeted hallway, and into a large gathering room flanked on one end by a large stone fireplace. The other end held floor to ceiling windows that overlooked the courtyard below. Above our heads, a glass dome showered light down upon us.

"Wow," I heard Roxie say.

Three seating areas split the room into different groupings. Leather sofas, chunky wooden coffee tables, and Oriental rugs helped to define each space. No expense was spared.

"I've closed off this area," Pippi said, "until work is done. I really want everyone to be surprised. They think the room is being painted." She laughed. "I can't wait to see their faces."

"You're doing the makeover in here?" Nels asked. "Inside?"

"An indoor sanctuary." Pippi's bun wobbled as she turned to face Nels. "With a waterfall and lush tropical plants, bromeliads, palms, and even a tree! A little bit of outdoors inside."

"How?" Roxie asked.

I pointed upward, to the atrium. "There will more than enough light for the plants to thrive. I brought the final plans, Pippi."

She motioned to a heavy oak table nearby, and I set out my design board.

Pippi studied it a good three minutes, even though she'd seen it before. "It's lovely, Nina. Just lovely. Everyone's going to adore it."

"Then we're all set. We'll be arriving here tomorrow at eight."

"That will be wonderful. I've planned a day trip to Columbus for everyone, so they'll be out of the house. I'll be in and out all day. I've many interviews set up this week to fill our vacancy." Her light blue eyes filled with tears. "It's always hard to bring in someone new."

"So soon?" Roxie asked.

Pippi folded her hands. "It seems harsh, doesn't it?"

Roxie nodded.

"There's a waiting list three pages long. The sooner I do interviews, the sooner another deserving soul can move in, and start living an enriched life—it's what I strive for here at Lowther House."

"Interviews, though?" Roxie asked.

"Absolutely, dear." She pulled a hankie from her sleeve, dabbed her eyes. "It's not just about money here. You have to fit in." To me, she said, "For you, Nina, I did make an exception to interview someone not on the waiting list."

Confused, I asked, "Me?"

"Yes." Her brows knit. "A gentleman called this morning inquiring about the vacancy. He gave you as a reference. He'll be along in a little bit."

"What's his name?"

"Oh my. I can't recall. I have it in my office. Did you not recommend him?"

"I don't remember telling anyone . . . "

"I'll be sure to clear the matter up before allowing him a tour."

Recommended by me? Odd.

"About tomorrow," Pippi continued. "Except for the east and north wings, you may have free reign of the place."

Roxie adjusted her glasses. "What's in the east and north wings?"

"Bedroom suites," Pippi said. "They're off-limits to respect our residents' privacy."

She led us out of the atrium, back toward the stairs. At the top of the stairs, laughter floated down the hallway. Pippi smiled. "Oh, do come meet Mr. William Umberry and his lovely wife Monique. I believe they're ensconced in a heated game of poker."

"Poker?" I couldn't help but think of Riley.

"High-stakes," she said.

She was sprightly, that Pippi. I had to fast-walk to keep up with her. We followed her into a large game room. A poker table sat in the center, and a handsome man and two women were seated there, mounds of peanut M&Ms piled in front of them.

Now those were my kind of stakes.

Pippi made introductions while Nels filmed. Monique Umberry was seventy, if a day, and must have been a heartbreaker when younger since she was still gorgeous, with healthy blonde hair, fair skin, brilliant green eyes. Mr. Umberry looked every inch of Clark Gable and fit the role to a T, complete with red satin ascot.

Next to him sat Minnie Baker, her big blue eyes somewhat blank, but her full cheeks rosy with health. Her wheelchair was barely noticeable beyond the flowing silk robe I noticed she wore after I tore my gaze from her turban, complete with giant ruby. A huge square cut diamond sparkled from her right hand. It had to be ten carats at least.

Pippi said, "This is Nina Quinn, the designer I told you about. She'll be working on the atrium tomorrow."

"Painting, correct?" Monique asked me.

I was a great liar. "A mural."

"I swear I've heard your name before," William said.

"Because I told it to you the other day, silly," Pippi said quickly. "When I explained about the camera crew being here."

"Ah yes. *Hitched or Ditched*," Monique said. "We watch it all the time. It's one of Pippi's favorites. Missed it last night, though—the cable went out." She popped an M&M into her mouth.

I noticed Pippi's sly smile. She'd told me all about her plan for the cable to "happen" to go out around 10:55 every night—so the residents wouldn't learn of my profession via HoD.

Monique set her chin in the palm of her hand as her elbow rested on the table. "Is that Thad Cochran as handsome in per—"

"Yes," Nels, Roxie, and I said at once.

Pippi laughed, color rising to her cheeks. "I'd love to have one steamy night with that man." She sighed. "The dreams of a lonely old woman."

"Oh stop now," William said dryly. "You're making me blush."

They all laughed. If they only knew that Thad might be up for Pippi's proposition.

The lot of them didn't appear to be too grief-stricken

by the death of a fellow resident. Since I lived in the Mill, which was highly comprised of a geriatric demographic, I wasn't alarmed. There apparently was a strange phenomenon in the older set where death was concerned. It became everyday. Commonplace. It was . . . accepted, I supposed. Certainly not something to fear, and certainly not something to dwell on. Life went on, and most of the older people I knew loved living it to the fullest.

Minnie studied us. "Who are you?" she asked, her voice hesitant.

Pippi bent down next to her chair, took Minnie's hand in her own. The huge diamond ring glinted from Minnie's ring finger. Pippi introduced us again, and I caught the flash of sadness in her eyes.

Minnie said, "Oh. Oh yes."

Alzheimer's?

"We should go," I said, checking my watch. "We'll let you get back to your game."

Blinking, Minnie twisted her ring. She looked up at me, caught my eye. "Who are you?"

"I'm Nina," I said. "But I really need to get going." I patted her hand. "Enjoy your game, Minnie."

As we left the room, I heard William and Monique explaining to Minnie that they were playing poker.

Pippi led us down the stairs, and I admired how she didn't apologize for Minnie. That kind of respect was hard to come by.

My phone rang and Pippi laughed aloud, apparently recognizing the song. I was going to kill Ana.

"Sorry," I said to Pippi after seeing the TBS number. "I need to get this."

"Go on," she said, waving a hand.

I stepped to the side and answered. "This is Nina."

I heard clucking. "What's wrong with Tam?" Brickhouse asked.

"Nothing's wrong with Tam," I said.

"What's this about needing to talk to your mother about her?"

I ran my hand along the walnut banister. "Did my mother call you?"

"Ach, why would she do that?"

Her voice was too high, too innocent.

"Because she's avoiding me."

"Why?"

"Something about construction workers and picketers."

Over my shoulder I heard Roxie ask, "How many people live here?"

Pippi said, "Seven, and we have a full-time staff of ten."

"Look," I told Brickhouse, "tell my mother to call me. I've got to go."

"But—"

I hung up. "Sorry," I said again.

Pippi led us down the stairs, telling us all about the original artwork on the walls, works she'd collected over the years.

On the ground floor we spotted a young woman in a tight-fitting business suit and three-inch heels hurrying away from us, down the long hallway leading to the kitchen at the west end of the house. Long red hair streamed out behind her.

Pippi watched her go but didn't explain who she was.

"Who was that?" Roxie asked.

I was beginning to like Roxie a lot.

"Just one of our . . . therapists. Perhaps you'll meet her tomorrow."

A buzzer sounded—the front door. Pippi crossed to the door. "This would be the gentleman I told you about earlier," she said to me. "The one who used your name as a recommendation." She pulled open the door.

I froze.

"Nina?" he said.

"Bobby? What are you doing here?"

Roxie motioned furiously to Nels, who hefted the camera onto his shoulder.

Bobby, I finally noticed, wasn't alone. "You remember Nina, Mac?"

Mac was tall like Bobby, but time had put a hunch in his back, and his injury had put a limp in his step. His bright blue Irish eyes shone with intelligence.

"I'm not senile," Mac griped, leaning in to kiss me. He grabbed my arm to steady himself.

He aimed for my lips, but I moved just in time so his kiss landed on my cheek.

"So you do know each other?" Pippi asked.

"Yes. Pippi Lowther, meet Bobby MacKenna and his grandfather, Patrick MacKenna."

"Call me Mac," he said, kissing Pippi's hand. "I hope you don't mind me using your name as a recommendation, Nina."

"You did what?" Bobby's gaze shot to mine. He hadn't known anything about it.

"It's all right," I said. "But how'd you know I was working here?"

"Word gets around." He winked.

Now I knew where Bobby had gotten it from. "It shouldn't," I said. "That's the whole idea of the surprise."

He leaned in, whispered, "Your mother is quite proud of your work."

I rolled my eyes. She was a blabbermouth, that's what she was.

Mac had completely charmed Pippi. Pink tinged her cheeks, and she smiled brightly. I wondered if I should tell her about his penchant for touching.

Probably she'd learn soon enough.

"Pippi, Bobby is my, ahem, boyfriend. My partner on *Hitched or Ditched*."

"Oh! How exciting!" Pippi looked around. "Where's your camera crew?"

"In the car. They didn't think anything exciting would happen in here," Bobby said.

I caught Roxie and Nels high-fiving. This would certainly be a coup for them.

"You're thinking about moving in here?" I asked Mac. I leaned in to Bobby. "Can he afford that?"

Bobby shrugged.

"Well, we should leave you to your tour, then."

I looked at Roxie, who was looking at Bobby and me expectantly.

Standing on tiptoes, I kissed Bobby's lips. He pulled me in close, anchored me against his chest and planted a kiss on me that curled my toes.

Whoa.

"Gets it from me," Mac boasted, shaking his cane.

Pippi fanned herself.

I needed a cool-down myself.

"I'll see you tonight," Bobby said with a wink.

Ohhh, that wink. It did things to me.

"O-Okay." I tried to walk, but my legs were still Jell-O.

Outside, I drew in fresh air, wished I had something chocolate to eat. One of those peanut M&Ms. Something.

I'd started the truck when Nels said, "Anyone else get a strange vibe in there?"

"Vibe?" I asked.

"Like something hinky is going on?"

"Yeah," Roxie said. "It's like the Stepford Inn."

"Exactly." Nels cleaned the camera lens. "Why's everyone so happy? Didn't someone just die?"

"Even still." I put the truck into Drive. "Wouldn't you be happy if you lived there?"

"What if Pippi Longstocking is giving everyone happy pills? Taking all their money?"

"Little Pippi?" I asked, shocked.

Roxie slumped back. "I guess you're right. She was too sweet to do anything evil."

"Hah!" Nels said. "I bet the east wing really leads to a secret laboratory . . ."

Roxie perked up. "There's one way to find out."

"No!" I said. "No snooping tomorrow. Lowther House is high class. Think old money country club. There's no secret labs, no happy pills being doled out. It's just a nice place to grow old."

"And die," Nels said.

Nels was really starting to get on my nerves.

"Yeah," Roxie perked up, "do we really know what happened to that poor old Mrs. Goldwin?"

"You two, stop." I turned onto 63. "There will be no snooping. Not so much as a voiced suspicion. It's my company and my reputation at stake if you two upset Pippi. I'm liable for you two. So behave yourselves tomorrow."

They both agreed, but I didn't believe them for a second.

Ten

I skipped out of work early and let everyone else go home too, since everything was set for the mini at Lowther House the following day. Our schedules were often topsy-turvy, so we had to take time off when we could.

I headed home hoping to catch up with my mother. Any other day she would have been at my house, overseeing the construction. With the picketers, I doubted any construction was going on today.

Flipping on the radio, I realized the old me would have been angry with her. Okay, so I wasn't thrilled construction had been delayed . . . again. But the new me was easygoing, care-free. Zenlike.

Note to self: Look up Zen ASAP.

"Do You Wanna Dance" played on the oldies station, and I sang along until I realized I always listened to the oldies station.

Impulsively, I turned the dial. The car thumped with the bass of a rap song. I listened for a minute before changing it. The new me could only handle so much. I stopped on a pop station. Someone was singing about the pain of breaking up. It hit a little too close to home. Another spin of the dial and I landed on the local country station. I stopped, listened. A man was singing about tequila and how it made "her" clothes fall off.

This had potential.

I liked tequila.

Could use some, as a matter of fact.

Wouldn't mind my clothes falling off with Bobby around.

No, no, no! Wrong.

Still, tequila sounded good. The old Nina would never drink at three-thirty in the afternoon, but the new me? Why not?

As I drove along, I thought about Deanna. Should I call her? I hated leaving things as they were. I just wished she'd given me the chance to explain about Weekend Warrior. But that wouldn't have changed the fact that she'd already set up another interview . . .

I sighed.

My thoughts switched over to *Hitched or Ditched*. I hadn't seen last night's show and didn't know if I wanted to. Probably, I did. I know Riley had taped it for me—maybe I'd watch it when I got home. Alone. With my tequila.

Sounded like a plan.

If I turned into a lush, it would be all Josh's fault. Him and his crazy plan. From what I'd seen so far, sexual harassment wasn't all that far-fetched an accusation. Not that anyone had hit on me, but there was enough hanky-panky going around.

Had I just said hanky-panky?

Note to self: Stop watching reruns of the *Newlywed Game* on the Game Show Network.

I hadn't seen even the barest hint of impropriety from Willie toward his staff. Now, with Sherry—that was a whole other deal. One I shouldn't worry myself about.

Who they slept around with was their issue. Not mine.

Mine was finding out about the sexual harassment.

I held the wheel with one hand, flipped open my phone

and dialed Josh's number with the other. It rang twice before switching to voice mail.

"Josh, it's Nina. I just wanted to talk to you about Jessica. If you could give me a call, I'd appreciate it."

Snapping the phone closed, I wondered when I'd hear
from him.

I left the radio dial on the country station and felt my
eyebrows dip as I turned onto my street. Cars lined both
sides, and I had to park four houses down, in front of Mr.
Weatherbee's place. I'm sure I'd hear about that later. He
hated anyone parking in front of his house, despite the
street being public property.

Walking back toward my place, I stopped short next to
the maple tree at the edge of my property, trying to take it
all in.

The Dave Matthews Band blasted from speakers set up
on my front porch. A buffet table had been set out on my
front lawn. The two picketers had their signs propped on
their shoulders. They each held plates loaded to their plastic edges. Several other men wearing hard hats, jeans, and
thermal long-sleeve T-shirts standing on the other side of
the table joked, laughed, and chowed down. All around,
residents of the Mill joined in, laughing, eating. I spotted
Mrs. Daasch doing the cha-cha with the foreman of the
construction crew.

It was an all-out block party.

At my house.

Screw Zen.

I was gonna kill my mother.

My backpack thumped my shoulder blades as I stomped
along the sidewalk. I slowed when I saw a familiar car pull
into the driveway across the street. It parked behind a dark
sedan I hadn't noticed before.

The door to the sedan opened, and I recognized Jennie
Nix, the Realtor selling the house. She greeted Brickhouse

Krauss as she stepped out of her brand new Camry hybrid.

Oh. My. God.

Was Brickhouse looking at the house? To buy it?

No, not poss—

They went inside.

Brickhouse Krauss. Living across the street from me.

Panic flared. Even though we'd been getting on okay, I didn't want to be living within a hundred feet of her.

Deep breath. In, out.

Zen.

Breathe.

I unclenched my hands just in time to be wrapped from behind in an intimate dance hold. His heart beat steadily against my spine. His strong arms held me firmly. By the way my stomach flopped around behind my belly button, I knew who it was; I didn't have to look at his face.

"Sigh, he'd be hot and steamy," Kevin singsonged, mocking my answer from the show the night before.

I jabbed him in his diaphragm with my elbow, then spun around as he bent double, gasping for breath.

Hitching my backpack onto my shoulder, I looked at him, feeling no remorse.

Okay, some remorse, but I didn't dwell. That was something the old me would have done.

"Serves you right for mocking me," I said.

Slowly, he stood upright. Though he had to still be hurting, a small grin tugged at the corners of his mouth. "It was worth it, holding you like that. You look great, by the way. Stunning."

I rolled my eyes. "What're you doing here, anyway?"

"Riley. We're doing a movie and dinner."

"Then do."

"He's getting ready."

"I'll spur him on." I headed toward the house, only to be stopped by my neighbor diagonally across the street, Flash Leonard.

"Hey cutie!" The neighborhood's geriatric playboy twirled me.

I broke into a smile, settled my right hand into his left and put my other arm around his back. Flash didn't move too fast these days, so I figured a little less spinning would probably be best.

Over his shoulder I spotted Kevin. He looked jealous. I smiled wider, feeling better.

"My sister is in town," Flash said. "Let me introduce you."

We tangoed across the lawn, over to a lovely woman speaking with the Molari brothers.

"Nina, this is my little sister, Sue Evans. She'll be staying with me until Christmas."

"It's a pleasure, Mrs. Evans." I shook her hand.

"Please call me Sue. Or Miss Sue, if you're one of those respectful types."

She had lovely hazel eyes, heavy on the green, that shone through her purple-rimmed glasses. Wavy white hair streaked with silver set off her beautiful complexion.

A little fluffy dog sat at her feet.

"That's Bear," she said, following my gaze.

"What breed?"

"Yorkie-poo. Part Yorkshire, part poodle."

"He's adorable." I scratched his ears, and he flopped over onto his back hoping I'd rub his belly.

He could keep on hoping.

"Great party, isn't it?" Flash said.

"It is."

"That mother of yours is one special mama."

I looked around at the construction workers mingling with the picketers mingling with my neighbors, all smiles and laughter. "Yeah, I guess she is."

"I love the hair, by the way. Very snazzy. Always did have a thing for blondes." He winked and twirled me again.

As I spun I caught sight of my mother on the front porch. She was smiling and tapping her foot. Her gaze met mine. She squinted, then her eyes widened and her mouth dropped open.

Right. The makeover.

She started down the steps toward me, then she must have remembered she was avoiding me. Like a startled deer, she froze, then turned and scurried into the house, slamming the door behind her.

"Miss Sue, it was nice to meet you! Flash, save me another dance! Gotta go!" I dashed after my mother.

The front door was locked. She must have forgotten I lived there. I stuck my key in the lock, let myself in.

"Mom!"

"No mama *aqui*," a squeaky muffled voice said.

I walked over to the hall closet, pulled open the door.

My mother waltzed out, fluffing her hair. "Hi *chérie*! Let me look at you. The hair! Divine. Oh lordy, lordy, is that a manicure?" she squealed. "Have I died and gone to heaven? I must tell Maria. I'll just grab my bag and go."

She was fast. She almost made it to the door before I said, "Stop right there!"

She stopped. Mid-stride. And slowly turned, giving me a little shrug. "It wasn't right that everyone was out there, just waiting. Hungry. I had to do something."

I held up a hand. "It's okay."

"It is?"

"It is."

Before I forgot, I said, "You need to call Tam. She doesn't want a baby shower—"

She held up her hand. "Already taken care of. I spoke to Tamara earlier. She also agrees that you look fabulous, but couldn't call, something about the cameras and hackers. I'm sure there's a story there, but I couldn't get it out of her. Anyhow, we've come up with something else."

I tossed my backpack on the couch. "Something else?"

"*Pah*, don't worry. It's all taken care of."

For some reason, I was suddenly worried.

"Now tell me all about this," she said, motioning to me with grand sweeps of her arm. "You look just gorgeous, Nina. Gorgeous."

"Thanks."

"Tell all."

"You've already heard it all from Ana."

"Secondhand hearsay. I want all the details."

"It's a long story," I said, heading into the kitchen.

"I have time. Where are you going?" she asked.

"To get some glasses—and tequila."

"Ooh! I'll get the limes."

After downing one shot of tequila (my limit), I felt much better.

"Have you heard anything about Mrs. Krauss moving in across the street?"

My mother poured her shot glass to the rim, her third. She held up the bottle, an offer to me. I shook my head. I was driving later.

"She might have mentioned something."

I looked out the kitchen window, over the heads of the revelers. A split story, the house across the street had been vacant for nearly two months, but only on the market for two weeks. It was overpriced, in my opinion, but since the housing market had skyrocketed in this area, even the older homes felt the boom.

I hoped and hoped Brickhouse Krauss couldn't afford the place. How much could a Catholic school teacher's pension be anyway?

I noticed one of the picketers, a chubby fellow with a grainy salt and pepper beard, buzz cut, and big, wide eyes glance over his shoulder toward the house. "Buzz" looked guarded, as if he was hiding something. Hard to hide something with a giant picket sign reading REALITY TV IS IMORAL written on it. And harder to be taken seriously with *immoral* spelled wrong.

What was he up to, that Buzz?

Footsteps pounded the stairs. Riley rarely did anything gracefully. Or quietly. Things were always being slammed around. "I'm leaving," he called out.

Before I could get a "'Bye" out of my mouth, the front door opened and then slammed shut.

My mother hadn't seemed to notice. "We've got to take you shopping," she declared. She licked salt off the top of her hand, then downed the tequila. "Your wardrobe has got to go." She snapped her fingers. "A bonfire! With marshmallows!"

"We are not burning my clothes."

"*Pah*. Fine. But we still must shop. My treat!"

"Sorry, I already have plans to shop with a friend."

"Wshtyrmma?"

Amused, I glanced at her. "The lime, Mom. The lime."

She took it out of her mouth, dabbed her lips with a napkin. "Without your mama?"

"Sorry. First come, first served."

She pouted. Then brightened.

Oh no.

"Handbag shopping, then! I've been waiting for years to get rid of that suitcase you carry around!"

"It's a leather backpack, not a suitcase."

"It has to go! It doesn't match the new you, *chérie*." She giggled.

The new me. People were noticing. That had to be a good thing. Or so I told myself. "Maybe we should put the tequila away."

She slapped my hand as I reached for the bottle.

"Then let me call Dad to come pick you up."

She giggled again.

Movement at the window caught my eye. I glanced out just in time to see a head bob past. A buzzed-cut head. I leaned farther and saw Buzz pull out a cell phone as he ducked around the corner of the house.

My nosiness got the better of me. "I'll be right back."

"No!"

"No?"

"Not until you promise me!"

"Promise what?"

"That you'll go shopping with me, *chérie*!" She burst into all-out laughter as she poured another finger of tequila. I couldn't help but laugh with her. My mother was a fun drunk. "To buy a nice bag, so you don't look like a hag!"

"All right. Just don't be a *nag*." I didn't say I promised. I rarely broke my promises.

She doubled over with laughter. "Bag, hag, nag!"

I left as she poured her shot glass to the rim again.

I stepped into the laundry room, slowly pulled open the back door, which was actually a side door, since it opened into the side yard facing Mr. Cabrera's house. I stuck my head out, but all I could hear was a hollow sounding "Ants Marching."

Creeping out, I went right, toward the backyard. Probably Buzz was calling home, checking on his family, making sure they were being moral. But something about the way he snuck away made me suspicious.

All my day lilies had begun to wilt, but my pansies still looked decent. Soon I'd be spending a whole weekend out here, pulling things up, getting everything ready for winter.

At the back corner of the house I paused. I heard Buzz say, " . . . not comfortable, nice people." After a second, he added, "I know I'm not getting paid to be comfortable."

Paid?

"Miz Quinn!"

I jumped, banging my elbow against the brick facade of the house. I lurched toward Mr. Cabrera, pulling him toward the front yard. I looked back over my shoulder. No sign that Buzz had seen me snooping.

"Is Celeste okay?" he asked. "She keeps talking about

Louis Vuitton and Chanel, the Wicked Witch of the West, and you."

"Bags and hags and nags," I said.

He raised a bushy eyebrow at me.

"Don't ask."

Today he wore a bright blue button-down with leaping dolphins, jeans, and those funny slip-on shoes that looked like something Aquaman would wear. "Have something to do with your hair?"

"Kinda."

"Well, I don't like it."

"Bags, hags, or nags?"

"Your hair! What's the deal, girlie? You can't just go and change without a word of warnin' to anyone."

Now I arched *my* eyebrow.

"First it's the hair, then it's the parties on the front lawn, what's next?" He harrumphed, crossed his arms, looked altogether put out. "Married and movin' away?"

I was about to debate the party comment, since it hadn't been my idea, but the look on his face stopped me. Mr. Cabrera puffed out his chest and his jaw jutted stubbornly, but his blue eyes were sad.

I saw through to the heart of his bravado. "Awww, I'm not going anywhere."

He huffed. "Never said you were."

I smiled. "Even if Bobby and I did get married, I wouldn't move, Mr. Cabrera. We'd live here."

"Hmmph." He stomped away—or tried to. His limp made it difficult. I couldn't help but notice the smile playing at the corner of his mouth.

Right about the time I noticed Brickhouse Krauss come out of the house across the street and shake the Realtor's hand.

Talk about wicked witches.

I spotted Riley doing a tango with Mrs. Greeble. He looked mortified. Mr. Cabrera cut in and Riley took off, jumping into Kevin's pickup. They slowly pulled away from the curve, Kevin giving me a nod as they passed. Riley didn't so much as look in my direction.

Sometimes I wondered why I loved that boy so much.

My cell rang. Madonna went quiet as I answered.

"Nina, it's Josh Drake. You called?"

"Josh, hi. I was hoping you could put me in touch with Jessica."

"Why?"

"I'd like to talk to her, get more details about the harassment." Searching for a quiet spot, I sat down on Mr. Cabrera's front steps. To block out noise, I covered my free ear with my hand.

"I don't think that's necessary, Nina."

"I'd like to know just how Willie came on to her, where, when. If anyone was around. If Thad's ever made a pass. What she might have seen around the set."

"All unnecessary."

My hackles went up. "Why's that?"

"I need your impression of the goings on at *Hitched or Ditched*. Not your impressions of Jessica's impressions."

It took me a second to decipher the double talk. "It would help me be more aware."

"It's not going to happen. Jessica is unreachable, doing a calendar shoot in Mexico. She won't be back until late tonight. Besides, this matter is probably all moot."

"How so?"

"Can't discuss it, but there's a settlement in the works."

"So Bobby and I are on the show, why?"

"Well, to find out if you should get hitched. Or ditched." He laughed and hung up.

I called him a few choice words, something the old me would have done too. There were some things I just wasn't ready to let go.

Eleven

Ana held up a pretend microphone and gleefully asked, "Which best describes Bobby's experience in the kitchen? Lukewarm, simmering, or boiling hot, hot, hot?"

I poured a glass of ice water. The studio had provided a little buffet table with cheese, crackers, fruit, and refreshments. Little did Ana know about the time Bobby and I had tried our hand at cooking together . . .

It was definitely in the scorching range.

"Stop," I said to her, taking a sip of the water, hoping for a cool down.

"Come on. These are questions that could be asked."

I prayed she was wrong. Questions like that tended to remind me of all I was resisting.

My stomach rolled. Maybe I should have eaten. Yeah, it had to be lack of food. Not the reminder that I'd made a horrible mistake letting Bobby move away. I grabbed a cracker, popped it into my mouth.

"Where is he, by the way?"

I spoke around the cracker. "Who?"

"Bobby!"

"Oh, I don't know." He wasn't there. I knew that immediately when I walked into the studio. That sizzle wasn't in the air. The zip, the zing I felt whenever he was around.

"What kind of fiancée are you?"

I gave her the evil eye. She laughed.

"Where's Carson?" I asked.

Ana adjusted the spaghetti strap of her barely there satin tank top. "Interviewing the production assistant," she said, pointing.

Ah. Louisa. The one who had the hots for Bobby.

I hated her, and didn't care that I did. The old me would have cared. The new me was making progress already.

I stabbed a cube of cheddar with a toothpick, popped it into my mouth, chewed and swallowed. "Where are you two going later?"

"Down to All Shook Up, the martini bar?"

How could I forget? I'd had an interesting experience there with Elvis impersonators.

"Then," she smiled, "who knows?" Her perfectly shaped eyebrows waggled.

"Oh, I think you know."

"I hope I know." She bit into a strawberry.

The set was still dark, and I'd yet to see Thad or Willie or even Genevieve. I didn't expect to see Sherry tonight, but who knew? Perry and Mario were also MIA, but it was early yet. Ambient light cast an eerie glow as we stood around, waiting for things to get under way.

The Channel 18 cameraman lowered his camera as Carson and Louisa shook hands and headed our way. Carson put his arm around Ana's shoulder, kissed her cheek. She looked up at him with adoration.

Yuck.

Louisa said, "Is Bobby not here yet?"

I wondered how she'd like a toothpick to the eye. "Not yet," I managed to say rather sweetly. But couldn't help adding, "He was still in the shower when I left."

I was right proud of my lie until she said, "You didn't drive together?"

Damn. I really hated her.

Ana tore her gaze away from Carson. "Separate cars. They aren't glued at the hip, you know."

Louisa looked like she wanted to argue, but decided against it.

Smart girl. A protective Ana was a dangerous Ana.

"Who are the suits?" Carson motioned with his head.

Three men in impeccable suits had walked into the room with Willie Sala.

"Network executives," Louisa said. "Surely you heard they'd be in this week? The deal to take *Hitched or Ditched* national is all but done."

Carson took out his notebook. "Why hadn't I heard about this? This is news! Big news!"

He was so excited I thought one of his veneers might pop off.

Louisa added, "Friday's the day they're supposed to sign the contracts."

Friday was shaping up to be a busy day for a lot of people.

Out of the corner of my eye I spotted Willie excusing himself from the group. He headed straight toward us, smoothing down the five measly stripes of hair on top of his head.

"Louisa," he said in a loud whisper, motioning her over.

Clipboard in hand, she hurried to his side.

Perry and Mario came in, holding hands. "What's going on?" Perry asked, referring to Willie's impromptu pow-wow.

"Don't know."

We eavesdropped as Willie, who may have been whispering, but his voice carried, said to Louisa, "Where's Genevieve?"

Louisa shrugged. "I don't know, sir."

Perry leaned in. "What I would do to buzz that comb-over off his head."

"Hideous," Mario agreed.

Willie's fists clenched. "She's supposed to be down here, schmoozing. Find her now!" he demanded.

Louisa scurried off. I looked around for Thad. No sign of him either. I thought I should probably tell Louisa to look in Willie's office bathroom for Genevieve, and that she'd probably find Thad in there too, but kept quiet. None of my business, I kept reminding myself.

"I need to go call my producer about this deal in the works," Carson said, tucking his notebook back into his jacket pocket.

Ana latched onto his arm. "I'll come with you."

He smiled, a thousand watts at least, and led her away.

"They'll be the cover story in the next *SoSceCinci*," Perry said. *SoSceCinci*, aka *Social Scene Cincinnati*, was the town's social, entertainment, and gossip paper, a weekly. Maria, my sister, an event planner, raved about the paper, especially since they loved to photograph her at her various events.

I tried to imagine how Ana would like the publicity. I quickly decided I should just go out and buy her a scrapbook—she was going to love the attention.

"When do you want to do our shopping trip?" Perry asked me. "You need new clothes in a desperate way."

"What's wrong with this?" I wore a classic black dress, nicely cut. It fit all the right places and hid all problem areas.

"My grandmother wore that same dress to my grandfather's funeral," Mario said. "In 1988. And I don't know much about clothes, that's Perry's thing, but I know you don't look so good."

Okay, that sealed it. Pulling out my day planner from my backpack, I looked at Perry. "When, exactly, is good for you?"

Perry wasn't listening. He was staring. "Well, hi-ho, silver! He looks hot tonight."

My skin danced. I didn't need to look over my shoulder to know who he was talking about.

Mario fanned his face. "You're not kidding. Nina, you're one lucky girl."

Bobby's hands settled on my shoulders, and his kiss lingered on my cheek. "Miss me?"

Mario and Perry watched us closely.

"As always." I tucked my day planner away and slipped my arm around his back. So natural, so easy. So contrived for Mario and Perry's sake.

Sneaking a peak, I saw Bobby wore dark trouser style jeans, scuffed loafers, a blue button-down, sleeves rolled up. Hi-ho, indeed. Hot didn't even come close.

"Who died?" he asked me, fingering the sleeve of my dress.

Perry opened his mouth.

"Ah-ah! Not a word," I warned. "We'll be right back." I pulled Bobby aside, stepping over wires, dodging hulking cameras. Someone ought to turn on the overhead lights, I thought, before somebody got hurt. "You don't like the dress?"

"Not really. Now, you out of it . . . "

Outwardly, I ignored his comment, but inwardly I was melting. "How's Mac?" I asked.

Bobby grinned—I assumed at my abrupt change of subject. His dimple popped out, and I fought the urge to kiss him. "Settled in front of the TV for the night," he said. "Watching a *COPS* marathon."

"How'd things go at Lowther House?"

"Great." His brows dipped.

"What?"

He hesitated. "Nothing."

"Does Mac have that much money?"

"Apparently he's been saving."

There was something in his tone. "What did Mac do for a living before he retired?"

"Long story."

The lights finally came up on the set, and I spotted Louisa rushing into the room, her cheeks flushed. Willie stepped away from the execs, leaned close as she whispered into his ear.

"What's going on there?" Bobby asked.

"No one can find Genevieve."

Smirking, he said, "Did they check Willie's office bathroom?"

"My thoughts exactly."

Willie's gestures were short, controlled. It was obvious by the strain in his face he was trying not to get angry in front of the network people.

"I spoke to Josh today," I said.

"You did?"

"Apparently there's a settlement in the works for Jessica."

"He's not the most savory of characters, but he's a good lawyer. He'll get her a good deal."

He'd totally missed the point. "A settlement means we didn't have to do this show."

His dimple came out as he smiled. "What? You're not having fun?"

Grrr.

"Just look at all the time we get to spend together this week," he said, moving in close.

I inhaled, smelled that soap/coffee/him scent again. My mouth went dry. "It's been, ah, a blast."

He laughed.

"What's so funny?"

"You should see the look on your face."

Heat climbed my neck.

With a fingertip, he lifted my chin. "Is it really so bad?" he asked, looking into my eyes.

I stared into his. The light blue seemed even brighter than usual. I sighed. "It's just . . . hard."

"For me too," he said, pulling me into a hug.

For a minute I let him hold me. In his arms, I forgot about the doubts, the questions, the regrets.

He let me go as Thad sauntered into the room in his robe. Carson dashed to his side and thrust a microphone to Thad's lips. The cameraman followed. Ana followed him.

"This is surreal," Bobby said.

I'd been thinking the same thing. For a reality show, nothing seemed to be real at all. Adultery, pretend contestants, phony death threats . . .

Louisa tore out of the room. Face flushed, Willie wiped his head, dislodging his comb-over. He returned to the execs, shrugging off the incident.

I turned away from the craziness, headed toward the hot tub. "While we have a second, maybe we should talk."

"About?"

"Us. That kiss today." I glanced up at him.

Arching an eyebrow, the corner of his lip curved up in a smile. "The audience will eat that stuff up, don't you think?"

"The audience? Oh! Right, right. The audience."

"We are pretend contestants, remember?"

"Of course. Pretend." Only there was nothing pretend about that kiss. He knew it. I knew it. Question was, what were we going to do about it?

Heat billowed up in plumes of steam as I leaned on the edge of the hot tub.

Moving in close, his body touched mine. He lowered his head, put it on my shoulder. "Wasn't it?" he whispered into my ear.

Did I want to get into this? To open this can of worms? He'd be gone in a week's time, back to Florida, back to his life.

I dipped my hand into the water, swirled it around. With a loud yelp, I suddenly yanked it out of the water while jumping backward, nearly knocking Bobby over.

He steadied me, keeping me from falling.

"Nina, what's wrong?"

I pointed a shaking, dripping finger toward the hot tub. "Someone . . . someone's in there."

"What?" He reached into the water, searched with his arm. His face paled as a body rose to the surface.

Looks like I'd found Genevieve.

Twelve

All was quiet in the Mill at one in the morning. My house sat in darkness as I pulled into the driveway and cut the engine. No evidence remained of the block party. If nothing else, my mother was a stickler for cleanliness.

Relief flooded me as I saw the house across the street still bore a FOR SALE sign and not a SOLD sign. I could take only so many traumas in one night.

I pushed open the truck door and gasped as I saw Mr. Cabrera standing there. "You just took ten years off my life," I said.

He helped me out of the truck. "Sorry, just wanted to talk with you."

Interrogate would probably be a better term. "And thought one in the morning would be a good time for a chat?"

"When better?" he asked, smiling. "Saw you pull in."

"You were waiting for me."

"I happened to be lookin' out the window."

"Happened?"

He grinned. I was glad to see he hadn't taken his dentures out for the night.

Glow from the street lamps lit the path up to my doorway. Riley hadn't bothered to leave the front light on. I unlocked the door and held it open for Mr. Cabrera to follow me in.

"Is anything wrong?" I asked, flipping on lights in the living room. Any hope my living room ceiling had been miraculously patched dissipated when I spotted the telltale hole above my head.

He followed me to the kitchen. "You tell me."

"What do you mean?" I asked, playing dumb. I held up a kettle. "Cocoa?"

"You have marshmallows?"

"Always."

He slid onto a stool, set his elbows on the island. "*Hitched or Ditched.*"

I heard a soft knock at the front door. I opened it to find Flash Leonard standing on my front porch, his sister Miss Sue and her dog Bear next to him. "We heard about the murder," Flash said. "You okay, darlin'?"

"I'm fine. Come on in." I led them to the kitchen. "Pull up a stool. I'll be right back."

Mr. Cabrera looked put-out that he wouldn't be the first to get the scoop. Poor guy.

I crept up the stairs as the three of them launched into a report on Genevieve's murder.

At the top of the steps, I switched on the hall light, tiptoed to Riley's room, slowly turned the knob and opened the door.

Sounds of deep breathing filled the air. He was a mouth breather, had been since I met him when he was eight years old.

Strong scent of boy filled my nose. Moonlight filtered in through his closed shades, lighting his face. Asleep, he looked so peaceful, even with one leg thrown over the edge of the bed and his iPod headphones dangerously wrapped around his neck. I untangled him and he stirred. He grabbed his pillow, thrust it under his arm.

I gently kissed his head—it was the only time I got to kiss him without complaint—and said, "Good-night." I backtracked out of his room, refusing to say good-night to Xena, Riley's pet snake. My love of Riley only went so far.

Back downstairs, Mr. Cabrera filled mugs with hot water. Bear woofed at me.

"He doesn't bite," Miss Sue said. She looked completely comfortable sitting at my counter in her pink button-down shirt and Levi's jeans.

After my encounters with BeBe, Bear looked like a dust bunny.

I grabbed a mug, poured in Swiss Miss and added water. Mr. Cabrera held up the Staypuff bag, but I bypassed it for the can of whipped cream sitting on the counter. I looked at the nutritional content. No carbs. Whew!

I didn't even look at the calories. I didn't want to know.

"So?" Flash prompted.

"Genevieve Hidalgo Sala is dead?" Miss Sue asked.

"Found drowned in Thad's heart-shaped hot tub?" Mr. Cabrera added.

"That about sums it up." I lifted my mug. "Cheers."

Mr. Cabrera popped three more mini-marshmallows into his mug. I didn't know why he bothered with the cocoa at all—he just wanted the marshmallows. "It's been all over the news."

I wasn't surprised. Everything that had happened tonight was a big blur, from finding Genevieve's body, to Louisa's screams, to Carson filming everything, to Willie's tears, to the police and the questions.

Through it all I felt guilty for not believing Genevieve's death threats.

Ana had been in cadaver heaven, trying to peek at Genevieve's body, weasel preliminary exam information from the medical examiner technician, and be the best eyewitness Carson Keyes had ever interviewed.

"What's going to happen with the show?" Bear had fallen asleep on Miss Sue's lap.

Cocoa burned my throat. "I don't know. Canceled, I guess."

Mr. Cabrera reached for more marshmallows. "This week's? Or forever?"

Good question. How did Genevieve's death factor into the sale of the show to the network? "I don't know."

"Do the police know who killed her?" Flash asked.

I shook my head. I'd had to tell the officials about me seeing Thad and Genevieve together, and me seeing Willie and Sherry together, and about the death threats. They had a lot of motives to sort through.

Mr. Cabrera tossed the empty bag of marshmallows in the trash can. "We should go, let Miz Quinn get some rest."

Basically, he was done with me because I didn't have any more information (or marshmallows). As it was, what he'd learned tonight would be spread across the Mill before my head hit my pillow.

I showed them out, their kisses on my cheek comforting, and locked the door behind them.

Pulling back the covers on the sofa bed, I was just about to slip in when the phone rang. I rushed to answer it before it woke Riley. Bobby's cell number glowed on the caller ID readout.

"Hey," I said.

"I just wanted to check in, make sure you're okay."

"I'm all right. You?"

"Okay. It's not every day I see a dead body."

For me it was becoming a common occurrence. I shuddered and noticed I had a voice mail waiting.

"You sure you're all right? It might not be good for you to be alone tonight. I can come over."

I saw right through him. "Riley's here."

He paused, and I swore I could *hear* him smiling. "Good night, Nina. Call me if you need me."

"Good night, Bobby."

Slowly, I hung up, trying not to think about needing him. I didn't want to need any man. Wasn't that the point of this self-discovery mission? Then why was I feeling as though I should pick up that phone and call him back? Even if it was just to talk?

I did pick up the phone, but only to dial into my voice mail.

"Nina Quinn, this is Duke reminding you that I'll see you at the Freedom High School track at five A.M. sharp. Don't be late or you'll regret it."

As I climbed into bed I was full of regrets. And none of them had to do with Duke.

"What happened to you?" Brickhouse asked as I hobbled into the office at 6:30 A.M., every muscle in my body aching.

I hadn't thought that possible—for every muscle in a person's body to ache. Had believed it was just a saying.

It *was* possible. Trust me.

"Duke," I said.

I heard a laugh come from Kit's office.

"Not funny!" I called out. I looked around. No drooling behemoth to be seen. "Where's BeBe?"

Brickhouse shoved an invoice into a file and placed it in the cabinet behind her desk. "That new one is out walking her."

"The new one?"

"Jeff."

Jeff. Right. The one I'd told specifically not to have anything to do with BeBe.

"Anyone else in yet?"

"Marty and Shay are out back loading the trucks. Coby's snoozing in the conference room. Who's Duke?"

Kit laughed again. I grit my teeth. "You don't want to know," I said. Carefully, I walked into my office, closed the door.

Gingerly, I sat. I woke up that morning barely able to move. And then, fearing Duke's wrath, dragged myself to the Freedom High track. There, I had run four laps—one piddly mile—and nearly needed CPR.

I pulled out a bottle of Advil and thanked my lucky stars Duke had given me tomorrow off.

My office door swung open and Brickhouse came in, carrying a steaming mug. She set it on my desk, said, "I bought a grinder for the office. Hope you don't mind," and walked back out again, leaving the door open.

If I didn't feel as though my skeletal system had wilted like the liriope outside TBS's front door, I would have gotten up and closed it.

Hopefully that ibuprofen would kick in soon, or I'd be of no use for Pippi's mini today.

Who knew self-discovery would be so painful?

From the office next door I heard the Nokia tune—Kit's boring ring tone. Straining, I tried to listen to his conversation, but no sooner had I deciphered his grumbled, "Daisy, I need to see you," than he strode out the front door, his cell phone held to his ear. The chimes crashed against the door as it closed behind him.

"Mrs. Krauss?" I called.

"What do you want?"

"Do you know what's going on with Kit and Daisy?"

"Not a clue? You?" she said loudly. Probably I should get up and go to the door. Or pick up the phone. Or use the intercom.

But shouting worked well enough.

"Nope. I'm worried, though."

She clucked. "Ach. Me too."

"If you hear something, will you tell me?"

"Only if you do the same."

"Deal."

She clucked again and said, "Don't you have work to do, Nina Ceceri?"

After flashing back to tenth grade, where I'd heard those exact words a lot, I opened the Lowther file, glanced at the master checklist Deanna had put together.

I'd been doing well not thinking about her, but knew eventually I was going to have to. I didn't want her to leave TBS, and I really didn't think she wanted to go.

My cell phone rang, and I heard Brickhouse singing along with Madonna.

Because I didn't want to get up, I chucked my well-worn stress ball at the door, hoping the door would close. It didn't budge. Giving up, I flipped open my phone, and wished I had my stress ball back, because I was starting to get a little stressed. I said hello to Ana. "You're up early."

She laughed. "Never went to bed."

I leaned back in my chair, thought about staying in that position until I could walk normally again. "Do I want to know?"

She giggled.

"Okay, that would be no, I don't."

"I went with Carson to the studio, and after he was done reporting on poor Genevieve, then we went back to his place and—"

Cutting in, I said, "Didn't want to hear about it."

"Party pooper."

I reached for my mug of coffee, hoping Brickhouse had made it like Roxie.

"Has Carson learned any more about Genevieve's death?" I asked.

"Carson? No, he's not an investigative reporter. He's just . . . "

"Fluff? Eye candy?"

"That works. Although I have to say he has a really nice—"

"Ana!"

"You're no fun, you know that?"

Was fun on my self-discovery list? I chose to ignore her

and said, "So we don't really know anything else about the murder?"

"Actually, we do. Well, I do. I'd make a great investigator, don't you think?"

I thought that sounded terrifying, but kept it to myself. "That would depend on what you'd learned."

"Remember that tech from the medical examiner's office I buddied up to last night?"

"You mean badgered?"

"Potato, potahto."

I smiled, sipped. Not too bad. I could get used to coffee drinking.

"He called a little bit ago."

"So early?"

"Okay, maybe I called him."

"To chitchat, I'm sure."

"I don't like your tone, Nina Colette Ceceri Quinn."

Setting the mug down, I grinned. "You're sounding like my mother."

Ana gasped. "I should hang up!"

"But you won't, because you're busting at the seams to tell me something."

She picked up where she'd left off. "After I agreed to meet him for lunch—"

"What about Carson?" I asked.

"It's not like we're exclusive."

"Oh. My mistake."

"Anyway, the tech—his name is Andy by the way—said that a prelim report on Genevieve came back and that he really shouldn't tell me, but . . . "

I leaned forward and regretted it immediately as my muscles cried in protest.

"Genevieve was dead before someone put her in that hot tub. Strangled."

"Wow."

"You're telling me. This is getting juicy, and it's just

about killed Carson that Willie's pulled the plug on him filming behind the scenes."

Genevieve's death probably wasn't the kind of publicity Willie needed or wanted right about now. "I don't blame him."

"I know, I know, but this could be the start of something big for Carson."

I thought of his big fish, little pond speech. "Is that something Carson wants or something you want for Carson?"

She hemmed and hawed. "Does it matter?"

Ditched. Their relationship was definitely headed toward ditched.

"I mean, really matter?" she went on. "He could be the next big entertainment reporter for the big names: *ET, Access Hollywood*, E! Oh my God, he would work for E! Think of the people I'd meet."

She'd gone off the deep end.

"Nina, you have to talk to Willie tonight. Get him to let Carson back on the set! This could be my big break!"

"Don't you mean his big break?"

"Isn't that what I said?"

"No."

"Oh. Slip of the tongue."

"Doesn't matter anyways. I won't be seeing Willie anymore."

"Why not? Won't you see him tonight at the taping of *Rendezvous*?"

Warmth flowed into my fingers as I gripped my mug. "Isn't the show canceled?"

"No one's called you?"

"No . . . "

"Willie wants to go on with the show. He's worried the network will back out if filming stops."

"Without a hostess?"

The chimes on the front door jangled, and I heard Brickhouse squeal in delight.

I don't think I'd ever heard her squeal before.

I craned my neck but couldn't see who'd come in, then I heard Tam say, "I hope you're not getting too comfortable behind that desk."

"Gotta go," I said to Ana, and clicked my phone closed.

I struggled to my feet, winced as I made my way out of my office.

Brickhouse had Tam in a big bear hug. When she finally pulled away, I saw little Nic strapped to Tam's chest in one of those newfangled strappy Baby Bjorn pouch things. How she hadn't been smothered by Brickhouse, I didn't know.

Brickhouse tickled Nic's chin, and the baby started crying.

"Stop scaring the poor girl," I said.

Brickhouse glared. "Ach."

"It's not you," Tam reassured. "She's been fussy all night. I can't get her to stop crying. My gosh, Nina, you look great. I mean, you looked good on TV, but look even better now."

"I've missed you around here," I said, sticking my tongue out at Brickhouse.

She clucked, and apparently chose to ignore me, instead saying, "My Claudia rarely cried."

I smiled at Nic. She snuffled. Redness streaked her blue eyes, and her bottom lip trembled and jutted out.

I turned to Brickhouse. "If you were my mother, I'd be too scared to cry too."

She ignored me. To Tam, she said, "What are you doing here? I told you I'd fill in for you this week."

"I thought it was safe to come in. No cameras now that Nina's gone and killed someone else."

"Hey! I didn't kill her!"

Folding meaty arms, Brickhouse glared at me. "Ach! What's this all about? Who died?"

I was surprised she hadn't heard the news from Mr. Cabrera. His gossip skills must be getting rusty in his old age. Tam filled her in. Nic's cries kicked up. Tam unhooked her, jiggled, wiggled.

Brickhouse shook her head at me.

"I didn't kill her!" I'd have stomped my foot, but I was too sore to move it with such force.

"You're as jinxed as my Donatelli."

"It's true," Tam said, jostling poor Nic.

Unfortunately, I was coming to believe the same thing.

Brickhouse made kissy noises at Nic and said, "I'd wondered where the Bobbsey twins had gotten off to."

"Who?" Tam asked.

"Roxie and Nels?" I guessed.

Brickhouse nodded.

Bobbsey twins. I liked it. It fit. Nic wailed.

Tam handed her to me. "Here, you try! Maybe it's me. Maybe she hates me."

Nic's cries escalated until her little face turned bright red.

"Nope, she hates Nina, though." Brickhouse perched on the edge of Tam's desk, beaming like the wicked witch she was.

"Is that normal?" I asked.

"She's a baby. Babies cry," Brickhouse said.

I gave her the Ceceri Evil Eye. "I meant the redness. She looks like a maraschino cherry!"

Brickhouse clucked. "She doesn't like you."

I gave her more of the evil eye and raised my voice to be heard over Nic's screaming. "Is she always this loud?"

The door opened and Harvey Goosey walked in, took one look at us and walked out again.

Tam nodded. "Day and night."

"What's going on?" Marty asked, walking in, Shay on his heels.

"Nic's upset. Won't stop crying," I explained, shouting.

"Might be colic," he said, dancing up and down, trying to distract the baby.

"Do you want her?" I asked him, holding Nic out.

He shook his head.

Shay stepped forward, took the squalling baby. She started singing softly in Spanish. It was so soothing I almost fell asleep, but Nic wasn't swayed. She passed her back.

I hadn't known Shay spoke Spanish. That could come in handy. Jean-Claude Reaux walked into the office, slipped off his sunglasses and took in the situation. He wore dark-washed skintight jeans, and a loose striped button-down, the buttons undone to show his six pack abs. Ever since he began moonlighting as an exotic dancer, Jean-Claude had been dressing like Fabio.

He bypassed the scene and went straight for the coffee machine, poured a mug and took a sip.

"Hot diggity! Fresh ground!" He sipped happily. "Why the change?" he asked, as though there weren't a screaming baby two feet from him and five people trying to make her happy.

We ignored him. "Thanks for trying," I said to Marty, who had broken a sweat dancing around, jumping up and down.

I bounced, I cooed, I even sang until everyone in the room begged me not to.

I'd have given her back to Tam, but she looked exhausted. I looked at Brickhouse and nixed that idea immediately. Poor little Nic was defenseless against Brickhouse's evil ways.

"Too bad Deanna's not here," Tam said.

Obviously no one had told her.

Brickhouse made a slashing motion on her neck. I saw Marty and Shay shaking their heads.

"What?" Tam said. "Is there something going on I don't know about?"

Nic wailed.

I shouted above the ruckus, "I'll tell you later."

I held out Nic. Her upper body had gone all tense, but her

tiny legs kicked like she was a professional soccer player. Coby came out of the conference room.

"You want to try?" I offered.

"No way." He headed straight for the fridge. "I don't do babies."

Jean-Claude set his mug down. "I'll give her a go."

He came over, took her, and held her at arm's length. Nic immediately stopped screaming. She looked at him long and hard.

"See? I've got a way with women," Jean-Claude said just as Nic's bottom lip jutted out. She opened her mouth and wailed.

Jean-Claude cooed and cuddled, to no avail.

"What a way you have with women," Coby teased.

"At least *I* tried."

The front door slammed open, the chimes jangling in agitation. Kit filled the doorway. "What are you doing to that child?"

He marched over, took her from Jean-Claude. "You," he said to Nic. "Shush."

Nic shushed. She stared at him, all big blue eyes.

"Give me that thing," he said to Tam, motioning to her Baby Bjorn.

Tam hooked it onto Kit, and he looked utterly ridiculous, but no one dared to laugh. He plopped Nic into the Bjorn. Adoringly, she gazed up at him.

Brickhouse said, "Now there's a man who has a way with women."

It was true. No arguing there. Poor Jean-Claude looked deflated.

Tam yawned.

"Why don't you take a nap in my office?" I said. "Looks like Kit's got Nic covered."

"What about the mini? He can't take her with him."

"We'll figure it out."

The chimes jangled as Nels and Roxie pushed open the

door. Tam took one look at them, snatched Nic out of the Bjorn and beelined for the door. To me, she said, "I'll see you later on." To Kit, she said, "Call me. I need a babysitter in a desperate way."

"What? Wait. Later on?" But she was gone. "Do you know what later on might be about," I asked Brickhouse.

She just smiled and sat in Tam's throne chair, looking like the Queen Mother.

"Do you know?" I asked Nels and Roxie.

They shook their heads and followed me as I limped back into my office. No sooner had I sat down than Roxie signaled Nels to start filming.

"Tell us your reaction, Nina."

"To Genevieve?"

"Cut," Roxie ordered Nels. To me, she said, "We're not supposed to mention Genevieve at all. Pretend it never happened."

"But that's creepy."

"Willie insists."

Willie didn't seem like a man in mourning, if you'd have asked me. Well, maybe of his deal falling through.

"Then my reaction to what?" I asked.

Nels started filming again as Roxie said, "About Bobby."

I took another sip of coffee. It was now lukewarm and had lost its appeal. "What about him?"

"You haven't heard?"

I felt like I'd already had this conversation that morning.

"Heard what?"

Roxie's eyes gleamed behind her glasses. "He's going back to Florida tomorrow."

Thirteen

Pippi swung open the door to Lowther House, all big smiles and open arms.

Worried, I took in her outfit. "Were you planning on helping?"

She looked down at her denim overalls, garden clogs, loose-fitting long sleeve tee, and laughed. "Heavens, no. I thought I'd spend the afternoon in the greenhouse. I've been inspired to try my hand at bromeliad hybrids. I'd love to add some of my own to your design. Are you limping?"

"Just a little sore this morning. Takes a while to work out the kinks." At this rate it would take a month. Maybe two.

And that wasn't the only pain I was in. My heart hurt. Physically ached. I couldn't believe Bobby hadn't told me about leaving. And would he leave without saying good-bye? Had I meant nothing at all? I tried not to think about it, to push it away, but it was there lurking in a dark corner of my mind.

Outside, my crew hustled and bustled, unloading. Nels and Roxie filmed everything, including Pippi asking me about Genevieve. "I bet it was simply horrible. Do you know if she was murdered or if the death was accidental?"

I really didn't want to talk about Genevieve. "I'm not

sure," I lied. "The medical examiner is supposed to release a preliminary report later today."

She nodded. "Just dreadful. Thad Cochran must be very upset."

I hadn't thought too much about Thad. I'd been focused on Willie's reaction to his wife's death. However, Thad had been involved with Genevieve. Had it been purely a sexual tryst or were there emotions involved? Pippi couldn't have known about the affair, though. Curious for her take, I asked, "Why?"

"The sale of the show, of course! Thad wouldn't do well without someone to play off of. It would be like having Sonny without Cher. Not so good."

We stepped to the side to allow Kit to pass by with the base of the planter box.

"Genevieve can be replaced," I ventured. "After all, she replaced Jessica Ayers."

This brought my speculation full circle. My original thought at who sent the death threats had been Jessica. For revenge. But according to Josh, she was in Mexico until late last night.

Not your business, my inner voice reminded.

I hated when it was right.

Nels had long since put down his camera. No use filming what couldn't be aired. Coby and Jeff each carried a side panel for the planter box. It had been crafted by Stanley Mack, my subcontractor for carpentry work. Made of solid oak, the raised panels were exact replicas of those in Lowther House's main entry.

Pippi smiled. "I cannot wait to see the finished product."

"Everyone is gone for the day, correct?"

"Off on their day trip. They won't be back until five. Except for Minnie, but she'll be in her quarters all day. I have a therapist coming in to look after her." Pippi clapped her hands together. "Come with me."

I followed her to the doors of the east wing, where the

residential suites and entrance to the greenhouse were located.

With a touch of her finger, a hidden panel opened. Behind
it there was a neatly labeled intercom system. I scanned
through the names until my gaze landed on the button with
GREENHOUSE marked next to it.

"If you need me, just buzz the greenhouse." She punched
a series of numbers into the keypad on the wooden door
and a lock was released. "I should be in there all day—
there's much to do."

"I'd love to have a look at what you're growing."

Her face paled, then brightened with a smile. "Perhaps
when you're done. Ciao," she said, pulling the door open.
I caught a glimpse of the tattoo on the back of her neck
as her bun bobbed. The door closed behind her with a re-
sounding click.

"She creeps me out," Roxie said.

"Sweet Pippi?"

"Do you think she's locked Minnie in her room?" Nels
asked. "Is that why you shouldn't worry that she'll inter-
rupt us?"

Roxie's eyes widened. "Do we even know Minnie's
alive?"

"Stop it, you two!"

Roxie cleaned her glasses with the hem of her shirt.
"Something weird is going on."

They shuddered in unison, and Nels hummed the theme
song for *The Twilight Zone.*

I shook my head. But as I hobbled out to help unload
supplies, I couldn't help but agree. Something weird was
going on.

But it wasn't any of my business to figure out what.

I must have a busybody gene or chromosome scientists had
yet to discover. It wasn't something I could change or shut
off on a whim.

From the second floor atrium I had a bird's-eye view of Lowther House's four wings. I noticed that only the residential suites had entrance to the courtyard, with small patios that opened into it. There were benches, a circular brick pathway, a nice bit of lawn, and expansive flower beds. In the center of the courtyard sat the greenhouse.

Nels caught me staring out the window. Again. "You know, I've got the combination to the door on tape . . . "

I faced him. "That would be wrong."

"We could be saving Minnie's life."

Through the opaque glass of the greenhouse, I could see Pippi's shadow moving back and forth amidst vegetation, but little else.

"Minnie's fine. See for yourself." At the far end of the courtyard, Minnie sat in her wheelchair, a blanket on her lap, a mug in her hands. She was accompanied by the redhead I'd seen the day before. The therapist Pippi had called in?

"How do we know she's alive? You can't make out features from here."

"He has a point," Roxie said, coming up behind us. She squinted. "That could be a decoy, a dummy, a mannequin. Or a dead Minnie used as a prop for our benefit."

Roxie had quite an imagination. "Holding a mug?" I asked.

She looked offended. "Didn't you ever see *Weekend at Bernie's*?"

"Minnie's fine." I jabbed Nels in his chest. "You keep that door combo to yourself."

Kit sauntered over. "I need to start the waterfall now that the base is together and filled. I figured in your present condition you don't want to be hauling fieldstone and river rock, but do you want to lay out the design?"

"Oh my God, are you pregnant?" Roxie cried.

Nels hefted his camera, zoomed in on my stomach.

I put my hand over the lens. "That would be no." To Kit, I said, "You have a good eye. Just follow the design board as much as possible."

He nodded. Dark circles rimmed his eyes, and I noticed he'd started wearing a belt. He'd definitely lost weight.

"What are you all staring at?" He looked out the window. "Exciting," he said dryly.

"We're trying to decide if Minnie's dead or alive," Roxie said.

One of his eyebrows jumped. "Minnie?"

"She's alive. She's right over there." I pointed. "See! Her mug moved."

Nels and Roxie deflated like day old latex balloons. "I was so sure," Nels said.

"You okay?" I asked Kit. He'd gone ashen—more than usual these days. "Kit?"

"What? Yeah. Fine."

"My foot," I said. Every muscle in his body—and there were a lot of them—had tensed. His hands were clenched into fists. I turned to look out the window, to see what I might have missed, and when I turned back, Kit was back at work. He'd climbed into the planter box and was fussing with the pump for the water feature.

What was with that?

"What's with him?" Roxie asked.

I smiled. I was going to miss Roxie when filming was over. Which reminded me . . .

"No clue. I need a minute, you guys."

I pretended to head for the restroom, detoured into the hallway, pulled out my cell phone and dialed Bobby's number. It was the sixth time I'd called. And like the five times before this one, he didn't answer.

So much for not thinking of him.

I gingerly pushed away from the wall, went back in to check on the makeover. Jean-Claude and Marty helped set rocks in place for the waterfall.

Roxie stood to one side, ogling Jean-Claude. And he knew it too—kept looking up, winking at her.

Jeff handed stone up to Kit, and Harvey and Coby were in and out, using a dolly to bring in more rocks. Once the stones were set, we could add the rest of the soil and the plants.

"I'm going to start bringing in the plants," I informed my camera crew. Roxie waved me on. Nels had slumped into a leather wingback, napping.

At the top of the stairs I took a deep breath. Trying not to moan, I made it down in one piece, my muscles aching. It took half an hour to load a cart with plants, everything from bird of paradise to liriope and the standard indoor palms. I'd come back for the weeping fig.

As I wrestled the cart up the ramp to the house, my phone rang.

Bobby?

I let go of the cart and gasped as it rolled down the ramp. I dove after the handle but was too slow and in too much pain to make it in time.

I braced myself for the impact of the cart against one of the TBS trucks, but once it hit the gravel drive, it slowed to a peaceful stop.

I, on the other hand, couldn't get up.

Madonna still sang. I didn't recognize the number on the caller ID.

Stretched out on my stomach, I said, "This is Nina Quinn."

"Nina, this is Louisa Thatcher, the production assistant at *Hitched or Ditched*. We need you to come in to the studio immediately for an emergency meeting."

"About?" I asked, rolling onto my back. The sky was a brilliant blue, streaked with wisps of white clouds.

"The future of the show. The meeting starts in an hour. Please be here." She hung up.

I did the same, closed my eyes and thought about taking a nap.

"Need help?"

I popped an eye open. Shay had her hand out to me. I slipped mine into it. She pulled.

"Thanks," I said, biting back a curse or four. There wasn't enough Advil in the world to help my pain.

"Do I want to know?" she asked, her light brown eyes shining with good humor.

I shook my head.

"Kit sent me out to help you."

That was nice of him, seeing as how it was his fault I was in this condition. "Go ahead and bring the cart upstairs. Go left just inside the doors and there's an elevator there."

Duke had mentioned that the more I used my sore muscles, the less they would hurt. Which was why I took the stairs. Slowly.

Waking Nels was easy, but pulling Roxie away from Jean-Claude wasn't.

"Where's Kit?" I asked.

Jean-Claude shrugged.

"I think he went out to the trailer," Jeff said.

I took the elevator down. Screw Duke. He was evil.

Pippi had to be informed I was leaving. I turned left out of the elevator, heading toward the east wing. The hidden panel was wide open.

"What?" Nels said. "Why're you looking at me like that?"

"Have you been down here?"

Roxie kept looking toward the stairs, perhaps hoping Jean-Claude would follow her to the ends of the earth. "He's been sound asleep."

Odd.

I pushed the greenhouse buzzer. Heard nothing in return. I pushed it again. "Pippi?"

We waited a good minute. "Well, okay, then. We can't wait here forever."

Nels shifted on his feet. "Pippi Longstocking is probably doing Minnie in right now."

"Minnie's fine! Why don't you two go out to the truck? I've got to find one of Pippi's employees to pass on the news that I'm leaving."

Backtracking, I headed down the west wing hallway, toward the dining room. I heard raised voices ahead and was surprised I recognized one.

"You're being ridiculous," a throaty female voice said.

"What you're doing is dangerous," Kit replied. "I'm worried about you."

I tried to pick up my pace. Damn Duke!

"Sometimes we have to do things to protect those we love."

"And what about you? Who protects you?"

"I'll be fine."

"I don't know how long we can go on like this." Kit's deep voice carried easily.

She said, "That's your choice."

"No, it's yours. Daisy, you need to think about what you're doing."

Daisy? I broke into a faltering jog.

"I don't have time for this, Kit. Good-bye."

I rounded the corner to the dining room just as the red-headed woman disappeared behind a swinging door leading into the kitchen.

Kit looked at me. "Did you need something?"

I saw the tears in his eyes and could barely find my voice. "I need to go . . . to the studio."

"I'll take care of things here. Don't worry." He brushed past me.

But after hearing that conversation, how could I not?

Fourteen

"You need to use more product," Perry whispered into my ear an hour later.

"Product?"

"For your hair, sugar. For volume. Lift. I'll bring you some tonight."

There was an odd sense of déjà vu floating around the studio. After all, it had been just three days since the last time we all gathered to talk about the show. We even sat in the same seats.

Although I couldn't help but notice the seat to my right remained empty.

Louisa informed us all that Bobby had been excused from this meeting. I wondered what he was doing. Packing?

"Thanks," I told Perry as I finger-combed my hair, trying to fluff it a little. I hadn't put much effort in doing it that morning, and it showed.

Always do your hair as if knowing you'll be seeing your hair stylist.

That little lesson was going straight onto my list of things I'd self-discovered.

No matter how my hair looked, Willie's looked worse. His five-strand comb-over stood on end as he paced the room.

Red streaked his eyes, day-old stubble covered his sunken cheeks, and he looked to be wearing the same clothes as yesterday—wrinkled Dockers, Converse sneakers, and a B52s' T-shirt that barely covered his slight beer belly.

"The show must go on," he said for the fifth time since the meeting started ten minutes ago.

Thad sat across from me. Unlike Willie, he looked great. Freshly shaved, bright-eyed, not a hair out of place. He didn't look like someone who grieved for the death of his mistress.

He rose to his feet, placed his hand on Willie's shoulders. "I agree with Willie. I'm fully prepared to take this show above and beyond as a solo host. The transition will be seamless."

Willie smoothed his strands. His tone came out more clipped than usual. "I appreciate the sentiment, Thad, but that's not necessary. A new hostess will take over tonight."

For a brief second Thad's mask slipped. I saw the pain, the hurt, the anger in his eyes. He blinked, and the emotion disappeared. Slowly, he pulled his hands away from Willie's shoulders. "Who?"

Louisa poked her head in the door before Willie could answer. "May I have a moment, sir?" she asked him.

He excused himself. Thad stalked over to the corner and pulled out his cell phone.

Perry said, "Thad seems a bit disappointed."

Mario leaned in. "I'm placing odds that he bumped off Genevieve so he could have a solo gig. He knew the show was about to go national and wanted the limelight to himself."

I shifted in my seat, keenly aware of Bobby's absence. "But he's the one who introduced her to Willie and suggested she'd make a great hostess."

"Maybe that was all talk on his part," Perry speculated. "What if he met Genevieve at that class he taught, introduced her to Willie, made an offhand comment, and next

thing he knew Willie and Gen were hitched and he had a
new hot tub buddy? He had to get rid of her."

"The question is," Mario added, "did Genevieve manipu-
late both of them to get her face in front of the camera?"

"So," I said, thinking out loud, "if you're right about
Thad, then he's really ticked right now that Willie's bringing in someone else."

All three of us stole a peek at Thad, who stood in the corner, his back to us. No one could hear what he was saying
as he spoke on the phone.

"Probably calling his agent," Perry surmised.

Louisa came back into the room, her cell phone to her
ear. No sign of Willie.

"No interviews, no comment. That's final," she said,
hanging up. She saw us looking at her. "Those reporters
won't let up."

"Was that Carson Keyes?" Mario asked. "I miss seeing
him around here."

Perry rolled his eyes. "Wipe the drool, Mario."

I smiled. They were very cute together.

Louisa sat down in Thad's empty chair. "No, Jim Hen-
man from Channel 6. He's not the only one. All the major networks are calling. As are the national entertainment
shows. As soon as Willie clammed up, they haven't left us
alone. I heard a rumor a reporter from E! was flying in."

"There's no such thing as bad publicity, right?" I said.

She glared at me.

Okay, maybe there was.

Her phone squawked. She answered. "Yes . . . Yes, I'll be
right down . . . No! Don't fill it yet. Let me check the place-
ment." She hung up, pushed her curly hair behind her ears.
"The new water bed," she said to our questioning looks.

"Water bed?" Mario ventured.

"Our signature hot tub had to go. That would be too morbid."

I shuddered.

She saw and said, "Exactly."

Madonna sang. Mario and Perry joined in, complete with arm gestures. I laughed and answered my cell phone. "Hey," I said to Ana.

"Did you talk to him?" she asked.

"Who?"

"Willie!"

"About?"

"Carson!"

"Oh. No."

She growled and hung up.

"Ana," I explained to Mario and Perry. "She's upset about Carson being booted off the set."

"She has amazing hair," Perry said.

"Nice bosom too," Mario added.

Perry arched an eyebrow. "Bosom?"

"It's a word."

"Not one you usually throw around."

"Well, it was hard not to notice when she was wearing that tank top last night."

"That's true," Perry said. "She did look good in it."

Both looked at me as if I'd have something to add. I didn't.

I noticed Thad had finished his call but still stood in the corner, looking out the window. I tried to wrap my head around all that had happened. There were so many people who might want Genevieve dead.

Willie, for one. On the surface, I wouldn't have thought it was because losing Genevieve might mean losing his TV deal. However, she had been cheating on him. It was a powerful motive to kill her—if he knew about the affair. Also, I couldn't help but notice the show was getting a lot of PR from her death. The network executives would take notice. They were after ratings, and the drama behind the scenes of the show were driving them higher than they'd ever been.

Had Genevieve been an expendable asset? Had Willie married her, made her hostess, all with the plan to kill her to get ratings for the show?

This was a morbid thought. What if he'd married out of love, found out she was cheating, then plotted to kill her for ratings? Two birds, one stone.

Sherry, Thad's wife, also had motive. What better way to get even with your cheating spouse than to kill his lover and ruin his career at the same time?

And Thad? What did he gain by Genevieve's death? Perhaps, like Mario suggested, he'd wanted to be the only host of *Hitched or Ditched*, have all the glory to himself. If that were true, then he'd killed in vain, because Willie was bringing in someone new.

Then I remembered . . . it wasn't my business. Police could more than handle it. Weren't they crawling all over the studio? Hadn't they interviewed anyone who'd come in contact with Genevieve?

I just needed to mind my own business, get through this week, and get on with my self-discovery.

I listened to Mario and Perry tick off their favorite Madonna videos before—thankfully—Willie came back into the room.

"I've put a lot of thought into this decision," he said. "I'd like to reintroduce you to Jessica Ayers, the original *Hitched or Ditched* hostess." He threw his arm wide, and Jessica Ayers stepped into the room.

I heard Perry whistle softly.

Jessica was beautiful, no doubt. Tall, short blonde hair, big blue eyes, flawless peaches and cream skin, mile high legs. No tan, I noticed. Had she really been in Mexico?

"No!" Thad shouted. "No, no, no!"

"Now, Thad," Willie cautioned.

Jessica's lips curved into a satisfied smile.

She might look innocent, but I saw the manipulator beneath the veneer.

"I will not work with her. She's a lying, cheating bitch."

Perry leaned in. "Rumor has it she left her boyfriend for Thad, who then refused to leave his wife. Things ended badly."

"Those who live in glass houses, Thad," Jessica purred.

"Meow," Mario whispered.

Thad turned as red as Jessica's lips. "Either she goes or I go," he said.

"Neither of you are going," Willie said. "The network execs will be here tonight. I expect a dynamite show. This is our last hope. So be good little children and play nice. Understood?"

Jessica folded her arms. "Perfectly."

"And if I refuse?" Thad said.

Willie's beady eyes narrowed. "Then your career is over."

Fifteen

 "Niiiiice."

"Work it, work it, work it."

"Yo, yo, lookin' good!"

I stopped halfway up my driveway and looked over at the four construction workers lounging on lawn chairs in my front yard. "Um, thanks. Still not crossing the picket line?"

"Sorry," said the guy who'd told me to "work it."

The same two picketers crisscrossed the sidewalk. One winked at me, and the other—the one I'd nicknamed Buzz—wouldn't look my way. I wanted to talk to him, see what I could find out about him being paid to picket, but it could wait a few minutes.

The fourth construction worker sitting there said, "You really ought to think about a new handbag. That thing looks like it's been run over by a semi."

Actually, it had been run over by a freight train, but I didn't want to dwell on the past.

"Yo, yo, he's right. Somethin' small and cute. Like you." This from a man sipping an IBC root beer with a straw.

One of the others, the only one wearing a hard hat, said, "Yeah, yeah. Chanel maybe."

"No, Kate Spade."

"Definitely Kate Spade. Hook yourself up."

I had a sneaking suspicion . . . "My sister's been here, hasn't she?"

"Has she ever. What a looker, that one," said Hard Hat.

"Except that dog," the IBC guy said. "Yappiest thing I ever did hear."

Oh no! I knew that dog! Gracie. She'd been, ah, a kinda-sorta gift from Kit. One that I regifted to my sister Maria as a wedding present.

Both being high maintenance and all, they got along well.

I rushed up the stairs, feeling every muscle in my legs.

"Don't forget—Kate Spade!"

"I'll keep that in mind," I called over my shoulder.

"Hey!" one shouted, "a little more product in your hair will do wonders!"

So I'd heard.

Pushing open my front door, I found my mother on all fours, a spray bottle filled with a mixture of water and white vinegar in one hand, a wadded up paper towel in the other.

I winced at the sharp smell. Yuck.

There were other smells too. Cleansers. Lemon Pledge, for one. The citrus of Mr. Clean. I looked around. Everything sparkled.

"Did Gracie go everywhere?" Gracie had bladder control issues, something I learned the hard way when she'd been staying with me.

"Don't be silly," my mother said. "Help me up."

Her hand grasped mine and I pulled. "Then why is my house so clean?"

"You should think about a housekeeper."

"I don't need a housekeeper."

"I beg to differ, *chérie*."

Deep breath. I smelled, I smelled . . . "Are those cream puffs?" I sprinted into the kitchen, my aches and pains all but a distant memory in light of freshly baked cream puffs. I reached for one.

"Ow!" I jumped, rubbing the love handle my mother had just pinched.

"Aren't you on a diet?"

"Why are you here?" I asked, ignoring her. "There's no construction going on, so you don't need to stay."

She tsked. "No need to snap at me just because you're hungry."

"Who are the cream puffs for?"

She dropped a cookie sheet into the double sink. "Oh, people."

"What kind of people?"

"People I know."

"Why are you being so evasive?"

"Why are you being so nosy?"

"It's my house!"

"Yes, it is. Did I mention you ought to think about a housekeeper?"

Deep, deep breath. I ignored the sinking feeling my mother was planning something. At this point there was nothing I could do or say that would change her mind—she knew it and I knew it, so I gave up the battle.

"Where's Riley?" I asked. School had been out for a while—I'd expected to see him camped out on the couch watching reruns of *Fear Factor*.

"At Mrs. Greeble's."

I looked out the window, down the road. "He's been doing a lot of work for her lately."

Riley had become the neighborhood go-to guy. He raked leaves, cleaned gutters, and did all sorts of odd jobs and errands. It was his new job—and so far he loved it.

"She needs the help. Such a big house for one person."

Mrs. Greeble's husband had passed away last spring, and she hadn't resigned herself to moving to a smaller place. The upkeep of her home was beginning to take a toll, both physically and financially. I hoped Riley kept that in mind when he charged her.

The picketers about-faced. I motioned to them. "Have they been out there all day?"

"Since eight."

"You've been here since eight?"

She waved a dishrag at me. "There was a lot of cleaning to do."

"Yeah, yeah. I need a housekeeper."

She smiled. We launched into a conversation about Maria enjoying her newlywedded life and about Gracie who needed medication. Then my mother needed to know every detail of Genevieve's death and what was going to happen with the show.

By the time I was done explaining, I longed for a cream puff.

"Kevin called," my mother said.

There went my appetite.

"Did he say why?"

"No, though I suspect it has something to do with the murder."

I suspected too. Note to self: Avoid Kevin at all costs.

"Anyone else call?" I asked. I'd noticed the light on my phone wasn't blinking. No messages.

"Like?"

"I don't know." I swung my foot back and forth.

"What are you not telling your mama?"

"Did you know I need a housekeeper?"

She grinned. "It's a good thing I love you, Nina Colette."

"Right back at ya."

Reaching across the counter, she handed me a cream puff. I'd like to say I took my time and enjoyed every morsel.

I fairly inhaled it.

"I'll need two of these for Buzz and Winky." I grabbed two more off the plate, set them on a napkin.

"Who?"

"The picketers."

"Ah. Honey and bees?" she asked.

She was referring to that old adage about attracting bees by using honey.

"Exactly."

Four webbed aluminum chairs sat vacant on my front lawn. Not a hard hat to be seen.

Which was probably a good thing since I hadn't thought to bring cream puffs for the construction workers.

Buzz and Winky circled the small island in my front yard like guppies that'd lost their school.

When they spotted me they swam a little slower—and came to a complete stop when they saw the cream puffs in my hand. "What happened to the guys?" I asked, motioning to the chairs.

"Clear out everyday at exactly four o'clock." Winky eyed the cream puff, practically drooling.

Buzz shifted from foot to foot. His worn-out Nikes skimmed across the ground as if doing a jig. Faded jeans hugged his ample waist, and a mustard yellow hoodie emblazoned with ST. BLAISE ELEMENTARY clung to his full-figured frame.

Since it was getting late and I needed to get to the studio, I decided to get to the point.

The point being my informal interrogation.

Using the cream puffs as an incentive.

Who, after all, could pass up a cream puff?

The great cream puff mission was all about information gathering. If my hunch was correct, someone had paid Winky and Buzz to picket my house. Their placards never mentioned any kind of organization, and I suspected there wasn't one. Well, one they belonged to.

This picketing was a PR stunt pure and simple. All I had to do was prove it. And find out who hired them.

Piece of . . . cream puff.

"Can I ask you two some questions?"

Buzz's Nikes skimmed faster. Put on some Celtic music and he could be the next big River Dancer. "Sure. I guess."

Winky never took his eyes off the cream puffs as he nodded.

"What organization do you work for?"

"Moral TV," Winky said at the same time Buzz said, "TV Morality."

They looked at each other, then at me. Color slowly crept into Buzz's cheeks.

"Moral TV," Buzz said.

"So, if I go inside, log onto the computer, and do a search for a group called Moral TV, will I find it?"

"Morality TV," Buzz quickly put in. "My bad."

My eyebrows arched. They were my built-in BS meters, and these two were seriously BSing me.

Someone had definitely paid them to picket. These guys had been on the news every night this week, garnering *Hitched or Ditched* a lot of PR.

"Have either of you met Thad Cochran?"

Buzz's feet stilled. Winky's nose twitched. Neither said anything.

"Willie Sala?"

Again, nothing.

"Sherry Cochran?"

"Never heard of 'em," Winky said.

Buzz wouldn't look me in the eye. "You?" I asked, point-blank.

"Me?"

"Do you know them?"

His left foot tapped. "Not personally."

"You sure?"

"Very."

My eyebrows jumped into my hairline. I didn't believe him for a second. But I also didn't know how to prove he was lying.

"Listen," I told them. "Do you know I have a gaping hole in my living room ceiling?"

They shook their heads.

"Do you know how hard it is to get construction workers here? On time? Willing to do the work?"

"No ma'am," Winky mumbled.

Ma'am. Hmmph. That made me angrier.

"Well, let me tell you what I do know. I know someone's paid you to stand out here. I know that my ex-husband is a cop. And I know that if you're here tomorrow on my front lawn, I will make a few phone calls and have you removed. You two are standing in the way of my house being put back together again, and I've had just about enough of it. So I don't know how much your boss is paying you, but is it worth getting hauled into jail? Do we understand each other?" I wasn't sure they *could* be arrested, but it sounded good.

Both nodded in unison.

"Good." I smiled and held up the napkin. "Cream puff?"

They each took one, dropped their pickets and ran.

I watched them jump into their car, a newer model Hyundai. And as Buzz drove off, I couldn't help but think I could get used to the new me.

Sixteen

"He'll be here, sugar."

Perry sounded so sure. I wasn't. I had yet to hear from Bobby. It was as if he'd dropped off the face of the earth. Gone. Poof.

I looked at my watch. Or rather, where my watch should be. I'd misplaced it somewhere and hadn't been able to find it. My mind hadn't quite accepted the fact that it wasn't on my wrist.

Perry held up his arm. "It's six-thirty."

"Thank you."

"How about tomorrow?" he asked.

"Tomorrow?"

"Shopping. I can't believe you're wearing linen at this time of year."

I smoothed my wrinkled pants. "Is there a time of year for linen?"

He shook his head. "We have a lot of work to do with you if you don't know the answer to that question."

Best to get started right away. I pulled out my date book. "Tomorrow afternoon is good."

He pulled out his PDA. "Twelve?"

I penciled it in. "Meet you at the mall?"

"In front of Macy's. And bring your credit card."

Thankfully, I was in a position where money wasn't an issue. I wasn't rich by any means, but my job provided well for me. Still, I had a few palpitations about spending large amounts of money on clothes. It was just something I'd never done.

The old me would have stressed over it. The new me still stressed over it, but pushed it to the back of my mind so I didn't think about it too much.

Louisa bustled around the set. The water bed had been made with red satin sheets and a red velvet bedspread.

Classy.

Jessica perched on the end of the bed, dressed in a tiny nightie sure to get men's blood pressures—and ratings—soaring.

Willie stood in the corner, talking to one of the executives. Technicians checked wires, cables, cameras and lights. Taping was set to begin in twenty minutes.

Still no sign of Bobby.

Don't care, don't care, I chanted to myself.

My phone rang, and I immediately flipped it open.

So much for not caring.

Only it wasn't Bobby. It was Kit. Something tightened in my chest when I remembered those tears in his eyes. I found a quiet corner to talk in peace.

"Hey," I said. "You okay?"

"Fine."

All right. I wouldn't push the issue—even though I wanted to.

"What's up?"

"We've got a problem."

"With the mini?"

"The mini's done, looks great, Pippi loved it."

I watched Louisa run back and forth across the set. She seemed to do more work than anyone else. "Then what's the problem?"

"Do you remember Minnie?"

"Oh no! She's not dead, is she?"

"No," he said in a way that made me sound crazy.

I'd been hanging around Nels and Roxie too long. I looked around for them. They must have gone home for the day—or were still in the editing room.

"She wheeled herself into the common room before the makeover was over."

"So, no surprise."

"Not for her."

"What am I hearing in your voice?"

"Nina, Minnie's ring is gone. Big diamond. And Pippi thinks one of us took it. She's going to be in the office at eight tomorrow morning to speak with you."

Yes, my employees all had rap sheets, but I trusted them. Every single one.

Except . . .

I hardly knew the new guy. Jeff Dannon. And hadn't he been arrested for theft?

Great.

"Had Jeff been around Minnie at all?"

"Wheeled her downstairs after she came in and found us."

His voice dropped off at the end of that sentence, his tone saying much more than his words.

"Did Pippi call the police?"

"No. Said she wanted to speak with you."

I wondered why. If a big expensive ring went missing, I'd want the police involved. But maybe she didn't want the PR, unlike some other people around here.

"Kit?"

"Yo."

"Are you okay?"

There was a long pause. "Dandy."

I sighed. "You know, I'm here if you need anything. Just gotta ask."

"Yeah."

I hoped he took me up on the offer, but doubted he would. He was the proud sort.

"Okay. Give me a call if anything else comes up."

"Will do."

I hung up just as Carson Keyes strutted into the room, a cameraman trailing him. I watched as he shook hands with Willie and the network guy.

Louisa bustled by. I grabbed her. "Do you know why Carson's here? I thought Willie banned all media."

"Changed his mind. Thought having someone behind the scenes would take the pressure off."

She hurried away.

From my spot in the corner, I could watch Willie unfettered. His comb-over had been plastered into submission. His dark eyes glistened and his teeth gleamed like those in a Crest ad. He looked like a salesman on the verge of landing the big one, and his hook was firmly lodged in the executive's lip.

Perry cozied up. "Just heard a rumor that ABC is interested in the show. Willie's got himself a bidding war."

Money. Had Genevieve's death been all about money?

Jessica lounged on the water bed. I couldn't forget she had a lot to gain from Genevieve's death too. Not only sweet revenge for being fired in the first place, but namely her job back, and a chance to get her name and face in a national market.

And Thad? He had the same motivation. I looked around for him. He wasn't here.

Mario stood at the buffet table with Louisa, chatting it up. I couldn't help myself. I said to Perry, "If Mario was an egg, would he be over-easy, scrambled, poached, or hard-boiled?"

Laughter bubbled out of him. "Oh, scrambled, definitely. Bobby?"

"Hard-boiled." I winked.

His laughter carried across the room, catching Mario's attention. He wandered over. "What's so funny?" he asked.

"Eggs," Perry and I said at the same time, then laughed.

One of Mario's eyebrows dipped. "I've got news for you," he said to me.

"Me?"

"You."

"About?"

"Bobby."

"Oh?"

I tried not to sound overeager but couldn't quite pull it off.

"He was a no-show today because he was looking for someone to take care of his grandfather tomorrow while he flies back to Florida to deal with his job."

So he hadn't left yet. That was good to know.

"What about his job?" Perry asked.

"I don't know," Mario said, then went on, "he's flying out first thing in the morning, though."

"How do you know all this?"

"Louisa."

"How does she know all this?"

"Bobby."

Perry scowled on my behalf. "What's he doing talking to her?"

"Well, originally for the show, to tell her he'd be gone tomorrow," Mario said. Then he leaned in and whispered, "But word is she's volunteered to watch over his grandfather while he's gone."

"Her?" I gasped, not sure whether I was relieved he hadn't asked me to help or hurt.

After all, Mac was a handful, but then again, Louisa was a complete stranger.

"Why would she do that?"

Mario arched his left eyebrow.

"Oh," Perry said. He turned a sorrowful look in my direction. "Ohhhh."

"It's okay. No big deal."

Both looked at me like they'd sealed my fate as "ditched" and were going to send me a sympathy bouquet pronto.

I couldn't very well tell them Bobby and I weren't really together and that we were on the show under false pretenses, now could I?

Actually, why couldn't I? Obviously Bobby and I weren't needed by Josh anymore. From the way Jessica lay sprawled on the water bed, there would be no lawsuit.

The only thing keeping me here was the contract I'd signed.

The sooner this farce was over, the better.

Hmmph. Asking Louisa to help him out.

What was that all about?

Out of the corner of my eye I watched Louisa dash across the set, all bouncy and trouncy, her curls flying out behind her.

Willie motioned her over, leaned in and whispered in his usual loud manner. They were about twenty feet away, however, and all I could make out was the name Thad.

Who wasn't to be seen. Was he off pouting somewhere, or had he quit the show in a tantrum?

Perry drew in a breath. "Well lookee-loo."

I turned. And lookee-looed.

"Hi," I said to Bobby as he kissed my cheek.

Mario and Perry gave him the evil eye. They did it quite well. My mother would be quite impressed with their efforts.

"Got a sec?" he asked me.

The old me wanted to shout, "Yes!" The new me, however, weakly said, "I think we're about to start."

"Just one, eensy second, Nina."

Don't give in, don't give in, the new me chanted.

I looked into his eyes and said, "Maybe later."

"Nina . . ."

My eyebrows snapped together. "Louisa? You asked Louisa?"

I'd surprised myself with my little outburst. Usually I hated confrontation, and now twice today I'd willingly thrown myself into it.

"Is that what you're mad about?"

"How about that I hear you're going back to Florida from Roxie, of all people. You won't answer my calls. Then I learn you're letting a complete stranger help you with Mac. What would I be mad about?"

"Well, I'm glad to hear you're not upset."

"Don't even."

"What?"

"Smirk."

"Who's smirking?" His eyes crinkled along with the corners of his mouth when he smiled. His dimple popped.

Ugh! I couldn't take it. "We're at least supposed to *pretend* we're in a relationship."

"Right. The pretend relationship. Because a real one is out of the question." He reached his hand up, and his thumb swept along my jawline.

I grabbed his hand. He had this way of touching me that made me forget all rational reason. "What kind of relationship could we have?" I asked. "With you there and me here?"

"Right. Me . . . there."

"Why do you say it like that?"

"Like what?"

"The way you did, all . . . dripping with undisclosed meaning."

He arched an eyebrow.

I punched him in the arm. "You know how you said it!"

Hurried footsteps turned our attention. Louisa whipped into the room, her face flushed. Willie strode over to her.

She didn't bother with the whispering, and we didn't

bother to pretend we weren't eavesdropping. "He's not in his dressing room."

Jessica slid off the water bed and slinked over to Willie. She seemed awfully chummy for someone who'd been claiming sexual harassment.

"I could do the show alone, Mr. Sala. I could be your next host," she gushed. "You don't need Thad."

Willie rubbed his stubble, smoothed the hairs on his head.

Behind him the execs whispered behind cupped hands.

Willie nodded. "You're absolutely right, Jessica. You're hired. Thad's out."

I could feel Bobby's body heat through my shirt, so I shuffled a little to my left, closer to Mario and Perry, who watched the goings-on with eager eyes.

They weren't the only ones. Carson and his cameraman were having their own cupped-hand meeting. Carson's eyes shone brighter than Jessica's Hollywood dreams.

If he hadn't been the biggest fish in the tristate pond before today, then this little coup sealed his fate.

Jessica squealed.

Louisa looked sick. "Should I let Thad know?"

Willie shook his head. "He'll figure it out."

Willie left Louisa open-mouthed and strode over to Jessica.

"Well, well," Perry said.

If Thad had been the one to kill Genevieve, then his nefarious plot hadn't just thickened—it had turned to quicksand and swallowed him whole.

Apprehension hung over the set, a silent buzz. Everyone's nerves were on edge, waiting for Thad to walk in and see he'd been replaced with Game Show Barbie.

Jessica knelt on the bed, the covers pulled up over her legs. Her cups runneth over her satin nightie. The execs had nothing but smiles. Thad's ousting must have sat well with them.

Actually, I could practically see the lead Carson would

take with his ten o'clock newscast. "Hostess with the mostest takes charge on *Hitched or Ditched* in wake of tragedy. Stay tuned."

And she definitely had the mostest too. That nightie left nothing to the imagination.

"Places for the intro, people." Willie clapped his hands.

I made a mental note to call home to ask Riley to tape the show tonight so I could see what Bobby had been up to all day, what his camera crew had captured on film.

Not because he wasn't telling me everything. Only because I was curious.

"What time do you fly out tomorrow?" I asked him as we sat in our seats on the set.

I couldn't help but watch Jessica as she flipped through her note cards for the show ahead. I hoped to heaven there weren't more sex questions. Where were the home decor questions? The obligatory wedding questions?

Enough about the sex! It just served to remind me about the lack of it in my life.

"At ten," he said.

I tried to smooth a wrinkle out of my pants. Darn linen. "Are you coming back?" I held my breath, waiting for the answer.

"Tomorrow night in time for the taping of *Rendezvous*." Something in me was so glad to hear that, despite the fact he'd be gone again in no time.

"There are a few things I need to take care of down there. Shouldn't take too long. Did you want to get dinner tonight?"

"Dinner or dessert?" I probed.

The corners of his eyes crinkled as he smiled. "I was thinking cookies might be good."

Outraged, I leaned forward, glared. "Perry! You told?"

"Sorry, sugar. I don't do well with secrets. I should have told you."

"Mario, you could have warned me."

He smiled. "I could have, but where's the fun in that?"

Sighing, I leaned back, crossed my arms.

"Remember the time with the double chocolate cookies and vanilla ice cream?"

"No."

"You lie like the rug Willie needs."

I couldn't help but smile. Willie really did need a toupee. Or to let nature take its course and allow his bald head to shine.

Overhead lights dimmed, cameramen took their places. A spotlight illuminated Jessica on the bed as she started Thad's usual greeting.

I wondered if he realized he'd been replaced yet. Or if he cared.

She greeted Mario and Perry, and I knew from previous nights that parts of their days would be pieced into this tape.

Jessica had trouble pronouncing *MacKenna* and stammered her way through my introduction too. Red filled her cheeks as she began speaking faster and faster, finally reading the closing line, a teaser about the next segment.

We took a break while Mario and Bobby went backstage to the soundproof booth closet.

I prepared myself for the night's double entendre questions.

"She's got great legs, doesn't she?" Perry said.

"Jealous?"

He laughed. "You're catching on, sug—"

Jessica's shriek cut him off. "You can't!"

Pulling her robe tightly around her waist, she stood over Willie, eyeing him like prey.

"Sorry, Jessie. You're no host. You're eye candy, not the nougat center."

Perry pretended to gag himself.

Willie clapped his hands. "Take ten. Louisa, find Thad. We need him back."

Reminding me of Riley, Louisa threw her arms into the air and stomped out of the room.

The new me didn't feel sorry for her one bit.

And little did she know what she was in for tomorrow, what with Mac's touchy-feely-ness.

Served her right.

Jessica wasn't through pleading her case. "Willie, this is outrageous. You can't do this to me. After all I've been through!"

"Life's tough, kid. Get over it."

Perry moved into Mario's empty seat. "This is better than *Dallas* the year J.R. was shot."

This whole week *had* felt like an eighties nighttime soap.

"Do you think Thad will come back?" I asked, watching Carson cross the room to interview one of the execs.

"Sugar, Willie's going to have some serious groveling to do."

If Willie knew Thad had been sleeping with Genevieve, then it would be a cold day in the netherworld before he kowtowed to him.

If.

That "if" was the hinge for many theories, including motivation for Willie to have killed Genevieve.

"You've got that faraway look again. Thinking about cookies?" Perry asked.

I laughed. "No. Far from it, and don't think I've forgiven you for blabbing. I was just thinking about Genevieve and who killed her. That person could be among us right now."

Perry whistled low and made a show of looking at each person milling about, his eyebrow raised.

There were at least fifteen people in the room, all of whom had been present last night. With the exception of Jessica.

Even though she hadn't been seen, it didn't mean she hadn't been there. Maybe Josh had made up her trip to Mexico.

My gaze stopped on the police detectives standing near the door. They were the same pair who'd interviewed Bobby and me last night. It made sense they were here, observing. Were they any closer to finding the killer? Had they found any solid evidence?

It was a relief to know Kevin wasn't working this case. He'd been involved in my life too often these days—it made it really hard to completely move on, away from him.

Toward Bobby?

I just wasn't sure what to do. Wasn't that the whole point of this self-discovery? To figure out who I was, what I wanted?

It hadn't even been two weeks, but I kept coming back to the same conclusion.

I wanted Bobby.

But I still couldn't tell if that was my heart or my libido talking. Or both.

"Ahh," Perry said. "Now you're thinking about cookies."

"I plead the Fifth."

"No reason why you shouldn't have a nibble."

Little did he know. "It's complicated."

"You want him, he wants you. You're definitely hitched material."

"You really think so?"

"Sugar, I'm never wrong."

"But you don't even know us."

"Don't have to. Sometimes things just are. No rhyme, no reason. Just are. If you nit and pick and dissect, the magic dies, and if there's one thing I know, sugar, it's the magic you want—and it's the magic you already have with Bobby. You don't need to be wearing a cape and pulling a bunny out of a hat to see it. It surrounds the two of you."

Louisa jogged into the room, pulled up short next to Willie.

"You find him?" Willie asked her.

Red-faced from exertion, she drew in deep breaths. "Not. Here."

I thought maybe I should give her Duke's number.

That'd serve her right too.

"Mr. Sala," Jessica purred. "Give me another chance."

"No."

"But—"

"No." The Channel 18 cameraman moved in. Willie covered the lens with his meaty hand. "Go. Away."

The camera guy backed up, bumping into Carson. I wondered if Ana and he had plans to meet later.

To Jessica, Willie said in short, breathless bursts, "You still want any job, sit down and be quiet. Unless you want to sue me again?"

"Sue him? What's that about?" Perry asked.

I figured it didn't hurt to spill the beans now. "Sexual harassment."

Perry's mouth formed a perfect little *o*. "No way."

"Way. Trumped-up charges, I'm guessing."

"Not exactly the way to get in the good graces of the boss. I wonder how she got her job back."

I wondered too.

"You're here only because I was desperate," Willie stated to Jessica. "Let's get that out in the open right now."

"Impeccable timing he has," Perry whispered, smiling.

Jessica glared at Willie, and it was easy to see the hatred in her eyes. Her Hollywood dreams must have outweighed her need to lash out because she turned on her heel, strutted to the water bed and climbed in, arranging herself in the middle. A spotlight from above lit her every curve as she leaned her head back against the padded headboard. She blinked against the bright light, squinted. A look of absolute horror came over her face.

"Jessica?" I rose. A chill swept down my spine. "Jessica?"

She tore her teary gaze from above, looked at me and started screaming.

Perry and I made it bedside at the same time as the detectives. No one knew quite what was going on. Jessica was too hysterical to speak.

I shaded my eyes against the spotlights and peered into the maze of catwalks above the studio, where she'd been looking when she'd gone pale.

It didn't take long to see what Jessica had spotted.

Thad Cochran's body dangled from a noose tied to a metal beam.

Seventeen

The local country station played softly in
the background as I drove home, a song about a man who'd
driven his big rig into a motel when he found out his wife
was in it with another man.

Life seemed so cut-and-dried in country songs. Jealous?
Just run down your wife, own up to it, and spend the rest of
your life in jail. No fuss, muss, or deception needed.

It was one pesky detail that had a way of interfering with
reality. People who killed didn't usually want to be caught.

Even if it meant taking their own life.

It sure looked as though Thad had committed suicide.
Had he killed Genevieve and couldn't live with the guilt?
Had his arrest been imminent?

Bobby didn't think so. We'd been back in the conference room, waiting to be interviewed by Cincinnati police
detectives, when he said, "Thad loved himself too much to
end his life."

"He's right," Perry added.

Mario nodded. "Thad loved Thad first and foremost."

All true.

The streets were quiet this time of night, and I'd made
every light. I couldn't wait to get home, crawl into the sofa
bed and try to figure out my life.

Tequila might help me figure things out faster, but that was probably taking the easy way out. The new me wasn't supposed to take the easy road.

I sighed. This self-discovery stuff was hard. Worse yet, I didn't even know if any of it would work.

So far I had a new look, a new diet, sore muscles, clean fingernails, and a whole lot of frustration and confusion. Not exactly a glowing endorsement of self-discovery, was it? I kept hoping that feeling of contentment, of knowing what the right thing to do with my life, would come over me.

No such luck.

I didn't know what to make of that. Do I keep on keeping on? Or go back . . . ?

Almost home, I decided to wait for the tequila to think about it.

Yeah, it was easy, but after the night I'd had, I needed it. A girl could take only so much.

As far as I knew, Thad's body remained dangling from the catwalk on the set of *Hitched or Ditched*. The police had been waiting for the arrival of the medical examiner before cutting him down.

And I couldn't help but wonder . . . If he didn't kill himself, how'd he get up there? It's not as though someone can lure a person onto a catwalk, slip a noose around their neck, and give a little nudge.

I rolled down my street, breathed in relief at the FOR SALE sign still up across the street, and slowed to a stop when I noticed the cars parked in front of my house. My mother's, Maria's, Ana's, Brickhouse's, Tam's . . .

Ah. Would this be the "later on" Tam had mentioned? Now I understood my mother's cleaning frenzy and the cream puffs.

Slowly, I pulled into my driveway. The shades were drawn, the inside dark, but I could see the flicker of the TV set.

Glancing next door, I noticed Mr. Cabrera's house sat

ablaze in light, and through his picture window I could easily see him and Riley playing a game of cards.

Not sure what to expect, I climbed out of my truck and up the front steps. I pushed open the front door, and the scent of popcorn, cream puffs, and strawberries filled my nose.

"Um, hello?" I said to the group gathered around the TV.

"Shh!" It was my mother who hushed me.

My couch had been pushed back, nearly into the kitchen. My living room, littered with pillows, sleeping bags, popcorn bowls, and margarita glasses, was a mess.

No one bothered to turn my way. Five pairs of eyes remained glued to the TV set, on the image of Carson Keyes, reporting from the parking lot of HoD.

" . . . examiner will have preliminary autopsy information by week's end, though by all accounts it appears as though *Hitched or Ditched* host Thad Cochran took his own life. No word from Cincinnati's finest on whether this tragedy is in any way related to the untimely death yesterday of Genevieve Sala, the show's hostess. For now, a source close to producer/director Willie Sala reports *Hitched or Ditched* has been put on temporary hiatus as the investigation continues. This is Carson Keyes, and I'll keep you informed and up-to-date. Back to you, Del."

Ana fanned herself. "Isn't he the cutest?"

"You should see him in person," Maria chimed in.

A smile crept across Ana's face. "You should see him naked."

Maria squealed and clapped. She'd been a cheerleader in high school. Old habits were hard to break. "Tell all!"

"I couldn't."

"You could too," my mother said, sipping her margarita.

"And has." Brickhouse chuckled. "Tell Maria about his tattoo."

Tam tossed popcorn into her mouth, talked around it. "A tattoo! No! Not Carson Keyes!"

Ana leaned forward, her breasts nearly spilling out of her V-neck nightshirt.

Wait. Whoa.

I took a good look around. Pillows. Sleeping bags. Sleepwear . . .

It was an honest to goodness slumber party.

At my house.

On a work night.

"It's a tiny pink ballet slipper on his right hip."

I noticed someone had put a piece of tape over the *Hitched or Ditched* camera in the living room. Probably my mother—she wouldn't have wanted anyone to see her clean.

Maria frowned. "A ballet slipper?"

"I know," Ana said. "Weird. He wouldn't tell me what it was about."

"Probably a tribute to an ex," Tam pointed out.

"Girlfriend or boyfriend?" Brickhouse clucked.

Ana drew herself up. "He is not gay! I can attest to that."

More clucking. "If the ballet slipper fits."

"Hi," I said again, still standing in the doorway. I thought it a good time to jump in, seeing as how Ana looked like she wanted to shove popcorn down Brickhouse's throat to permanently end her clucking.

"You're home!" Tam cried.

My mother smiled as though she hadn't shushed me minutes before. "Welcome to Tam's slumber party!"

"Nina!" Maria shrieked.

Oh no—I'd forgotten the earplugs.

"You look . . . you look . . . amazing! Are your eyebrows plucked? Are those highlights? Oh. My. God! Do you have a manicure?"

"And a pedicure."

She squealed.

Everyone launched into a discussion on my new look

as I set my backpack and keys down and made my way to the margarita pitcher. Tequila in its best form. If I'd had any hesitation about taking the easy road, it'd been washed out by the presence of five crazy women in my living room.

"This is just what I needed," Tam said. "A night away. Listen." She cocked an ear.

I listened. The news anchor waxed on, outraged at the cost of heating bills.

"It's quiet. No crying." She sipped her margarita, smiled. "It's heaven."

Okay, so I'd been put out by my own plans being thwarted. I'd been looking forward to the quiet night in bed, the chance to sort things out, but seeing Tam so happy . . . It was worth a little inconvenience.

"You don't seem all that upset by Thad's death," I said to my mother.

"*Pah*. I was over him the minute I heard about him and Genevieve. No one likes a slimeball."

"Amen," Maria said.

"Was he blue?" Ana asked. "Did his eyes bulge out? Had he wet himself? I've heard that when you're hung, you lose control of your bodily functions. True?"

I gulped my margarita.

Brickhouse clucked. "Thad Cochran would hate it to get around that he wee-weed on himself."

Maria nodded. "Most egotistical man I'd ever met."

My mother looked aghast.

Tam looked enthralled.

"So?" Ana asked.

"I didn't see him," I lied.

"But you must have heard."

"Nope, not a thing. I was locked in the soundproof booth." My fibbing skills never ceased to amaze me.

"Hmmph," she grunted, clearly disappointed.

Gingerly, I plopped down onto the cushion of sleeping

bags. Ibuprofen had worked miracles on my aching muscles. "Is Riley gone for the whole night?"

"Sleeping at Donatelli's." Brickhouse stretched out her legs. She wore a two-piece Tinker Bell flannel pajama set. I didn't know if I'd ever be able to look at her the same way again.

Maria examined her pedicure. "He mumbled something about too much estrogen before he bolted out the back door."

Can't say I blamed him.

Tam frowned. "Do you think she misses me? Maybe I should call home. Do you think I should call home?" She tugged on her roomy Beatles T-shirt. Plaid lounging pants and floppy-eared bunny slippers completed her pj's.

My mother patted her hand. "You know where the phone is, *chérie*."

Tam sprinted into the kitchen. She moved really well for a woman who'd recently had a baby.

"Oh look! Look! It's Carson again." Ana sighed.

I'd never seen her so giddy over someone. Could it be that she was finally ready to settle down? Or did she just have stars in her eyes?

I hoped Carson wasn't hurt in the cross fire. He seemed the sensitive sort, especially if he'd succumbed under pressure to have a ballet slipper tattooed on his hip. He'd never see Steamroller Ana coming.

Brickhouse aimed the remote at the TV, turned up the volume. I refilled my glass.

"Sources on scene have confirmed Sherry Cochran, the widow of *Hitched or Ditched* host Thad Cochran, has been taken to University Hospital following a collapse after hearing the news of her husband's death."

The screen cut to footage of an ambulance pulling up to the front door of the HoD building, then flashed ahead to Sherry being wheeled out of the building.

I hadn't realized Sherry was there. Did she arrive after hearing the news about Thad? Or had she been there all along?

I took another strawberry-filled sip.

None of my business. The detectives were quite capable of sorting this all out.

"Who's that?" Maria asked, squinting at the TV. She was nearsighted but refused to buy a pair of glasses.

I put my glass down, reached for the popcorn. The cream puff plate was empty. "Who?"

"The blonde with the pixie cut. That style is really all wrong for her. Who does she think she is, Twiggy?"

"Her name is Jessica Ayers."

"She looks familiar."

"She was the hostess of *Hitched or Ditched* for two years, before Genevieve came in."

Maria shook her head. "No. Never watched the show before you were on it."

"You probably met her at some charity shindig or another."

"Nope. I'd have remembered that hair."

Brickhouse clucked. "Ach. Perhaps she probably wore it in a different style when you met her."

My mother said, "She's had that same style for as long as she's been on *Hitched or Ditched.*"

"It'll come to me," Maria said.

And it would. She had a talent for remembering faces.

Ana held her fingers to her lips. "Shh! I can't hear Carson."

Coochie-cooing noises came from the kitchen—Tam obviously having a conversation with Nic. Well, I hoped it was Nic. If it was Ian she was talking to like that, then I'd be worried.

My mother sipped her drink. "I give her till midnight."

"Who? Nic?"

"Tam."

"Shhh!" Ana glared.

Brickhouse nodded. "I say one."

"That long, Ursula?" My mother tsked.

Maria snapped open her Chanel handbag. "I've got five dollars that says, oh, four-thirty."

Brickhouse reached for her tote, my mother for her Louis Vuitton. Ana pulled a five from the depths of her cleavage, and without ever taking her eyes off the TV, passed it behind her and said, "Three."

My mother looked at me just as Tam paced by the kitchen doorway. The light from the TV caught the tears in her eyes. "Closest without going over?"

Everyone nodded.

"Eleven," I said, knee-walking to my backpack on the table near the door.

"But it's ten-thirty now," Brickhouse felt the need to point out.

"I'm aware." I pulled a five out of my wallet just as Tam came back into the living room.

"I think she misses me," Tam said. "Ian says she's okay, but I don't know. There was something in her voice when I spoke with her."

We all nodded, though I personally thought she might have had a little too much to drink.

"Maybe I should go home," Tam said, dropping onto the floor.

My mother, dressed in silk pajamas, easily slid across the sleeping bags and wrapped an arm around Tam. "It's okay, *chérie*. Why don't you give it a little time." She caught my eye, winked. "At least another hour or so."

"Or two!" Brickhouse shouted.

"Or four!" Ana threw over her shoulder.

Tam's eyebrows dipped. "What's going on?"

"A little pool." I tossed my money at my mother, who glowered at me for telling.

Tam threw her head back and laughed. "This is just what

I needed," she said. She dug around in her canvas bag and pulled out a five dollar bill. "I take six A.M. By then I'll be able to get home in time to say good morning to Nic when she wakes up."

"See what you did," my mother said to me. "I'd have won that bet."

Brickhouse clucked. "Not likely."

Maria yawned. She wore one of those long flowing Mommy Dearest peignoirs, with the feathers along the bottom hem and the high heel slippers. A sleep mask sat atop her head. "Do you have a vacuum?"

I eyed the popcorn bits on the floor. "Since when do you do housekeeping?"

"It's for my bed."

"Bed?"

Brickhouse smirked, and nodded to the box in the corner. It was one of those inflatable mattresses. Queen size.

"And could you fill it up for me?" Maria batted her eyelashes.

That would be no. Oooh—my new self could even withstand Maria. That alone made the process worth it.

Ana turned off the TV. "Maybe I'll call Andy the tech at the M.E.'s office tomorrow morning, see what he knows about Thad's death."

My mother rose. "I'm going to need another pitcher of margaritas if she's going to keep talking about dead bodies."

Tam leaned back on her pillow, set her travel alarm clock. "Easiest money I'll ever make."

"Oh," my mother said. "The construction foreman called. He won't be able to make it tomorrow."

I groaned. It figured. I finally got rid of the picketers, and now the construction guys were going to be a no-show.

"Someone put on the movie," Brickhouse said.

"Movie?" I asked.

Maria sighed. "*Love Story.*"

I wondered if Mr. Cabrera would mind if I bunked on his couch.

I couldn't sleep.

Between Brickhouse's and my mother's snoring, Maria's tossing and turning on her squeaky inflatable mattress, and Tam getting up every half hour to call home, I'd maybe dozed five minutes.

I blinked to clear my vision. The digital readout on the VCR told me it was 3:53 A.M.

My head swam with information. As much as I'd tried to drown it out with the margaritas, it floated there on the edge of my consciousness.

Neither Thad's nor Genevieve's deaths were any of my business. It was happenstance that I'd been thrown into the situation, bad luck that I'd stumbled on the two of them in the bathroom, and Willie and Sherry in each other's arms.

However, as I lay there, staring at the hole in my ceiling, I couldn't help going over everything again, the events that had happened in the last couple of days.

First the death threats, then the death of Genevieve, then Thad.

If I looked from the outside in, and asked who gained from their deaths, there was no clear answer.

If Willie was the murderer, what did he gain? His freedom, sure. Maybe even revenge. But he lost so much more. Genevieve was the ink in his network deal.

If Sherry killed them, what did she gain? The same as Willie, I supposed. But she also lost her meal ticket. I couldn't imagine that Thad made much money on HoD—his star was just rising, fame and fortune within his grasp.

But now Willie and Sherry had each other. Maybe that was the ultimate gain. Not money. Or fame. Or fortune. Or the show. Love.

Had they plotted and planned their spouses' deaths?

I couldn't forget about Thad and his apparent suicide. If

he'd committed suicide, why? Out of guilt? Had he killed Genevieve? A lover's spat gone wrong? Or did he kill himself out of despair? Over losing her and possibly his job?

The sound of a big truck outside filtered through the quiet night. I sat up as the engine idled, then shut off.

People were rarely out and about at that time of night in the Mill. I bit back a groan as I climbed out of my sleeping bag.

Outside, a car door closed.

Muscles ached as I peeked out the window. My stomach immediately knotted.

Rushing to the door, I pulled it open and slipped out.

"What are you doing here?" I asked Kit, wrapping my arms around myself to ward off the cold. BeBe slurped my hand. Her tail slammed against my orange mums, sending petals flying.

"You said if I needed anything to let you know. I need a place to stay. Can't find a hotel that'll take BeBe."

"You can take Riley's room."

"I can't—"

"He's not home."

"On a school night?"

"You'll see why soon enough."

BeBe followed obediently as we walked up the front steps.

"Is that Tam's car?"

"Yep."

"Is everything okay?"

"Yep." I pushed open the front door. Light spilled across the living room floor.

"Good God. Maybe I should just sleep in the truck."

"Nonsense," I whispered. "You're more than welcome here."

BeBe was in sniffing heaven. She licked Maria's toes, and I heard her mumble Nate's name.

I shuddered. Too much information.

"What's on her face?" Kit asked.

"Sleep mask. Keeps the light out."

"Oh."

Kit and BeBe followed me up the stairs. I hoped Kit didn't notice how slowly I was taking them. BeBe slipped a few times on the hardwood but finally made it up. "Let me change the sheets."

"I'll do it."

"You sure?"

He nodded. I popped open the linen closet, pulled out a clean set of sheets. "Towels are in here too," I said.

"All right."

"You okay?" I asked.

"Been better."

I didn't know what to say to that. "Need to talk?"

"Nope." He had tomorrow off, and I hoped he slept in.

My heart breaking for him, I sighed. "You sure you don't want to talk?"

"Not yet."

I backed out the door. "Good night, then."

"Oh, Nina?"

"Yeah?"

"I might need to stay here for a few days while I find a place."

"Stay as long as you need, Kit."

I crept back down the stairs, wincing with each step. Tam was slipping into her jeans. "Is he okay?" she asked me.

"I guess. Doesn't want to talk about it."

My mother's snores filled the room. I motioned to the kitchen. "I heard him fighting with Daisy at Lowther House yesterday. About her doing something dangerous."

I filled Tam in while I rooted around for something to eat. I settled on a low-carb granola bar.

Tam read the wrapper. "What's up with you?"

"What?"

"Low-carb? Ursula says you've been drinking coffee,

Ana says you haven't been sleeping with Bobby, your mother says you're on a diet, and Mr. Cabrera says he heard you listening to country music."

"Chatty bunch."

"They're worried."

"I'm fine. Just trying new things." I glanced at her jeans. "Leaving?"

"Yeah. I miss them. Is that sappy?"

"Completely." I gave her a hug.

"You know this means Maria wins the bet. We'll never hear the end of it."

I smiled. "She won't gloat for long once she finds out BeBe was licking her toes."

She smiled, then the corners of her lips turned down, into a frown. "There were supposed to be six of us here tonight, Nina."

"Six?" I polished off the granola bar.

"Deanna."

I choked. Tam whumped my back.

"I spoke with her today," she said once I could breathe again.

I wiped down the already clean countertop. "Oh?"

"Listen. She was convinced you were letting her go. She made up that interview at The Grass Is Always Greener."

"So she says."

"I called over there and checked it out."

"Sometimes it's scary how thorough you are."

"Nina . . ."

"Why would she make it up?"

"She's young, foolish. And would like a second chance."

"I don't know, Tam."

"I saw someone on TV recently who said she believes in second chances."

Pulling in a deep breath, I said, "Okay. I'll talk to her."

Tam beamed. "I'll call her first thing."

"Don't have her come in first thing, though. I have to deal with the whole missing diamond ring situation first."

"Diamond ring?" Tam asked. "From Lowther House?"

Nodding, I draped the dish towel over the bar of the oven.

Tam whistled low. "The new guy?"

I shrugged. "Don't know."

"The police interview him yet?"

"The police weren't called."

Her eyebrows dipped, her shoulders straightened. "What? Why not?"

"I'm not sure. I meet with Pippi at eight. Maybe she'll have some answers for me."

And hopefully not leave me with more questions.

Eighteen

"This just came for you." Brickhouse handed me a FedEx package.

"Thanks," I said.

She shifted on her feet. "How's Kit?"

"I don't know."

"I'm going to kill that Daisy with my bare hands."

"I'll help."

Smiling, she clucked. I don't know how she did both at the same time, but she managed.

"Do you think he knows how much we care?"

I lifted an eyebrow. "We? Are you going soft on me, Mrs. Krauss?"

"Never."

"That's what I thought. But yes, I think he knows. I hope he knows." I peered up at her. "Maybe we should tell him?"

"He probably wouldn't take too well to that."

"You're right. His bald head would get all red."

"He'd stammer."

"Glare."

"Bolt," we said at the same time.

"We'll keep it between us," I said.

"Deal."

The chimes on the front door rang out. "Pip's here," Brickhouse whispered over her shoulder.

"Give me a few minutes."

She closed the door on the way out.

I ripped open the FedEx package. Inside was a document from the legal department at *Hitched or Ditched*, releasing me from my contract.

The episodes featuring me and Bobby, Mario and Perry, would never again see the light of day. It was as if the show was trying to erase this week from its memory.

Can't say I blamed them.

Glancing down, I looked at my schedule for the day, and wondered about my appointment with Sherry. I crossed it off. There was no way she was going to keep it, if she even remembered she had one after all that had happened.

I set my new handbag on my desk. My mother had given it to me this morning before I left for work. My backpack had disappeared sometime during the night.

It was a nice bag, Coach, but it didn't feel right.

I flipped the flap, pulled out my cell phone, checked the readout.

Bobby hadn't called since the last time I'd checked it.

I jumped in surprise as it suddenly rang in my hand. I ground my teeth at the strains of "Like a Virgin." Today while I was at the mall with Perry, I would find someone to change that tune.

I recognized Kevin's cell number and answered, trying to sound peppier than I felt. "Good morning."

"What's wrong?"

"Why does something have to be wrong?" I was worried sick about Bobby, but Kevin didn't need to know that.

"You're never chipper in the morning."

"Maybe I'm just happy to hear from you."

He laughed. "Now I know something's wrong."

Really, what wasn't? My life was a mess. "I'm okay."

"Does this have anything to do with that reality show?"

Most, but not all. "Nope."

"Then I don't suppose you want to know what I found out about the case?"

The old me would have jumped at the chance to know. The new me said, "Nope."

"Now I know something is terribly wrong. Is it about *Booby*?" He laughed.

I rolled my eyes at his immaturity, though I supposed I was just as bad, never calling his girlfriend Ginger by the right name. "Bobby's fine."

"But you still don't want to know? I called in a favor, got the inside scoop . . ."

I felt myself caving. "Oh, all right."

"That's the Nina I know and loved."

I noticed the past tense. "Well?"

"Feisty this morning," he said.

I did feel on edge. A lot had happened over the last few days. I was stressed. "Kevin, I've got a client waiting."

"Fine. As I said, I called in a favor—"

"Yeah, yeah."

"You're one of a kind, Nina. You know that?"

"Are you buttering me up?" I had the sneaking suspicion he didn't just call to share news.

"Me? Never!"

Now I knew he was.

"As I was saying, I called in a favor. The M.E. is awaiting some tox screens and such, but the case is all but closed. Thad Cochran killed Genevieve."

"Are they sure? There's an awful lot of behind-the-scenes stuff going on there."

"So I've heard on the news, but the evidence points in that direction. I guess they interviewed Thad, and he confessed to having been with Genevieve in the hot tub the day she died. They'd been doing this near-asphyxiation sex game."

"Did he confess he'd killed her?"

"Actually, no. Said she was fine when he left her in the hot tub, but there had been an arrest warrant issued for Thad yesterday. That's why the detectives were at the studio last night—waiting to take him in."

I guess he did have good sources. "So, the case is closed."

"Unofficially."

It did make sense. I supposed. Except the part about Thad killing himself. He wasn't the type, and if it had really been a sex game gone wrong, then was it truly murder?

"Stop," Kevin said.

"Stop what?"

"Thinking about the case. Let the police handle it, stay out of it. No snooping."

"Me, snoop?"

"Nina . . . "

"Kevin . . . " I was just giving him a hard time. Truth be told, I was beyond glad to have the case closed. I never wanted anything to do with *Hitched or Ditched* again.

"So, is that all?" I asked.

"All?"

"You just called to tell me about the case?"

"Well, now that you bring it up, there is something else."

Hah! I'd known it. "What?"

"I need to go no contact."

My stomach dropped. "Why?"

"I can't talk about it."

"I'm not understanding, Kevin. You're a homicide detective. Since when do you go undercover at all?"

There was a long silence before he said, "Since I started doing some work for Ian."

Ian the DEA agent? Oh good God.

"Nina?"

"I'm here." A thousand questions popped into my head.

"I can't answer any questions."

"I wish you'd stop doing that!"

"What?"

"Reading my mind. I hate it."

"I know."

I groaned.

"I'll be okay."

"I'm not worried about you."

He laughed. "Liar."

"I'm not," I lied. "It's Riley." Which was actually true.

"I'll be okay, Nina."

"If you're going no contact, then you're in danger, right?"

He didn't say anything.

"Shit." My hand shook. How come hearing his voice, worrying about him, still happened after all this time?

"Since when do you swear?"

"I've just taken up the habit. Does Tam know you're working with Ian?"

"No."

"Does Allspice?" I was referring to Detective Ginger Barlow. Kevin's partner both in and out of the bedroom.

I could hear his smile. "Running out of spices?"

"Maybe. Does she?"

"No. No one but the DEA, my immediate supervisor, and you now."

"Why'd you have to go and tell me? This is just what I need, one more stress in my life."

"Because of Riley, Nina."

Right. Riley. Who'd be wondering where his dad was.

"What do I tell him?" I asked.

"You don't have to tell him anything. I'll call when he gets out of school and let him know I have to go away for a while."

I drew in a deep breath. Outside, I caught sight of snow-flakes starting to fall.

October was a crazy month here in Cincinnati. Eighty degrees one day, snow the next.

My intercom buzzed. "Ms. Lowther here to see you," Brickhouse said.

I held my cell to my chest. "Give me just a minute more, please." I waited a beat and said to Kevin, "I've got to go."

"Don't worry about me."

A lump had lodged in my throat. "I won't," I lied.

"Yeah, and I won't worry about you snooping into the *Hitched or Ditched* case."

"Actually, you won't have to."

He snorted. "I'll call if I can. 'Bye, Nina," he said, then hung up.

I closed my phone, dropped it into my backpack. It immediately rang again. Ana's cell number lit up the screen. I pressed the silence button, dropped it again. I wasn't in the mood to talk to her right now.

Automatically, my hand reached for my bottom drawer, to my chocolate stash. Just as I pulled it open, I remembered it was empty.

Only . . . it wasn't.

Confused, I pulled the box of Almond Joys from the drawer. A note was taped to the top of the box.

Since you're fresh out of cookies, I thought you might be getting hungry.
—Bobby

My eyes and nose stung with held in tears.

I took a minute to compose myself, then buzzed Brickhouse. "Please send Pippi in."

"Right away," she answered.

"Oh, and Mrs. Krauss?"

"Yes?"

"Did Bobby happen to stop by yesterday?"

She clucked. "Oh, did I forget to tell you?"

"Must have slipped your mind."

"Must have."

A minute later Pippi was settled across from me, worry in her eyes, a frown on her lips. "I don't know what to say."

"We don't know for certain any of my people were involved."

"Fair enough. However, there's never been a single incidence of theft at Lowther House in its existence. The day you and your workers come in, a valuable ring goes missing?"

It did seem a little coincidental, and everyone knew how I felt about that.

"When was the last time the ring was seen?"

She fidgeted. "No one is absolutely sure. Definitely a hundred percent Tuesday. Saw it myself when Minnie was watching the poker game."

I'd seen it then too.

"Perhaps she simply misplaced it?"

"We've looked everywhere."

"Pippi, I think we should call the police."

"No! I mean, that's not necessary. We should be able to work this out between ourselves."

"May I ask why not?"

"I don't want to drag Lowther House's reputation through the mud, Nina. People pay me a lot of money for their privacy. I feel responsible for bringing your company in, and feel I must try to resolve this issue myself before alerting the authorities."

My eyebrows inched upward. That answer sounded too pat, too practiced to be completely true. "I cannot go around accusing my employees without proof."

"Have you spoken to the young man who brought Minnie back to her room yesterday?"

"He was in her room?"

"Yes. She has a pass card for the alarm system, so she doesn't have to remember the code for the east wing."

"No, I haven't had a chance to speak with him yet."

"I've heard your employees—"

"I vouch for all my employees and their character." Even Jeff Dannon, though I didn't know why. I'd had very few employees revert to their illegal ways after I took them on.

She rose. "Please speak with him and get back to me. I'll be waiting for your call."

I walked her out, watched her settle into her Lexus and drive away.

"Mrs. Krauss, could you please call together an emergency employee meeting?" I didn't want to ruin everyone's day off, so I said, "Tomorrow, nine A.M. sharp."

Brickhouse clucked. "Who's she accusing of what?"

I tipped my head. "Was that sentence grammatically correct?"

"Don't start with me, Nina Ceceri."

"Jeff. Missing diamond."

"I don't believe it."

"It's not for us to decide. Just call the meeting."

I poured myself a cup of coffee, dumped in some creamer, some sugar, and carried it back to my office. Checking my phone, I saw Ana had called three times, my mother once. Nothing from Bobby.

He'd be taking off just about now . . .

I wasn't in the mood to talk to Ana or my mother, so I busied myself with invoices for the next hour. The office was quiet. Everyone except Brickhouse had the day off. The chimes on the front door jangled loudly.

"Well, well," Brickhouse said.

Curious, I went to the doorway. My muscles were slowly forgiving me. Deanna stood there, holding two nine-by-thirteen-inch trays.

"German chocolate cupcakes," she said, holding them out.

"Bees and honey," I mumbled, hearing my mother's voice.

"There's one for every hour I've been gone. I know they're your favorite." She held them out with such a look of sincerity that I couldn't help forgive her on the spot.

"Come on," I said, holding out my arms. "Let's get this over with."

She stepped into my hug, tears in her eyes.

Brickhouse clucked and mumbled something about me being a softie.

I guess there were just some things I couldn't change about myself. "Let's just forget the last couple of days and move forward."

Deanna nodded. It was the first time I'd seen her speechless.

I led her into my office, took the pans of German chocolate cupcakes, removed the foil off the top pan, plucked out a cupcake and bit into it.

Duke would have had a fit if he could see me, but since my butt was still sore from the treadmill incident, I figured I'd earned the calories.

Deanna sat across from me, still a jumble of nerves. Her leg bounced, her thumbs rotated around each other, her left eye twitched.

"With the current setup of TBS, there's not a need for more than one designer," I started out.

"Not this again," Deanna mumbled.

I smiled. "That's why I'm going to start a new division of Taken by Surprise."

Her thumbs stilled. Her knee still bounced. "New division?"

"Weekend Warrior, and you, Deanna, will be in complete charge of it."

Her eyes widened. "What is it?"

"There aren't many people who can afford TBS's services. I realize that, and I feel bad they're not more available to everyone. So, I got to thinking, what's the most expensive part of our services?"

"The labor," Deanna said.

I knew she was smart.

"Right. So, what if TBS offered a special service? We—rather, you—design the landscape and pull together all the materials needed for the design. Everything will be delivered to the homeowner's front step. Then the homeowner does all the work to see the design come to fruition. It will be a fraction of the cost we charge now, people can do it on their own time schedule, and there's a sense of accomplishment they receive by doing the yard themselves, without the hassle of searching for the right type of stone, the perfect plant, liners, pumps, all the tedious, time-consuming details."

Her face lit. "I love it!"

"I knew you would."

"I'm so sor—"

"Ah!" I shook a finger. "We weren't going to dwell, remember?"

"Okay. Can I say thank you?"

"You just did."

"When do I start?"

"Now." I pulled a file from my drawer. "Here are some names I've accumulated over the last month or so of people who were interested in a makeover but couldn't swing it for one reason or another. You should contact them, offer this new service. I guarantee your spring will be busy."

Slowly, she stood, clutching the folder. "I'll make you proud, Nina."

I didn't tell her she already had.

Looking up at the wall clock, I noted that Sherry Cochran's appointment time had come and gone. I'd stuck around just in case.

I ate another cupcake as I tidied my desk, gathered up my handbag. "Why don't you go home, Mrs. Krauss?" I asked, headed for the door. "I'll be out all afternoon, and there's really no need for you to stay."

"Where are you going?"

"Out."

"Where?"

"If you must know, to the mall." I was due to meet Perry there in forty-five minutes.

She grabbed her purse. "Good timing. I need a few things myself."

"But—"

"Close your mouth, Nina Ceceri. We'll take my car."

"But—"

"No arguments."

"And to think I was just beginning to like you."

"Ach. We can't be having that, can we?" She pushed me out the door.

Nineteen

Lips pursed, eyebrows dipped, Perry said, "No, no! Get it off right now! My eyes!"

I pointed at Brickhouse's cleavage. "You could hurt someone with those. Poke someone's eyes out."

"Donatelli's going to love it," she said, admiring the leather bustier in the dressing room's full-length mirror.

Perry cupped his mouth, directing his words so only I could hear him. "I hope this Donatelli doesn't have a heart condition."

"If he doesn't now," I whispered, "he will after he gets a look at that."

Brickhouse spun. "I wonder if they have a matching skirt."

"No!" Perry and I shouted at the same time.

An older woman popped her head out of the adjacent dressing room at all the commotion. She took one look at Brickhouse's outfit and darted back inside, a huge grin on her face. Thank goodness I didn't recognize the woman from the Mill. News that Brickhouse had turned hootchie mama would have been all over the neighborhood by the time we left the mall.

"Ach. No fun, you two."

My cell phone rang.

Perry said, "How appropriate. A Madonna song for a Madonna kind of outfit. Perhaps you should have it for your ring tone, Ursula."

Brickhouse said, "For a gay guy you're no fun."

Eyebrows dipped and mouth open in outrage, Perry said, "No fun? Me? Not true!"

She jabbed him in the chest. "I haven't heard a show tune since I met you."

I rolled my eyes, checked my caller ID. It was Bobby. I hesitated for just a second before I answered it.

"Bobby?"

"Hi, Nina," he said.

Perry said, "I don't sing show tunes until I've had one drink, maybe two."

"Ach. You know songs from *West Side Story*?"

"Has Joan Rivers had too much plastic surgery?"

She let out a laugh. "It's karaoke night at Out of Tune, a little place near me."

"I've heard of it," he said warily.

"Are you game?"

"Darlin', if you promise not to buy that bustier, I'm there."

I stepped away from the conversation. "Bobby, you still there?"

"Where are you? And did I just hear the word 'bustier'?"

I moseyed over to the lingerie. A beautiful sheer camisole/panty set caught my eye. "I'm at the mall with Perry and Brickhouse."

"Dare I hope the bustier is for you?"

"You daren't," I said, flipping through the hangers to see if they had my size.

"Just my luck."

I pulled a hanger off the rack, held the camisole up to my chest. Tiny embroidered flowers were stitched along the V-neck seam and along the waistband of the panties. It was a gorgeous set. Glancing up, I saw Perry across the way giving me a thumbs-up. Then he fanned himself.

I shook my head at him.

He nodded at me.

Unable to believe I was even contemplating buying it, I set the lingerie back on the rack, stared at it.

I knew Bobby would love it.

He cleared his throat. "I said, 'Just my luck.'"

"I heard."

"Usually you have a snappy comeback for me."

"Sorry."

His voice dropped a notch. "Are you okay?"

I checked the price tag on the cami set. Eighty dollars. I'd really want to own it for that price.

Or really want Bobby to see me in it.

"I'm okay, Bobby." I sighed, took a deep breath, and was about to tell him how much I missed him. Not only right now, but for the past six weeks. Of how I went to bed thinking about him, woke up thinking about him.

Damn it.

I just couldn't admit to myself that he wasn't a rebound relationship. Because then I'd have to open myself up once again to pain and heartache and possible rejection.

It was nice to see that my self-discovery had finally allowed me to see that.

But what did I do about it?

Searching, I found a place to sit, at the base of a mannequin wearing a barely there fur-trimmed teddy. Maria would have loved it.

"For some reason, I don't believe you," he said softly.

He was perceptive, that Bobby.

"Is this about the murders?" he asked.

Okay, maybe not that perceptive.

"Maybe," I said.

"Any news there?"

I told him what I knew, about the case being unofficially closed.

"I still can't believe Thad would kill himself," he said.

"Me either."

I found I didn't want to talk about it anymore. "Where are you?" I asked.

"Just landed in Tampa—I'm on my way to my place. I have a couple of meetings, then I'm heading back."

"Important meetings?"

My cell phone crackled. My battery was low, and reception in the mall wasn't the greatest.

"You could say that. I know what I want, Nina," he said softly. "And I'm going to get it."

I smiled. "With that attitude, who could say no?"

He laughed. "That's what I'm banking on. Listen, I need a favor, Nina. I know you're busy . . . "

"What's wrong?"

"It's Mac. Louisa can't stay with him."

Imagining Mac chasing Louisa around the house, playing grabby-grab, I smiled. "Oh?"

"Louisa has to go, something about emergency meetings with Willie. I'll be back later tonight, but I don't want Mac to be alone for that long."

I hoped Mac had gotten in one pinch at least. "I'll head over there now."

"You sure? What about your shopping?"

"I've bought too much already." I spotted Brickhouse waddling toward me, Perry behind her carrying my numerous shopping bags.

"Thanks, Nina. I'll let Mac know you're on your way. Call me if you need anything."

"I will."

"I'll be getting in around nine tonight. Will you be able to stay around and talk?"

"Talk?"

"Talk, though where that goes . . . "

I laughed.

"I can't believe the thought of *that* made you laugh."

"You never give up."

"Never. You'll cave. 'Bye, Nina."

I might. I was feeling weaker by the minute.

Hanging up, I watched Brickhouse eye the teddy on the mannequin standing behind me. "No leather, but how about this?" she asked Perry.

He set the shopping bags down. "Tasteful, pretty . . . all right, give it a go."

Her eyes lit and she went in search of her size.

"That's an image of her I really don't need in my head," I said.

"Was that Bobby on the phone?"

"How could you tell?"

"Your face. It glows when you talk to him. Does he know how much you love him?"

I shrugged.

"Do you know how much you love him?"

"I'm just starting to figure that out."

"Maybe you two could figure it out together?"

"Maybe."

Brickhouse returned and held up the teddy on a hanger. "Should I try it on?"

"No!" we shouted at the same time.

She headed toward the register.

"I've got to cut our shopping trip short," I said, and explained about Mac.

"You sure you don't want to buy just one more thing?"

I followed his gaze to the sheer camisole set.

To buy it would be admitting I did want a future with Bobby, long distance or not. That I was ready to take that leap of faith, to open my heart up again, to love again. And accept all the risks that came with it.

I walked over, picked it up. "Maybe just one more thing."

Twenty

Mac was more a kisser than a pincher. Every time I turned around, he was there, trying to steal a smooch. I'd finally gotten him settled in front of the baseball playoff game.

He and Bobby were currently staying together at Mac's place, a small run-down apartment in Springdale, about fifteen miles south of the Mill. For someone who could afford Lowther House, Mac sure didn't live like he had money.

He sat on a worn couch, circa the year I was born, watched TV on one of those old sets that didn't have remotes, and even had a rotary phone.

The kitchen was dated but spotless. I washed down the counter, dried the dishes in the sink, and went to make sure Mac was okay.

He was sound asleep on the couch, his head tipped back. He snored almost as loud as my mother.

Almost.

I opened the slider on the back patio and stepped outside. The snow had stopped and had melted almost immediately, leaving everything slick.

Pulling out my phone, I dialed into TBS's voice-mail system. Most calls were not urgent. I'd get back to them tomorrow. One, however, caught my attention. It was from

Sherry Cochran, and she wanted me to call her back as soon as possible.

Over my shoulder, I checked on Mac. Still asleep. Mentally, I repeated Sherry's number until I punched it into the phone. She answered on the third ring.

"Thank you for getting back to me so soon," she said after the standard hellos. "I'm so sorry I missed my appointment today."

I leaned over the railing. Mac lived on the third floor. It was a long way down. "It's perfectly understandable. No need to worry. We can reschedule when you're ready."

She breathed a sigh. "I'm so glad to hear that. I'd been afraid I missed my chance."

"Not at all. I'm so sorry about what happened, Sherry." I felt the need to say it, though I barely knew her.

"Don't be. I'm not."

I straightened so fast I nearly lost my footing. I grabbed hold of the railing. The cool air soothed my burning cheeks. "You're not?"

"No."

"Oh."

"That sounds harsh, I know, but Thad and I haven't been in love for a long time. He was an egotistical ass."

Ohh-kay. I didn't ask why she'd stayed with him. None of my business.

"However," she said, "he didn't deserve to be murdered."

"But I thought—"

"They're wrong. Thad would never kill himself. I've been at the police station all day trying to convince the detectives someone killed Thad. No one listened. They thought I was just being hysterical. Do I sound hysterical to you?"

Maybe a little, but I said, "Um, no."

"Thank you. Thad had already put down a deposit on a house in California, had a meeting with a decorator lined up. He had plans, Nina. He didn't care one whit that Genevieve had died, no matter how the police try to paint it. Thad wanted the spotlight for himself anyway."

"Do you, uh, think Thad killed her?"

"Maybe," she said. "I really don't know. I wouldn't put it past him."

"So you, uh, knew about the affair?"

"All of them. He made a point of telling me."

Nice guy.

"Did he, uh, know about yours?"

There was silence for a second. "How did you know about mine?"

I came clean. "I saw you and Willie together Monday night."

"Ah."

"Sorry. I just happened to be walking outside, getting fresh air."

"No, Thad didn't know. Neither did Genevieve."

"Did Willie know about Thad and Genevieve?"

"Yes. I went to him and told him. That's when we became close."

"Do you, um, think Willie killed Genevieve?"

"He didn't. We had our own plans for Thad and Genevieve."

Did I dare ask? It was something the old Nina would have done. The new one, though? Some things just couldn't be helped. "If you don't mind me asking, what kind of plans?"

"It's no secret now—I've told the police everything. Willie was going to finalize the deal with the network people, then cut Gen and Thad loose and hire new hosts. Willie and I were going to file for divorces and live happily ever after in Malibu. Genevieve and Thad would have had their worlds pulled out from under them. Come this Friday, when Willie was supposed to sign the final contracts, they would have had nothing but each other. It was the ultimate revenge."

Willie's comment about everything being over on Friday now made sense. But it seemed to me Genevieve and Thad had paid the ultimate price—but by whose hand?

"Let me tell you this, though. In their deaths, they gave us the greatest retribution. A bidding war has erupted. Three networks now want the show. Like they say, there's no such thing as bad PR."

The PR comment reminded me. "Were Genevieve's death threats real?"

She laughed. "Lord, no. Completely made up for the benefit of that reporter. Worked like a charm too."

Too well—someone had capitalized on the PR those threats had gotten.

"Did you hire the picketers to boost ratings too?"

"Actually, we had nothing to do with the picketers. Just some morality group out to sabotage the show."

Not from what I'd overheard. Interesting.

"I've got to go, Nina. I'll call to reschedule our appointment."

"Any time."

I hung up, pulled my hand off the railing and felt a metal spur bite into my skin. "Yowch!"

Blood pooled along the cut. From the kitchen, I grabbed a paper towel and wrapped my finger. It was just a tiny slice, but wouldn't stop bleeding. I applied pressure and went in search of a Band-Aid.

Mac still snored as I passed by. I froze in the doorway of the hallway, though, when I heard Carson's voice coming from the TV.

"This is Carson Keyes, stay tuned to Fox 18 after the game to see my exclusive interview with Thad Cochran's widow, Sherry." He arched an eyebrow. "Hear why she believes her husband was murdered."

So, Sherry was taking her case public. I wondered what the police would think of that. I couldn't imagine they'd be pleased.

I checked the medicine cabinet for Band-Aids, but didn't see any. Crouching, I searched the vanity drawers, then under the sink.

Success! I pulled out the heavy first aid box, flipped the top, and felt the air whoosh from my lungs.

The box wasn't filled with Band-Aids or gauze at all. Instead there was a stash of valuables. Gold, silver, rubies, sapphires. Right on top of the pile was my watch. Next to it lay Minnie's diamond ring.

I sat down on the floor, replayed seeing Mac at Lowther House. He'd grabbed my hand while trying to kiss my cheek. He could have gotten my watch then.

A voice called out from the front room. "Nina?"

It was Bobby. Sudden happiness at hearing his voice vanished at the thought of bringing this to his attention.

I jumped up, spilling jewels across the floor. "Just a sec."

What to do? What to do?

Jeez.

Taking a deep breath, I pulled open the door. "Could I see you a minute?"

"In the bathroom?"

My smile quivered. "Privacy?"

"My room—" He pointed across the hall.

I tugged him inside, closed the door. "Look!"

He looked down, noticed he was stepping on a gold chain, and pressed himself against the wall.

"My watch," I said, holding it up. "Minnie's ring too!"

"Your hand!" He grabbed hold of it. "What happened?"

"Just a little cut. I was looking for a Band-Aid and found Mac's cache."

He rubbed his hand down his face. "I didn't know he was still doing this."

"Still?"

"Long story."

"Do you know that Pippi thinks one of my employees stole this ring?" My eyes widened. "Oh my gosh! Did Mac go to Lowther House just to rob the place? And used my name to get in?" Oh, Lord. How was I going to explain this to Pippi?

"I don't know," Bobby said. "Seems so. Are you going to the police?"

I put my watch and Minnie's ring in my pocket, stuffed the jewels back into the first aid box, and shoved it into his chest. "I don't know what I'm going to do."

Pulling open the door, I came face-to-face with Mac. He took one look at me, at Bobby, and at the first aid box, and said, "Oops."

"I'm going to go," I said. In the living room, I shrugged on my coat, grabbed my purse. I checked it before I left. "Mac?"

Mac strode across the room, pulled my wallet from the cushion of the couch, handed it over.

Bobby hung his head.

Then I noticed something else. "You're not limping," I said to Mac.

"Oh, that. I, uh . . . "

Bobby's mouth dropped open. "Mac?"

"It was never hurt, was it?" I accused.

Like a little boy caught with his hand in the cookie jar, he shuffled his feet. "No."

"Why?" was all Bobby said.

"Missed you," Mac murmured.

Okay, it would have been kind of sweet, if he weren't a lying klepto.

"I'm going. You two can sort this out."

"I'll call," Bobby said.

I nodded and left.

Ana found me sitting in the dark.

Thankfully, Kit, Riley, and BeBe hadn't been home when I'd gotten back. They'd left a note—something about shopping.

Ana flipped on the floor lamp, looked at me and tsked. "This looks familiar."

"Don't start."

She was referring to my month-long pity party, where I'd spent long hours sitting in the dark with only a tube of cookie dough to keep me company.

I didn't even have cookie dough today. And I really wished I hadn't left my cupcakes at the office.

Flopping down next to me, she picked up my hand.

I pulled it away, crossed my arms.

"You're snippy, and you haven't been answering your phone, and I've been worried."

My lip trembled. A tear fell.

"Oh no!" Ana cried. "Stop! Stop!"

I sniffled. "I can't help it. Look at me! I'm a mess."

"You're not a mess. You look beautiful."

"You're delusional."

"What's going on, Nina? You haven't been yourself lately at all."

"My life is horrible."

"No it's not!"

"It is! I'm just a mess. I've been on a self-discovery quest that's thrown me for a loop. I don't know what I want. I love Bobby, I really do. Heart, soul, and all that goopy stuff. I can finally admit that, and that I want him in my life. But tonight I find out I barely know him. I don't know anything about his family, his upbringing. And Kevin! I mean, how can I still care so much? Why don't I hate him? That's messed up, right? We're divorced, for crying out loud. He *cheated* on me with Ginger Ho. I mean Barlow. I need to stop calling her a ho. That's wrong of me, right?"

"Whoa!" Ana jumped up, pulled me to my feet.

I gasped. "What are you doing?"

"That's it!" She grabbed my down vest, shoved it at me. "What?"

"Your self-discovery has come to an end. It's done. Your journey is over."

"What? Why?"

"You've clearly lost your mind."

I barely had time to grab my purse before she hauled me out the front door, pushed me into the front seat of her car. "Where are we going?"

"Detox." She stepped on the gas, reversed out of my driveway and zigzagged onto the road. "The day you tell me that Ginger Barlow is not a ho is the day I put you into an asylum. What else?"

"What else what?"

"What other crazy things have you been telling yourself? Better yet, what have you done?"

"I've been dieting."

Ana's mouth dropped open.

"That's right. No cookie dough." I didn't tell her how many cream puffs I'd had, about the cupcakes, or the doughnuts. I was a lousy dieter—no doubt about that.

She stepped on the gas pedal. The car shot forward. I didn't even buckle my seat belt. That was something the old Nina would do. I kind of missed the old Nina.

"Come on, Nina. What else? I know there's more."

"I gave up Dr Pepper."

"What!"

"I've been drinking coffee."

"Shit. This is worse than I thought."

"There's more."

"Spill."

"I've been jogging."

Ana's long hair swayed as she shook her head. "Can this get any worse?"

"It can." I pulled a CD out of my brand new purse, held it up.

Ana gasped. "Is that a purse?"

"Like it?"

"No! Where's your leather backpack?"

"My mother took it away."

"Okay . . . " She took a deep breath. "Give me that thing." She pulled the purse out of my hands, let go of the steering wheel and dumped all my stuff onto her lap. She powered down the window and tossed the purse into the night. "What's the CD?"

"Wynonna Judd."

"Hand it over."

"Wait!"

"What?"

"I kind of like it."

She made the sign of the cross. "Fine. We'll work on this a little at a time."

She lurched into a parking spot in the Kroger lot.

"Kroger?" I said.

"Don't ask questions."

Inside the store, she tugged me along like I was a temperamental two-year-old. She flung items into the cart, starting with a roll of cookie dough and a case of Dr Pepper.

"Put something in," she said to me.

"I—"

"Do it."

I marched over to the ice cream case, reached in and pulled out three pints of Graeters's Coconut Chip.

I looked at Ana, who smiled. My lip trembled again.

"Stop!" she said, pulling me into a hug.

"Thank you, Ana."

"Hey, it's what I'm here for. Come on, let's go pick out some Clairol."

I grabbed hold of the cart. "Actually . . . "

She drew in a deep breath. "Yes?"

"I, um, kind of really like the hair."

She slumped in relief. "I'm so glad you said that! Me too! It looks so good."

"Then why . . . ?"

"Desperate times, Nina. However, it seems like you're on the right track now. You just need to find a balance. Mix this new stuff with the old. Don't replace it altogether."

She was right.

"But, Nina, we've got to do something about those nails. You're just not a manicure kind of girl."

I'd been feeling the same way. "I know just the thing." I speed-walked the cart to the floral section of the store. Grinning, I stuck my hands into the soil of a potted ivy, wiggled my fingers in the dirt.

It felt good to be back.

Twenty-One

By the time I got home, Kit was there, his Hummer parked in front of my house.

Ana kissed my cheek. "I'll call later and check on you. Right now I've got a date."

"With Carson?"

"Nope, Johan."

"No! Not Dr. Feelgood. I thought you were over him. He's so needy, clingy, and—"

"I was kidding." She laughed. "Just testing to see if you're really back to your old self. You are. I'm meeting Carson at his apartment. He said he has big news to share with me. Think he's going to propose?"

"No."

"Me either, but how cool would it be if he did?"

"You haven't even known him for a week."

"Sometimes," she sniffed, "you just know."

"Yeah, know that you're going to break his heart."

"Hey!" Then she smiled. "That technician at the M.E.'s office is kind of cute. And I bet he has tons of stories about dead bodies."

"You need help," I said, grabbing my bags and pushing open the door.

"Probably."

I wrestled with the Dr Pepper carton. "There's no 'probably' about it."

"How's Kit?" she asked.

"Heartbroken. Not that he's said so. You can just tell."

"Give him a hug for me," Ana said, shifting into reverse.

I closed my door, waved as she drove off. I turned to walk into the house just as Flash and Miss Sue descended on me.

"Did you hear?" Flash said.

"What?"

He pointed across the street. There was now a SOLD sticker slapped over the top of the words FOR SALE.

My heart sunk. "Anyone know who bought it?"

"Nope," Miss Sue said. "I asked the Realtor, but she wouldn't say. Quite rude of her."

"Quite," Flash added.

"Well, as soon as you know, would you please tell me?" Hopefully it wouldn't be Brickhouse. *Please, let it not be Brickhouse.*

The sound of a power saw split the quiet night. I tipped my head. "Was that coming from my house?"

"Someone's been working in there all day," Miss Sue supplied.

"Really?" I hadn't noticed anything different inside. Of course, I'd been sitting in the dark, moping.

"Mr. Weatherbee has already called to complain about the noise."

I checked my watch now that I had it back. It was creeping up on eleven. "I'll see what I can do to quiet things down."

The pair ambled off. I balanced my Kroger bags, Dr Pepper carton, and pushed open my front door. Almost immediately BeBe nearly pushed me back outside.

I dropped my haul and managed to keep my balance.

"What took you so long?" Riley asked. "She's been

waiting by the door since Ana pulled in the driveway."

"I—" BeBe's tongue swished my face like those hanging rags at a car wash.

Riley made a face. "Gross."

Kit whistled and BeBe sat.

I needed to learn how to do that, but couldn't whistle to save my life. I used my sleeve to dry my face.

"What do you think?" Riley asked, motioning upward.

Kit drilled a screw into the drywall above his head.

"Oh! There's no hole!" I even clapped—Maria would have been so proud.

Riley beamed with pride. "The upstairs is completely fixed too."

"You've been busy on your day off," I said to Kit.

Sure enough, a whole slew of tools were lined up against the back wall of the house, near the stairs. I don't know how I could have missed them before—I must've been really out of it.

"Riley helped as soon as he got home from school. Kid can wield a mean wrench."

I flopped BeBe's ears to and fro. She looked up at me with happy brown eyes. It was nice to feel so loved. "Kit, you didn't have to . . ."

"If I'm going to be staying here for a while, then you need your bedroom back."

I felt such a rush of emotion, I ran over and threw my arms around his neck and kissed his cheek. "I completely forgive you for siccing Duke on me."

"Notice you didn't huff or puff once running over here."

"Yeah, but my muscles ached."

BeBe jumped in on the love fest, prancing, slurping, and drooling. Riley laughed until there were tears in his eyes. I pulled him into the fold.

BeBe licked his face from chin to forehead. "Yuck!"

I laughed. It felt good.

Finally, I pulled away. Riley helped me bring the groceries into the kitchen. "Are you two just about done for the night?" I asked. "There's been some complaints about the noise."

Riley put the ice cream in the freezer. The fact that there were three pints of it didn't faze him in the least. "Mr. Weatherbee?"

"Of course," I said.

"We're done for the night." Kit wandered in, sat at the island. "Some mud, tape, and a little paint, and your ceiling will be as good as new."

"I owe you," I said to him.

He shook his head. "You've got that turned the wrong way 'round."

Riley said, "Should I keep this out?" He held the cookie dough.

I looked at the two of them. "Want to split it?"

Both nodded.

I cut the tube into three chunks. I peeled back the wrapper and bit in.

Riley broke off a hunk with his finger, stuck it in his cheek like a squirrel would store an acorn. "Before I forget," he said, "Grandma Cel called, Maria called, and Bobby just called about ten minutes ago. Dad called too. Said he's going out of town for a while, which probably means he's going deep undercover and just doesn't want me to worry about him."

I choked on a chocolate chip. Sometimes I forgot how perceptive Riley was.

He pounded my back. "I thought so."

Kit grinned.

"You didn't hear it from me," I said.

"Do you know what he's doing?" Riley pushed another wad of cookie dough into his mouth.

I shook my head. "He didn't say."

"Because I thought maybe it had something to do with the increased mob presence downtown?"

"You're good," I said. "But I really don't know. He wouldn't say."

"Damn."

"Language!"

He gave me a look like I was a crazy woman. "Damn's not bad."

I sighed, looked to Kit. He said, "I know you're not looking for my opinion on 'damn.' "

Riley said, "See?"

"Just don't say it around Grandma Cel."

"Jeez, give me some credit." He finished off his cookie dough and said, "I'm gonna shower, then go to bed."

"I'll get my stuff from your room," Kit said.

Riley paused on the stairs. "No rush."

BeBe looked between Riley and Kit and followed Riley.

"Loyalty is hard to come by these days," Kit mumbled.

What did that mean? I wondered. Had Daisy been disloyal? "Do you want to talk about it yet?" I asked him.

"Not yet."

"Ana says to give you a hug."

"Tell her thanks."

"All right. Well, I'm going to make a few calls, head to bed. You need anything?"

"Nope."

"And my room really is safe?"

He smiled. "Are you questioning my craftsmanship?"

"Never!"

"Your bathroom is good as new too."

"You're a miracle worker."

"If you want to say so."

"I do." I kissed his cheek on my way up the stairs.

"Oh Nina?"

"Yeah?"

"I put your shopping bags in your room. Some interesting items in there."

I felt my cheeks color.

"Do I sense a hitched in your future?"

I tossed a chunk of cookie dough at his head. His laughter followed me up the stairs.

I marveled at my room for a good fifteen minutes. The wood floors looked amazing, the tile in the bathroom sparkled. All the fixtures were attached and worked. I flushed the toilet three times just because I could.

Happy, I ran and jumped into my feather bed and picked up the cordless phone from the nightstand. First I called my mother. She gushed for ten minutes about how wonderful Kit was, how she'd fired the construction crew, and speculated about who was moving in across the street. Her money was on Brickhouse.

I fluffed a down pillow. "This is going to sound strange, but do you know the real name of the picketer with the buzz cut?"

"Ralph Insprucker. Why?"

I rooted around the nightstand drawer for paper and a pencil, and finally found both. I jotted Ralph's name down. "Just curious."

"You're lying to your mama!"

"Am not. I've got to go, I need to return Maria's call."

"She's in bed for the night, *chérie*."

Okay, I crossed her off my list. "Then I need to call Bobby."

"Are you lying to your mama?"

I smiled. "I'd never."

Before I tried Bobby, though, I called Tam. "Did I wake you?"

"Do you hear that?"

Nic screamed in the background. "Yeah. Maybe I should call back tomorrow."

"No! Ian has her while I'm on the phone. Make this call as long as possible. I can't believe I missed all this. What was I thinking?"

I laughed. "That you love them?"

"Right. That."

"Well, I was just wondering if you were up for a little freelance computer work?"

"Work?" she said really loudly. "Sure, I'd love to do some work for you right now." She sounded positively giddy.

"It doesn't have to be right now," I said.

"Shhhh!"

Smiling, I gave her two names to do background searches on. She was whistling hi-ho, hi-ho, off to work I go as she hung up.

I rooted through the plastic Kroger bag that now acted as my purse and found my cell phone. I scrolled through the numbers, found the one I was looking for. He answered on the third ring. "Nels? This is Nina Quinn. I need a favor . . ."

When I was done with him, I stared at the phone, wondering about calling Bobby.

Finally, I dialed, then hung up before the call went through.

Dialed again a minute later.

Hung up.

I did that three more times before I let the phone ring. Mac answered. "Hi, Mac. It's Nina. Is Bobby there?"

"In the shower, sweetie pie. Want me to have him call you back?"

"Yeah."

"And Nina?"

"Yeah, Mac?"

"I'm sorry about everything."

"It's okay."

"Bobby's done good for himself with you. Good night."

"Good night."

I stretched out on my bed, more comfortable than I'd been in months, and waited for Bobby to call.

He never did.

Twenty-Two

Early the next morning I found myself on the road to Lowther House, my cell phone pressed to my ear.

"You'd be amazed at how many Ralph Inspruckers there are," Tam said. My cell phone crackled. "Good tip on St. Blaise. I hacked into their accounts, and sure enough Ralph has a couple of kids who attend. Got a pen?"

I rooted around my Kroger bag, pulled out a pen and notepad. "Yep."

She ticked off all the essentials I needed to track Ralph down. I had a plan to find out exactly who hired him to picket my house, because it sure as heck hadn't been any morality group.

"And, Nina . . . ?"

"Yeah?"

"Bobby's grandfather has a rap sheet dating back to 1934. Lots of petty theft, fraud. Looks like the quintessential con man to me."

I'd figured, but it was nice to have the confirmation. "I'm almost at Lowther House now. I need to get this all straightened out."

"What are you going to do?" Tam asked.

"I'm not sure."

"Good plan," Tam mocked.

"Don't you need a nap or something?"

She yawned. "Now that is a good plan."

I thanked her, hung up, and put my truck into park.

I'd canceled my 9:00 A.M. emergency meeting at TBS. Now I just had to return Minnie's ring. It took a while of arguing with my conscience, but I finally decided what Pippi didn't know wouldn't hurt her. The ring would be back in Minnie's possession before I left.

As I walked up the front steps, I had to admit Roxie and Nels's speculation had gotten to me, and maybe a little bit of Ana's morbidity too. I couldn't figure out why Pippi was so adamant the police not be called to investigate. What did she not want them to see? To find out?

I punched in the code Pippi had given me for the front door and was grateful it still worked. I climbed the stairs slowly, quietly. If anyone asked why I was there, I was simply checking to see how the mini turned out.

In the atrium, I smiled. The mini had turned out beautifully. Water cascaded down shimmering stone and pooled in the pond. The plants would fill in over time, creating more of a natural look, but even as it was, it was relaxing and peaceful, a hint at the great outdoors inside.

"Ms. Quinn, good to see you," Monique Umberry said.

"Hello there."

Her husband stood by her side. "Beautiful job you did."

I looked around for Minnie. She wasn't with them. "Thank you."

"Very sneaky of Pippi to trick us so," she added.

"Yes, well, it's the nature of the surprise."

"And I do so love surprises!" Monique gushed. "Especially this one. The indoor garden in so very wonderful. A year-round oasis of tranquility."

Smiling, I realized this was exactly why I loved my job. "I'm glad you're enjoying it."

"Would you care to join us for a game of poker?" William held up a bag of peanut M&Ms.

"Those are my kind of stakes, but I really can't stay. Do you know if Pippi is around?"

"She's in the greenhouse last I heard. Do you want me to get her for you?" Monique asked.

"Thank you, but stay, enjoy your game. I'll buzz her on the intercom."

I left the pair to their game. Downstairs, I looked at the intercom. To push or not to push?

For some reason I felt the need to surprise Pippi, to catch her off guard. I slipped a small piece of paper out of my pocket, typed the numbers into the keypad.

Nels had come through for me.

The door released, and I pushed it open. Oak flooring gleamed under recessed lights. Beautiful artwork graced the walls. There were no tables or chairs lining the hallway, probably in deference to Minnie's wheelchair.

A sweet smell lingered in the air as I walked along, and I couldn't quite place the scent. I counted four thick wood doors with raised panels and brass numbers. The one farthest on my left was open. Minnie sat in front of the TV, watching SportsCenter. I knocked.

She looked up, tipped her head. "Do I know you?"

"We met the other day? My name is Nina."

"Oh."

I held out my hand and she looked at it for a second before taking it. In a blink, I used my left hand to cover hers. I slipped the ring onto her finger, much like Mac had probably gotten it off.

"Your hands are cold," she said.

"Cold hands, warm heart?"

A flash of clarity filled her eyes. "Cold hands, need mittens."

I laughed. And breathed out in relief. She hadn't noticed.

Luxuriously appointed with silk fabrics, pricy antiques, and even a flat screen TV, no expense had been spared on Minnie's room.

A large picture window looked out into the courtyard from her kitchenette. There was a perfect view of the greenhouse. From where I sat, I could see Pippi moving about, back and forth.

"Minnie, it was nice seeing you again."

The distant look returned to her gaze. "Who are you?"

"I'm Nina."

"Oh. Did the Cubs win last night? I can't recall."

I checked the ticker running along the bottom of the screen. "Three to one."

"Good."

She continued to watch the newscast as I slipped out the door, feeling all at once sad for her yet relieved too. She didn't seem frustrated by her condition, and from my quick perusal, she had the best of care.

I turned left at the end of the hall and came to a pair of French doors leading to the courtyard. They weren't locked.

Following the cobblestone path to the door of the greenhouse, I took a deep breath and walked in.

Pippi turned in alarm, spraying water in my direction. Once she realized what she was doing, she turned off the hose.

I wiped my face with the back of my hand.

"Oh my! I'm so sorry. You startled me."

I took a look around. My mouth dropped open.

"Oh my," Pippi said again.

This time it had nothing to do with getting me wet.

I immediately knew why Pippi hadn't wanted the police involved.

Ana, Roxie, and Nels would be disappointed—there weren't any dead bodies. There were, however, several marijuana plants. I suddenly placed the sweet smell I'd noticed earlier.

I couldn't believe my eyes. "Pippi . . . "

She dropped the hose, wrung her hands. "I can explain."

* * *

Fussing with the clasp on her overalls, Pippi wouldn't look at me. "It's only a matter of time before medicinal marijuana becomes legalized. Here at Lowther House we strive to make our residents' lives as comfortable as possible, especially when they are in pain. This is a natural solution to taking three, four, sometimes five prescription painkillers."

I fingered a marijuana leaf. The plants were full, healthy. "This is why you didn't want the police involved in the disappearance of Minnie's ring?"

"They wouldn't understand, Nina."

Trying to imagine Kevin's reaction to this stash, I bit back a smile. He was a stickler for Just Say No.

"I've long been a supporter of alternative therapy. And it's not just me. There's a lot of support in the community, all on a hush-hush basis, of course."

Of course. I remembered Kit once telling me Daisy's job involved pharmaceuticals. "Is Daisy one of your supporters?"

Pippi finally met my gaze. Curiosity burned in her blue eyes. "Daisy Bedinghaus? I wasn't aware you knew her."

"We have a mutual friend." Bedinghaus. I hadn't known her last name until now.

"Daisy is an ardent supporter. She makes it her business to be."

"Her business?"

"Yes, through her Heavenly Hope Holistic Healing center."

"Right, right," I murmured.

"What are you going to do, Nina?" Pippi wrung her hands.

Just call me Nina Colette Progressive Thinking Ceceri Quinn, but I didn't mind the marijuana so much, as long as it was being used medicinally. I'd heard a lot about its benefits to those in pain. Who was I to decide whether it was right or wrong? That was up to some Supreme Court somewhere or another.

Checking my watch, I edged toward the door. "I need to be going, Pippi." I pulled a card from my wallet. "I know you're more than capable, but if you need help with your indoor garden, give this company a call." It was a blatant plug for my friend Lea's indoor landscaping maintenance business. She was just starting out and needed the word of mouth.

Pippi took the card. "What are you going to do, Nina?"

"Do?" Actually, I was going to go home, grab Riley, and implement Operation Buzz.

"About," she motioned around us, "all this?"

My eyebrows dropped. "All what?"

She opened her mouth to explain, then caught on. "Oh." The corners of her mouth pulled tight in a wide smile. "Thank you. I owe you one, Nina."

A cool blast of autumn air whooshed into the greenhouse as I pushed open the door. "Good-bye, Pippi."

"Nina?"

Over my shoulder I noticed Pippi worried her lip.

"I hate to bring this up right now, but feel I must. Did you speak to your employees about Minnie's ring?"

"I did," I lied.

"And?"

"Nothing."

"Oh dear."

The small courtyard acted as a minivortex. Leaves swirled around and around. I pushed the hair out of my eyes. "I'll call you if I learn anything."

She breathed deeply. "Please do. It's an heirloom."

"I'm sure it will turn up."

She looked skeptical. I smiled as I walked out the door.

* * *

I was on my way home when my cell rang. I never did have my ring tone changed. Now it was growing on me.

I didn't recognize the number but answered just in case. "Hello?"

"Ms. Quinn, this is Duke."

Uh-oh.

I had a good idea who'd given him my cell number.

"Meet me tonight, five-thirty, at the gym. Don't be late."

He hung up.

My muscles quivered in fear at the sound of his voice. What had I gotten myself into?

Madonna's voice filled the cab of my truck again. Fearing it might be Duke, calling back, I almost didn't answer. Good thing my sensible side kicked in and looked at the caller ID: Bobby. "Hi," I said.

"Mac just now told me you called last night," he said. "I'm sorry."

"I wasn't worried," I lied. I'd been up half the night worrying why he wasn't calling, and spent most of the morning trying to dissect our relationship.

Then I'd remembered Perry's advice.

It was time to let the magic happen. On its own. One day at a time. I decided to go along for the ride, bumpy as it might be.

"About Mac—" he started.

I cut him off. "Did I ever tell you my cousin Lou is wanted in four states for hijacking semi trailers and selling the goods at interstate flea markets? Or that my great-uncle Joe has done time for insurance fraud, or that my nana Ceceri once spent a night in jail for feeding money into downtown parking meters?"

"You can go to jail for that?"

"Well, I think the charge came from hitting the meter maid upside the head when she tried to stop Nana."

He laughed.

"My point is, there's a lot we still need to learn about each other, and each others' families. There's time."

"More now."

"Why's that?"

"Are you driving?" he asked.

Dread tickled the nape of my neck. Hairs there stood on end. "Yes."

"Pull over."

Without using my blinker, I cut across two lanes of traffic on 75 south and pulled onto the berm. I hit the button for my hazard lights. "I'm over."

"I didn't get a chance to tell you last night, and I'd really like to tell you in person—"

"Now. Now would be good."

His laughter came through the phone loud and clear. "I quit my job, Nina."

My heart leapt into my throat. "You what?"

"I realized the most important things in my life were here. This is where I need to be."

Cars whooshed past. My heart rate beat just as fast. "Oh."

"I've bought a place."

"What's that I hear in your voice?"

"What?"

"Mischievous . . . ness," I added. Brickhouse would have a field day if she'd heard me. I had a sudden thought, about the SOLD sign across the street from me. "You didn't!"

"Oh, I did. Just what kind of welcome wagon reception should I expect?" There was a tinge of trepidation in his voice.

I immediately thought of the sheer camisole set I'd bought. "Definitely friendly. There are some things we should probably talk through, though."

"Mac and I are flying to Florida later today. We're going to rent a U-Haul, pack everything up, and be back late next week. How about a date? Next Saturday night at my place. It'll be a mess, but—"

"You're moving in so soon?"

"Immediate occupancy."

"All right, then. I'll bring the pizza."

I hung up, smiling like a fool.

Twenty-Three

"I can't believe you're recruiting a poor innocent child into helping you."

I rolled my eyes. "You cannot help, Mom. Buzz knows who you are."

"He knows Riley too."

"He's only seen Riley once or twice, and he'll never recognize him in that getup. I don't recognize him in that getup."

"I don't recognize me either," Riley said, taking in the drooping sweatpants, zippered hooded sweatshirt, aviator sunglasses. "I can't believe I'm wearing a Dr Pepper hat. What's my life come to?"

From the closet, I pulled out my down vest. "Hey. Don't knock my hat."

My mother shook her head. "*I* cannot believe you own a Dr Pepper hat. Where have I gone wrong?"

I ignored her. "Buzz's kids will be getting out of school soon, so we've got to hurry. Hopefully he'll be outside waiting for them, if not walking them home."

Riley pulled open the front door. "Is it sad that this is the most exciting thing to happen to me since I came back from nothing to w—" He cut himself off, then finished lamely, "—to win a cribbage match against Mr. C last summer?"

I arched an eyebrow.

He grinned.

My mother said, *"Pah."*

No use in pushing. I wouldn't get anything else out of Riley. When pressed, he clammed up tighter than Ana when she was asked how many one-night stands she'd had.

My mother picked up her handbag. "Well, I'll come with you."

"There's really no need."

She gave me the Ceceri Evil Eye.

"Fine. Suit yourself."

Riley said, "Can you teach me how to do that?"

"What?" I asked, grabbing my Kroger bag and locking the door.

"The eye thing." He tried, and looked so funny I couldn't help but laugh.

"We'll work on it, Ry," my mother said. "It must come from deep within." She eyed my bag.

"Like that?" he asked.

"Yes," I said, climbing into the cab of my TBS truck. "Except it's usually used on people."

Riley settled himself in the small backseat.

My mother poked the Kroger bag with the tip of her acrylic nail. "What, pray tell, is that? Where is your Coach bag?"

I couldn't very well tell her about Ana's method of detox.

"Ana chucked it out the window," Riley said from the backseat.

Readjusting the rearview mirror, I gave him the evil eye.

"I've really got to learn that," he muttered.

My mother fussed with her fingernails, probably thinking about filing them into daggers. "I must have a word with Ana."

I had to warn her ASAP.

"Chérie, you certainly can't go around carrying your things in a plastic sack."

I drove slowly through the Mill. "It's quite sturdy."

"And what happened to your hands?" She grabbed my right hand off the steering wheel, tsked over the state of my fingernails. "We must schedule an appointment for a manicure. This won't do."

I tugged back my hand. "Actually, I like it just fine the way it is."

My mother's eyes widened. "Oh no."

"What?" Riley leaned forward.

Fear tinged my mother's voice. "She's regressing."

"Re-what?"

"Regressing," I said. "Maybe if you paid attention in English class, you'd know what it meant."

"Like you did in tenth grade?" he threw back.

Touché. I'd had Brickhouse Krauss for tenth grade English. "Maybe I'll see if Mrs. Krauss is interested in a little tutoring."

Riley's eyes widened in fear. "You wouldn't."

I waggled my eyebrows. "Geese and gander, kid." I'd used a cliché and actually didn't mind! Maybe my self-discovery had been beneficial after all. I'd learned to finally accept my little quirks and oddball traits.

"What's that mean?" he asked.

Suddenly feeling old, I sighed.

"Stop torturing the poor boy, *chérie*. And despite how much you're trying to detour from it, I'm not going to forget the original subject."

Damn, I thought, as she said, "By regressing, I meant that she's acting as she used to, going back to the way she was."

"Good," Riley said. "I liked her better the old way. Except for the hair. The hair is much better now."

I almost forgave him for ratting Ana out.

My mother sighed heavily. "I should have known it wouldn't last."

"You still have Maria," I told her.

"This is true."

I turned down Buzz's street. Riley and I had gone over all the details, all the scenarios. He was well-prepared, and I knew from experience he was a great liar. He shouldn't have any trouble at all.

Buzz, aka Ralph Insprucker, lived in a newer development not even a half mile from St. Blaise. It was just about four o'clock. Any minute now his elementary school kids would be on their way home. I was hoping an out of work dad would, at the very least, meet his kids at the sidewalk.

Church bells tolled. We watched in silence as kids ran down the sidewalks, backpacks thumping their spines. Had I ever been so eager to go home from school? Maybe. In tenth grade.

A pair of children, two girls, skipped up Buzz's front walk, pulled open the door and disappeared inside.

So much for being Father of the Year.

Shifting in my seat, I thought aloud. "Okay, plan B."

"Plan B never works," Riley said.

"You've done this before?" my mother asked.

"Maybe once or twice," I murmured. "And this time it will work."

My mother tsked at me. There goes my Stepmother of the Year award.

"You know what to do," I said to Riley.

He hopped out of the truck, crossed the street without looking both ways (*Grr*), walked up Buzz's front walk and knocked on the door.

My mother's nose pressed against the glass. "This isn't safe."

"It's perfectly safe."

"What if this man is a pedophile?"

Now I knew where I'd gotten my worry-wart genes. "Riley's not going inside."

"How do you know?"

"Because I told him not to."

"*Pah*. As if he always listens to you."

All right. She had a point there. A knot formed in my stomach as the younger girl who'd gone skipping up the walkway appeared in the doorway, held up a wait-a-minute finger to Riley.

"He'll follow the plan." Now I was trying to reassure myself as much as her.

"Who came up with this plan?" Little clouds of condensation formed on her window as she spoke.

"I did." Buzz filled the doorway. "There he is."

My mother sat up, her hand on the door handle as if ready to jump out and save Riley at a moment's notice. Then I noticed my hand on my door handle and made myself relax.

I'd been hanging around my mother too much.

As if I were a play-by-play announcer, I said, "Right now Riley's telling Buzz that his car broke down around the corner and could he please use Buzz's cell phone to call for help."

"Won't Ralph question why he didn't walk over to the gas station?" She pointed to the Shell down the road.

"Does Buzz seem like the sharpest tool in the shed to you?"

"You've a good point, *chérie*."

Buzz motioned Riley inside. I heard my mother's breath catch.

Okay, mine did too—until Riley shook his head. "Now Riley's telling him that he's not allowed to enter people's houses, and could he just use his cell phone."

It must have worked, because Buzz unclipped a phone from his waistband and handed it out the door. He watched Riley like a hawk.

"Riley's the only one I know who can figure out how to retrieve the number that called him on Tuesday around four, and he's sneaky enough to do it without Buzz knowing it."

Riley turned his back to Ralph. Within a second he'd returned the phone and strode down the walkway and up the street.

Buzz looked after him for a minute but didn't follow.

I reversed the truck, turned around in someone's driveway.

"What are you hoping to accomplish with this phone number?"

"I'm not sure," I said. "It's just a hunch."

"A hunch about what?"

"Murder."

There'd been no time to do much with the phone number Riley had gotten except to jot it down and tuck it in my plastic Kroger bag.

I'd hoped the number would have an accompanying name, but Riley hadn't found one.

He'd made plans to sleep at a friend's house, and I dropped him and my mother off at my place before doing a quick change into workout clothes. I hotfooted it to the gym.

If there was one place I didn't want to be, it was on Duke's hit list.

Huffing, I made it inside with one minute to spare. Duke waited just inside the door. He made a show of eyeing the clock but didn't say anything as he turned. I followed.

The gym was packed for five-thirty on a Friday night. Every machine was taken, and I was heartened to see people struggling just like I had. Maybe there was hope for me yet.

"There's no hope for you," Duke said, stopping so abruptly I barreled into him.

"What?"

"With these traditional machines, or with conventional exercise. I've never seen a more pitiful performance as I did at the track the other morning."

"So . . . I fail?" Was I destined to have a stomach roll hanging over my jeans for the rest of my life?

He folded his arms, peered down at me. "Duke never fails. You, Ms. Quinn, do not have the patience, the motivation, or the discipline to stick to a regimented training program. Therefore, I suggest something a bit unconventional."

"Such as . . . ?"

"Fun."

"Fun?"

He pushed open a thick metal door. Inside, two groups of women stood on opposite sides of a high net, their gym shoes squeaking on a freshly waxed floor. Laughter filled the air as a ball flew across the net and ricocheted off several hands before being sent back over to the other side.

My cheeks rose as I smiled. "Volleyball!"

"You said you enjoyed playing it as a teenager."

I hugged him. He didn't hug back.

He tossed me a bag with elbow and knee pads, and sat at the end of a bleacher. "Give it a go."

The group gave me a rowdy welcome. I played two sets, trying to remember the nuances of the game. I was terrible but had a blast.

Afterward, dripping sweat, I walked over to Duke. He sat like Buddha amidst the chaos.

He said, "You'll hurt tomorrow. Sunday too. Rest and let your muscles heal. Come Monday, meet me back here, other side of the hallway. Indoor soccer."

I smiled wide. "I love soccer!"

He nodded. "They're going to eat you alive. After that, you can decide which you like better, and we'll get you on a team."

I didn't dare hug him again. "Thanks, Duke. You're not so bad after all."

Sternly, he said, "Don't let it get around."

Twenty-Four

The front door slammed open, and Kit nearly toppled off the ladder. I held it steady as BeBe leapt to her feet to greet Ana.

"Big news, big news," she said, tossing a Macy's shopping bag at me.

"What?" I asked, peeking inside.

She danced around the living room. "Remember the news Carson had to share with me? He's joining *Inside Edition* as a roving correspondent. He's going national!" She sang this last part and did a two-step with BeBe, who stood on her hind legs.

BeBe's tongue lolled out in sheer delight.

"There's a party tonight to celebrate." She let go of BeBe, perched on the back of the sofa. Her short skirt showed off her great legs. A sequined top shimmered beneath a velvet blazer. "You're both invited as my guests!"

Kit continued to plaster my ceiling. "No thanks."

"Oh, come on." Her voice held a joy I hadn't heard in a long time. "You could use a night out."

"Nope. Thanks." He balanced precariously. "I'm good here."

She wouldn't let up. "With some goop and a trowel?"

"All the excitement I need." He smoothed the mud along the ceiling, feathered it out.

Kit still wasn't interested in talking about Daisy. I wondered exactly what she was up to at Heavenly Hope Holistic Healing that was so dangerous.

There was nothing I could say or do to get him to spill. So, he had listened while I told him all about Pippi, Minnie, Mac, and Bobby.

He'd muttered something about getting his own place as soon as possible. I wished he wouldn't—I kind of liked having him around, and not just because he knew how to fix things.

I thought maybe it was the mama hen in me. Here, I could keep an eye on him, protect him from whatever danger Daisy presented.

"Okay, then, you!"

Ana pointed to me as I pulled a new handbag out of the Macy's bag. "Me?" I held up her gift. "This is cute." It was a black leather Fossil bag, half tote, half purse. As Goldilocks was wont to say, it was just right. "Thank you."

"No problem. And yes, you. Now, go get dressed."

I hedged. "I'm not really in the mood for a party." Truth be told, I was exhausted. I'd forgotten how tiring volleyball could be. Besides, I still had to figure out what to do with that phone number. I wished I could just hand it over to Kevin, but there was no way to reach him. The Cincinnati detectives would probably think I was just as crazy as Sherry Cochran.

Ana blinked her big brown eyes at me, stuck out her bottom lip and let it quiver.

BeBe took this as an invitation. She jumped up and lathered her face with doggy kisses.

She laughed.

Okay, she was in a really good mood.

"It'll be fun, Nina." Holding BeBe at bay, she did the lip thing again.

"All right, all right. Just put that lip away before BeBe falls in love."

I rushed upstairs to change into some of the clothes Perry had picked out for me. I chose black slacks, a satin tank top, and a beautiful teal jacket. I slipped on black high-heeled boots, zipped them up, and wobbled into the bathroom. It took me ten minutes to put on my makeup, five to slick my hair back into the evening 'do Perry had taught me.

I nearly tripped as I walked down the stairs. "Well?" I said.

Kit wobbled on the ladder. "Holy mother."

Ana's jaw dropped. "Okay, you can't go."

"What? Why?"

"Carson's going to take one look at you and forget all about me."

"Stop!"

"Okay, maybe not, but only because it's me. Anyone else he'd dump in a heartbeat."

"There's nothing like a humble woman," Kit intoned sarcastically from atop the ladder.

Ana stuck her tongue out at him. "Don't make me come up there and spackle your lips closed."

His eyebrow lifted. "I dare you."

Ana jumped to her feet. She had no problem walking in three-inch heels. "If I weren't all gussied up . . . "

"All talk." Kit smiled as he slathered.

I barely made it down the stairs without breaking an ankle. "All right, all right, you two. That's enough. What time is this party?"

"Nine."

"But it's ten now."

Ana dumped the contents of my Kroger sack into my new handbag. "You've so much to learn."

"Oh no! I'm done learning for now. I've had enough of that this past week to last me until the end of the year at least."

We said our good-byes to Kit and BeBe. Ana had barely buckled her seat belt and started the car before saying, "Kit told me about the picket guy's phone number. Let's call it!"

"I don't know. What do we say?"

She reversed. "If someone answers, just ask who you're talking to. And if they don't answer, even better, because then their name will probably be on the voice mail."

It sounded logical to me. Pulling the number out of my bag, I punched it into my cell phone. Butterflies filled my stomach. The phone rang and rang, then switched to voice mail. I hung up.

"Well?"

"Nothing. Just that canned voice-mail voice reciting the number I called."

Excited, she said, "Maybe we can flush him out."

I shifted to face her. "Are you nuts?"

"Some, but so are you. What's the harm in it?"

"Oh, let me think." I tapped my chin. "This person could be a serial killer?"

She laughed. "We're not going to let him see us! Listen. We call, say something like, we know what you did, tell him to meet us at, oh, Eden Park at eleven P.M. We go, we park at the art museum and hide out until he arrives. Then we see who it is, get back in our car, and go from there."

"You know, you've been watching way too many criminal shows. Things never work out like that. Besides, all we know for sure is that the person who owns this number hired the picketers. Nothing else. Could be completely innocent. Heck, maybe Thad did kill Genevieve, then himself."

Ana flew down the on ramp to 75 south. "You haven't heard?"

"Heard what?"

"Where have you been all day?"

"Out! What happened?"

"The autopsy on Thad was done this morning. Thad was

murdered. Strangled, just like Genevieve. The noose was just a ruse." She laughed. "That rhymes."

"You haven't been drinking tequila, have you?" I was suddenly reminded of bags, hags, and nags.

"What? No. Why?"

"Just curious."

"And now the police are saying that Thad wasn't a suspect in Genevieve's death. Louisa came forward and said she'd seen Genevieve alive after Thad had left her in the hot tub. She signed some papers for the FedEx guy—they have the exact time. Apparently Louisa knew all about the love fest going on at *Hitched or Ditched*. They paid her well to keep her mouth shut."

If Louisa could resist telling all to Bobby, then she was paid really well. "This is just bizarre."

She changed lanes, sped up. "I guess Sherry was right after all. I wonder if her appearance with Carson last night led to the M.E. taking a good look."

"I'd like to think the M.E. would have figured it out on his own."

"I think Carson deserves some of the credit."

"I think you're too gaga over Carson to see straight."

"He's really cute."

"And leaving town."

"I could use a new job . . . "

"Analise Maria Bertoli! Would you leave here?"

"I don't know. Maybe. If he asked."

"Do you really love him?"

"Is there such a thing as love?"

"Don't you sound jaded."

She shrugged. "I like him a lot."

By the way he looked at her, he liked her too. I decided not to think about her moving. Denial was a good place in my book. "So, Thad was murdered."

"That means whoever that phone number belongs to could be our killer."

"But Sherry said no one at *Hitched or Ditched* hired the picketers."

"Do you believe her?"

"Why wouldn't I?"

"Maybe she's trying to hide her involvement? Maybe she offed good old Thad because he was boffing Gen."

"Then why would she go on TV?"

"To try and deflect the blame. Right now, Carson's painted her as a grieving widow, but we know better."

That we did.

My toes were squished inside my boots. They started to ache. "She's not strong enough to get Thad up on that catwalk."

"Willie is."

"Willie? Maybe? But I don't know if he had time. He was with the TV execs . . . But who else could it be?"

"Jessica?"

"She did want Thad's limelight. And revenge against Genevieve."

"The look of horror on her face was too real. She's not that good of an actress, trust me."

"Louisa?"

I loved that theory. I had no evidence whatsoever to back it up, but I loved it.

"Let's call the number!" Ana said.

Just then my cell phone rang. Saved by Madonna. Or rather, Maria. "Hello?"

"I figured it out, Nina!"

"What?"

"How I know that Jessica girl."

"Oh?"

"Remember I did the Cincinnati Ballet's bicentennial party a few years ago?"

"Vaguely."

"That's where I know her from. She was one of their prima ballerinas. I didn't recognize her hair because she had one of those little caps on her head, with her hair pulled back in a bun that only prima ballerinas can get away with wearing. Anyhoo, that's not the interesting part."

"Oh?"

"What's with the ohs?" Ana asked. "Who's that?"

"Maria," I said.

"What?" Maria asked.

Not this again. "Ana's with me. She was wondering who I was talking to."

"Maybe I should call back later when she's not there."

At her guarded tone, my stomach started to ache. "Why?"

She said, "I went back through my scrapbook. *SoSceCinci* did a huge spread on that party. In one of my pictures, there's a ballerina in the background kissing a man." She paused for dramatic effect. "The ballerina was Jessica, the man Carson Keyes."

I gasped. "The ballet slipper tattoo!"

"Right."

"What are you two talking about?" Ana demanded. "Carson?"

"Shh!" I said to Ana.

Maria went on. "I did some checking and found out they've been dating for a couple of years and have always been hush-hush about their relationship. Only a few people knew about it. My contact said they really wanted to keep their private lives private."

I stole a look at Ana, my heart sinking.

"And get this," Maria said, "they broke up about two months ago, right before Jessica was fired from *Hitched or Ditched*."

Suddenly I remembered what Perry had said. That she had broken up with her boyfriend for Thad . . .

That boyfriend must have been Carson.

Maria said, "My contact at the station said Jessica dumped Carson because she has big dreams and wants a big budget to achieve them. Carson wasn't cutting it.

How's that for irony, just before she gets canned? Cosmic justice, that's what that is."

I didn't share the news about Jess's relationship with Thad, and wondered about this new twist. "Failing? I thought his career was thriving? Most popular, blah blah . . . "

"Damn it!" Ana whined.

"Shhh!"

"Hype," Maria said. "His career had been stagnating for a while now. Too much of the same old, same old. They wanted someone younger, hipper. Before these murders, Carson was about to be fired from Channel 18, according to the news director there."

"And you know this how?"

"The news director is Nate's racquetball buddy. Now Channel 18 is racing to keep Carson from leaving."

"They lost that race," I said, thinking of *Inside Edition*.

"Well, maybe now Carson will get Jessica back. Sounds like they deserve each other. Tell Ana I said sorry. Gotta go. Nate's waiting in the hot tub. *Au revoir*!"

Ana pounded the steering wheel. "What is going on?"

"Let's, ah, pull off the highway."

She looked at me like she was about to argue, then took the next off ramp. She sped into the parking lot of a movie theater, slammed on the brakes, unbuckled her seat belt and turned to face me.

I unbuckled my seat belt too. Just in case I needed to make a run for it.

Slowly, I told her what Maria had told me.

Ana slumped in her seat. After a long quiet minute she said, "Maria didn't see the bigger picture, did she?"

It was more statement than question. "No."

"Hand it over," Ana said.

I knew what she was talking about. I rummaged around my handbag, found the phone number. I passed it over to her.

She took one look at it and a tear slipped out of her eye. She nodded. "He hired the picketers."

I speculated. "To boost the ratings of *Hitched or Ditched*, which in turn would boost his ratings on Channel 18 since he was behind the scenes all week." A desperate attempt to secure his job.

"Or get Jessica back, but why kill anyone?"

"Maybe he saw his opportunity to go national, to maybe get that big job Jessica wanted him to have. Genevieve made it easy with the death threats."

"And," Ana said, "killing Genevieve got Jessica her job back too, didn't it?"

"Why kill Thad, though?" I wondered aloud.

"He was the only media outlet on scene when Thad died. Can you get much more of a scoop than that? It's probably what propelled *Inside Edition* to hire him, to capitalize on his current popularity. Do you think Jessica knew what he was doing?"

I shook my head. "You should have seen her face when she saw Thad dangling above her. She didn't know. About that, at least. About the other stuff? I'm not sure."

Ana drew in a deep breath. "Wait. I thought you didn't see Thad, that you were in the soundproof room?"

"Now's not the time to get into that . . . You okay?"

She must not have been, because she didn't press about Thad's body. Instead, she said, "Yeah. Let's go."

"To the party?" Was she crazy?

"To the police station."

Twenty-Five

A week later I sat on my couch, watching the breaking news coverage of Carson's arrest on MSNBC.

He'd finally gone national.

It was late, well past nine. BeBe's head rested on my lap. Kit was out (I didn't know where), and Riley was down at Mrs. Greeble's, changing a lightbulb. She was paying him altogether too much—he was flashing cash left and right, and he'd promised not to accept anything from her tonight.

BeBe's ears perked as my phone rang. Reaching over her massive body, I plucked the phone from the coffee table, looked at the caller ID, and answered by saying, "Are you watching it?"

"I hate that he looks so good," Ana said.

"I know."

"Men suck."

"Not all."

"Like who?"

"Bobby."

"He's different."

"How?"

"I don't know, he just is."

"Kit," I pointed out.

"He's different too."

I sighed. "Fine. All men suck."

"Thank you."

"You okay?" I muted the TV.

"Yeah. I'm gonna go take a hot bath."

"No date tonight?"

"Nah. I've sworn off men. I think I'm going to try some self-discovery stuff."

"Lord help us all."

She laughed. "Overall, it seems to have worked for you."

It had. "You know I love you just the way you are."

"I know. I'll call tomorrow. Have fun tonight!" she said before hanging up.

Tonight. My Big Night with Bobby.

My phone rang again. I smiled at the caller ID. "Hello?"

"Do you see the tie Carson Keyes is wearing? Hideous."

"Perry, not everyone has the taste you do."

"Very very true. He does look good, though. Pity he's a murderer." I heard someone in the background. "What? Can't you see I'm on the phone . . . Fine. Nina?"

"I'm here."

"Mario says hello."

I laughed. "Hi back."

"What?" he hollered. "Yes! She says hi back."

"Perry, I've been thinking."

"Scary."

"I know. You and Mario have done so much for me, making me over and all, let me do a garden makeover for you both next spring, my treat of course."

"Thank the Lord! We never thought you'd volunteer! Mario! Mario! She offered!" I heard whooping in the background, and I laughed.

"You two are crazy."

"We know. You still coming for dinner tomorrow night?"

"I'll be there."

"I'll set an extra place just in case."

"Thanks."

"Good luck, sugar."

I hung up. BeBe looked at me. "It's almost time," I said to her.

She licked my chin.

"Thanks, I needed that."

I turned up the volume on the news, trying to drown out my nerves.

The anchor recapped the case against Carson, including some newly disclosed DNA evidence from the noose that pretty much sealed it. The reporter said sources inside Cincinnati's police department believed Carson had lured Thad up on the catwalk under the pretense of taping a teaser for his segment that night.

Jessica was still being investigated as an accomplice, but had thus far been cleared of any wrongdoing. She'd just signed a big contract to stay on with *Hitched or Ditched*. Fox had picked up the show for the fall season and was going to have an *American Idol* type show this winter to find a new host.

Ana and I had been right on the money regarding Carson's motive. The murders had been about cementing his career and getting his name in the limelight.

Apparently, the motivation had nothing to do with winning Jessica back. Rather, he'd been trying to show her up. Show her what she'd lost. An in-your-face kind of thing.

Looked like that plan backfired.

The doorbell rang and BeBe leapt to her feet, woofing so loud the whole neighborhood probably heard.

Peeking out, I saw the pizza delivery man fairly shaking on the porch. Cracking the door, I heard him say, "Please tell me that's one of those recorded barks?"

A big black paw reached out through the crack.

He jumped back, nearly dropping the pizza.

"Here," I said, handing him twenty bucks. "Do me a favor—deliver the pizza across the street. The house with the U-haul and Harley in the driveway."

"I'm thinking you're doing me the favor!" He took off down the stairs.

Stronger, thanks to my new soccer league, I pushed BeBe backward and closed the door. She rose up, putting her paws on my shoulders.

"Down," I said.

She slurped my face.

"Hungry?"

She plopped down, raced to the kitchen. I filled her bowl with kibble. It flew across the floor as she gobbled it up.

"I'm going now," I said to her.

She wasn't listening.

Taking a deep breath, I smoothed down my zippered sweatshirt and felt the embroidery of the camisole beneath it.

I was definitely weak where Bobby was concerned, but I didn't care.

I smiled and took the plate of cookies I'd made down from the top of the refrigerator—out of BeBe's reach. I left a note for Riley and Kit.

Outside, the wind whipped down the street. Fallen leaves rustled along the ground.

Lights blazed in Bobby's house. He hadn't yet hung blinds or curtains, so I could easily see inside. I made a mental note to have him do it after we ate. I knew Mr. Cabrera had a telescope.

There was a spring in my step despite the chill in the air. I was halfway across the street when I saw Bobby step out of the kitchen. He wasn't alone.

I stumbled to a stop.

Louisa leaned in and gave him a hug. A long one.

It was probably a good ten seconds that I stood there staring at them before I made a decision.

It's true that I may be weak where Bobby is concerned, but I'm not stupid.

I turned around. By the time I reached my front door, I figured I was being irrational. There could be any number of reasons Louisa was with Bobby. Hugging him.

No reasons I liked, but there could be.

I just needed some time to think before I headed back over there. Sans cookies. Sans cami.

I pushed open the front door. BeBe galloped toward me. I heard the phone ringing above the sound of my pounding heart.

BeBe and I two-stepped to the coffee table. I grabbed the phone, dislodged the dog, and pushed the Talk button before I had a chance to look at the caller ID or catch my breath.

"Hello?"

"Nina?"

It was a woman's voice, one I didn't recognize. "Yes?"

"This is Ginger Barlow." She paused, then said, "Kevin's been shot."

From the Desk of Nina Quinn

As fall slips into winter, don't trade in your gardening gloves for mittens just yet. Before it gets too cold, think about planting a bulb garden to bloom the following spring.

Decisions, Decisions

There's no lack of choice when it comes to choosing spring-blooming bulbs. Each variety offers something unique and different for your garden, whether it be height, color, texture, or scent. Mix it up to add interest to your bulb garden.

Your local garden center or nursery will have a variety of choices. Some great bulbs to look for: common snowdrop, allium, amaryllis, common bluebell, crocus, grape hyacinth, daffodil, English iris.

The best place to store bulbs until you can plant them is in the refrigerator, and never store them in a plastic bag—they'll die.

Home Sweet Home

Most bulbs need to be planted at a depth three times the

size of the bulb itself. Think about planting in clusters for added visual appeal. Keep in mind that most bulbs require lots of sun, so if you have a shady area in mind for your bulb garden, look specifically for the few bulbs that will tolerate shade.

Full-figured

When looking for bulbs at the local garden center, choose healthy bulbs that are firm to the touch and have a good solid shape. Be careful not to handle them too much—they bruise easily.

Going Up

It's important to plant your bulbs the right way up, with the growing tip pointing upward, the roots at the bottom. If your bulb lacks these obvious characteristics, lay it on its side. Nature will take over.

Divide and Conquer

Over time, bulbs will clump together. It's important to dig them up and divide them so they won't rot. To do this, wait until the bulb has stopped blooming or has gone into dormancy. Once that happens, dig up the clumps and carefully separate each bulb. Then simply replant.

Au Natural

Naturalizing bulbs is a great way to spruce up your lawn and add early color to your spring landscape. The key to naturalizing is for the bulbs to look . . . natural, as if Mother Nature herself had simply dropped the bulb in your yard. Plant bulbs randomly about your landscape and look for bulbs that will quickly form colonies for greater visual appeal. If you plant bulbs in your lawn, make sure you wait several weeks after flowering to mow.

As the winter turns to spring, and you see that first burst of color emerging from the chilly ground, you'll be glad you took the time the previous fall to do a little extra gardening. The payoff will be well worth the effort.

Best wishes for happy gardening!

Investigate the Hottest New Mysteries!

Sign up for the FREE HarperCollins monthly mystery newsletter,

The Scene of the Crime,

and get to know your favorite authors, win free books, and be the first to learn about the best new mysteries going on sale.

To register, simply go to www.HarperCollins.com, visit our mystery channel page, and at the bottom of the page, enter your email address where it states "Sign up for our mystery newsletter." Then you can tap into monthly Hot Reads, check out our award nominees, sneak a peek at upcoming titles, and discover the best whodunits each and every month.

Get to know the magnificent mystery authors of HarperCollins and sign up today!